In the Lion's Mouth

IN THE LION'S MOUTH

JEAN HARRINGTON

Kenmore, WA

A Camel Press book published by Epicenter Press

Epicenter Press
6524 NE 181st St.
Suite 2
Kenmore, WA 98028

For more information go to:
www.Camelpress.com
www.Coffeetownpress.com
www.Epicenterpress.com
www.AuthorJeanHarrington.Weebly.com

Cover design by Scott Book
Design by Melissa Vail Coffman

ISBN: 978-1-94207-856-2 (Trade Paper)
ISBN: 978-1-94207-857-9 (eBook)

Printed in the United States of America

*To America, may she always
remain a land of welcome.*

Acknowledgments

For publishing *In the Lion's Mouth*, the second book in my Irish series, my thanks to Camel Press Editor Jennifer McCord and Publisher Phil Garrett who believed Grace O'Malley's story deserved a retelling. The third book, the previously untold adventures of *A Wild Colonial Girl*, is also due for release within the year.

PROLOGUE

The West of Ireland, 1667

"Tell me, love, what have you always longed for?" Owen asked.

"You."

He laughed, sending the birds scattering from the treetops. "Besides me, what else is your heart's desire?"

"Shoes."

"Am I hearing you aright?"

Grace nodded. "With buckles, and stockings to go with them." She looked down at her long, slim legs dangling at the horse's sides, to her bare ankles and the worn moleskin brogues covering her feet. "To my knowledge, no woman in Ballybanree has ever had shoes. But I saw shoes once. On Lady Anne Rushmount's feet. What a glorious sight! They had silver buckles over the arch, and heels that lifted the foot clear off the ground." She sighed, remembering. "But shoes like that are for a lady only."

"Are you not a lady?" Owen asked.

She turned in the saddle to smile over her shoulder at him. "Indeed, I am. In moleskin brogues," she added ruefully.

"As soon as we reach Galway and sell the horse, shoes are the first thing we'll buy. Then we'll seek out a trading vessel bound for Cork City. The farther away we get the better."

She leaned back against him, letting the chestnut's easy canter lull her into a happy reverie. Shoes. Love. Freedom. A whole new world awaiting them. Surely this day had been made possible by God alone.

By God and by stealing the horse.

Chapter One

GRACE CUPPED A HAND OVER HER eyes, the better to watch the tall man stride along Galway's Claddagh dock. Even as their boat pulled away, she kept staring at the shoreline. Only when they rode the tide into the bay and no sail followed did she breathe a sigh of relief and relax in Owen's arms.

"That's Lord Rushmount back there, Owen. I swear it is."

"I think you're right, lass. The man's treading the wharf like a cock o' the walk. Few Irishmen have such an arrogant strut."

"Did he see us, I wonder?"

"He may have. Whoever it is peered out to sea."

"You think he'll come after us?"

"If he does, he'll see me hanged for the horse. But before I let that happen, I'll kill him. You know that, love."

Still intent on the dock, Grace said, "If you don't, I'll kill him myself." At the sound of her own words, she tore her gaze from the receding shore and looked at Owen with dismay. "Listen to us. Talking murder and meaning every bit of it." She dropped to the rough plank deck and covered her face with her hands. "Dear God."

Owen sank next to her. He put an arm around her shoulder, drawing her close to his chest. "We're not murderers. We're decent people forced to the edge of a cliff. Should we leap to our deaths or fight for life?"

She lifted her tear-streaked face and grinned up at him. "Fight, of course. As long as it's not with each other."

He grinned back. "We're both stubborn and bound to disagree from time to time. 'Twill add to life's excitement, I'm thinking." Still smiling, he stood and held out his hand. "But we'll not argue now, not on this day. Come, love, let's watch Galway fade from views. We may never again see—"

A shot rang out, the ball whizzing by his head, singeing the hair over his right ear. As it flashed past, it grazed the mast, sending shards of wood flying about the boat.

Owen dropped to the deck. "Stay down, Grace. It's Rushmount."

Hearing musket fire, the captain came racing along the deck. At the sight of the splintered mast, he stopped in his tracks. "'Twas a bloody ball! I can't believe it. Who'd shoot at us?"

"An Englishman," Owen said. "He was aiming at me."

"Why you?"

"He wants her . . . my wife."

In the same instant, both men looked down at Grace lying quietly at Owen's side.

"Oh my God." The words were as close to a scream as any Owen had ever uttered. "Grace! Dear God, Grace."

Blood ran from her temple down her cheek trickling into the corner of her mouth and along her neck. Already the stream had soaked into her linen waist, staining the cloth wine red.

"Grace. *Mavourneen.*" Owen lifted her quiet form in his arms, searching for the blood's source. His hand trembling, he brushed her hair back from her forehead. A splinter of wood, sharp and lethal as a spike, had pierced the flesh above her left eye. He looked up at the captain in horror. "It nearly took her eye. Thank God, it went no farther . . . it must be removed."

Now, before she awakens.

Just enough of the wood jutted out to give him a purchase. One fast pull only would he allow himself. Ordering his hand not to tremble, he hesitated for a moment, then with fingers of steel he pulled—hard. The shard came free and with it a fresh gush of blood.

Grace lay against him without moving. *He had to stop the blood.*

"Wait, I've something might help." The captain hurried below deck, soon returning with a jug, a tin cup and a soiled piece of cloth. He handed Owen the jug. "*Uisce beatha,* a cure for everything under the sun. Dab some on her wound. 'Twill staunch the bleeding, and the sharp feel of it will bring her round."

Owen poured a little of the whiskey into the cup, his terror mounting with each second Grace remained unconscious. He rejected the man's cloth.

"I have my own, sir." From his breeches pocket, Owen removed his greatest treasure, the square of embroidered linen Grace had given him the summer last.

He dipped the linen into the whiskey. His hand above her face shook. This would cause her pain. How could he?

How could he not?

Dabbing the wet cloth on her temple, he pressed it to the wound. At his touch, she moaned, rocking her head back and forth as though to escape the sting. He lifted his hand. The bleeding had slowed. Again he pressed on the wound, his touch lighter this time. After what seemed an eternity, she rewarded him with a flash of green eyes. "Owen," she murmured. "What are you doing?"

"I'm tending to you."

"What happened?"

"Rushmount shot at us. He aimed for me, but missed."

"I can see that," she said, a little smile lifting her lips.

He helped her to sit against the side of the boat. To his relief, when she raised her head, the bleeding did not increase. He dabbed at the few drops beading the gash as gently as he could, but still she winced.

"Sorry," Owen said, all the anguish in the world in his eyes. "So sorry."

"Don't be sorry, Owen O'Donnell. He could have killed you."

"He could have killed *you*!"

"But he didn't. And here we are alive and well and loving each other more than ever. What have we to feel sorrow for?"

"Will you always be so wise? Throughout our entire lives?"

"Aye," she said, her chin firm, her eyes asparkle. "And glad I am you know it."

He laughed, and tossing the whiskey in the tin cup overboard, he poured a fresh tot from the jug before easing down beside her. "Sip this, love. 'Twill do you good."

They passed the cup between them sipping slowly, warmed by the drink and the sun and the sweet, salt air. When Grace dozed, her head against his shoulder, Owen scanned the horizon. Possibly Rushmount would board another vessel and give chase. But no sail hove into view. A good thing, that. Grace had gone through enough already and the day not yet high noon. She had no need to see her husband kill a man before sunset.

"'Twas the first time in my life I ever fainted," Grace said an hour later. She yawned, stretched, then stood and gazed over the side at the surrounding sea. "It makes one hungry."

"That and the lack of food. You've eaten nothing since yesterday," Owen said. "We have the meat pasties we bought on the dock. Will you have one?"

She nodded. "And a drink of water, if there is such on board. I have a terrible thirst as well."

"There's a barrel of fresh water. I'll fetch you some."

"And is there a little place I can go to clean off the blood and change into my other waist? I shouldn't like to walk about Cork City like this." She dropped her voice to whisper in his ear. "When I change, I need to switch the coins to my clean clothing." Her cheeks flooded pink of a sudden. "And I'll need to use the privy in a while. I hope there's one of those as well."

"I'll speak to the captain. After you eat," he added firmly.

"Aye, husband," she answered, her eyelashes fluttering down submissively.

He laughed, relieved she felt well enough to jest. Later, while Grace went into the cubby below deck to freshen herself, Owen approached the helm, ignoring the captain's sour look and curt grunt of greeting. *He has every right to be vexed*, Owen thought. *As I would be in his place.*

"I'm a blacksmith," he began. "I can repair the mast for you. But I'll need a fire."

"I allow no fires on board," the captain said, his face flinty. "Some vessels do, but there'll be none on the *Moira McGee*. Too dangerous. While at sea, the men eat cold food. They know that when they sign on."

Sign on. If the crew made their marks on a piece of parchment, Owen knew that was all the signing they did. More likely they just nodded in agreement at the terms. But that was none of his affair. "I can fashion a metal collar and secure it to the mast, making the wood stronger than new."

"Is that so?" The captain still had no smile for him, but he pulled his gaze from the horizon and held out a hand. "Jeremy Dean's the name."

"Owen O'Donnell."

"From whereabouts, Owen O'Donnell?"

He hesitated. The less anyone knew the better, but hell, he reasoned, Rushmount knew they were aboard. What difference would it make if he told this man the truth? "We're from the village of Ballybanree. North of Galway."

"And this Englishman as well?"

"In a manner of speaking. His manor house is there. On ancient O'Malley land."

"Ah, you have an old grievance then."

"My wife does. The land belonged to her family."

"Your Mistress O'Malley, now, is passing fair, but 'tis not every day an Englishman seeks an Irish woman at musket point."

"There's more to the tale."

A smile creased Dean's weather-worn face. "Spoken like a true son of Erin. An Irishman's tales are never simple."

"We took his horse."

Dean's mouth dropped open. "Christ! That's a hanging offense!"

"A man for a horse, then? You call that justice?"

"I call it theft."

"Not so. We left Grace's crop as payment. And the blood of her father and brother." Owen's voice took on a hard edge. "And now her own blood as well."

"This Englishman, he killed her family?"

"Hanged her father for poaching deer . . . the villagers are kept half starved . . . he tried to help. Her brother died by his own hand. A broken man."

Dean let go of the helm long enough to bless himself. "Jesus, Mary and Joseph, his immortal soul is lost."

"Along with his family's land."

How bitter I sound. Release anger to the air and it gains strength. He would have to make certain he never allowed it to overwhelm him. That was a weak man's path. But having aroused the captain's curiosity, he'd finish his tale.

"What Elizabeth and her heirs didn't seize, Cromwell did. The horse is nothing in comparison." A smile flirted with Owen's mouth. "The steed was Rushmount's favorite. It gives me pleasure, I will admit, to think on that."

A frown creased Jeremy Dean's forehead. "But a man doesn't steal a horse merely for the amusement of it."

"I told you the tale was not simple."

"Go on, O'Donnell. You have me captive to it."

"Rushmount . . . for that's his name . . . couldn't endure being bested by a lass. He wouldn't believe Grace was the poacher—"

"Wait, now. You said her da—"

"After Rushmount hanged him, she took up her da's crusade in secret."

"A slip of a lass like that? A deer slayer? Bloody unbelievable."

"But true. She's a fine marksman."

"With a flintlock musket?"

Owen shook his head. "If ever there were firearms about the village, they were seized long ago. She used a bow and arrow. But once she confessed to Rushmount—"

"Confessed? Why would she place herself in danger that way?" Ignoring his compass entirely, Jeremy Dean hung on Owen's next words.

"I had a proposition for his lordship she knew nothing of."

"*You* did?"

"Aye. For distilling *uisce beatha*, a plan to aid the whole village. And make Rushmount even richer than he is today. But not knowing of this, Grace took another deer. When Rushmount discovered the remains, he went mad. He refused to go ahead with the villagers' plan until the poacher confessed. When he learned Grace had defied him like her da before her, he came after her."

"So that's when you took the horse."

Owen nodded, his jaw tightening at the memories his tale unleashed. "You've got the whole of it now."

With his eyes refocused on his compass, Dean corrected course a bit. "Except for one wee fact. How long, may I ask, since you two were wed?"

"Three days ago."

"And two nights without a bed to call your own?"

A grin took over the captain's features, but Owen knew he meant no offense. "There will be other nights. Many of them, God willing."

WITH A BUCKET OF WATER THE MATE PROVIDED, Grace washed off the blood and slipped out of her stained waist and shift. She reknotted the sovereigns from the sale of the horse in her clean clothes, donned them and dropped the bloodied garments in the water to soak clean.

Taking one of the high copper combs from her bundle, she stroked it through her hair careful to avoid her throbbing temple. After her tresses were tangle free, she'd use both combs to lift her hair from her face and away from the wound until it healed. She *was* lucky the splinter had missed her eye. Aye, lucky, she exulted, to be here with her love, speeding away from old hurts, old grievances, making ready for a new and wondrous life.

With each angry throb at her temple, her heart throbbed also, but eagerly with a power far stronger than the pulsing wound. No minor injury could mar the happiness flooding her being. Free, they were, and with a whole New World awaiting them.

Her heart light, she made her way up the ladder to the deck. The salt-laden air of late afternoon blew soft but steady, lifting her hair from her shoulders, keeping the boat skimming toward freedom.

"Grace, over here!" Owen called.

She walked to the bow where he stood beside the captain who gave her as wide and white a smile as any she had ever seen. "Take over for a minute," he said to Owen. "I must salute your valiant bride."

Owen grasped the helm, watching as Jeremy Dean engulfed Grace in a body hug that left no doubt of his admiration. Before letting her go, he held her at arm's length. "You're a beauty, Mistress O'Malley O'Donnell. You've the face of an angel and the heart of a warrior."

"Ah, so you know of the poaching."

"I do that, and I know most men would quail at the thought. You're like the storied women of old . . . Deirdre and Brigid and—"

"Grace O'Malley?" she interrupted with an impish grin. "The first one, Granuaile, I mean." The captain's praise was high, indeed. She wasn't about to take it to heart, but she could play with it, and with him a wee bit.

"The pirate queen? Who defied Elizabeth? Sank her ships? And Spanish ships as well? Ah, now there's a tale worth repeating."

"My da descended from Granuaile. It's been many generations now, but I love hearing of her, too." She touched the combs in her hair with their intricate, convoluted coils of copper wire. "These were hers. They're my greatest treasure. After my husband, of course. He's the best gift I'll ever receive."

Receive. Her face turned scarlet at the implication of the word. To hide her confusion and escape, a little, from Owen's knowing glance, she looked out over the water. The sea air would cool her cheeks.

If Captain Dean understood, he concealed his awareness well. "You're a rare woman, Grace O'Malley, and glad I am you both outwitted this Rushmount." He let out a short bark of laughter. "I'd be a poor Irishman now, wouldn't I, to feel otherwise for the great granddaughter of a woman who went to sea like a man and took on the whole bloody English empire. And you carrying on today with her same spirit."

Still laughing, he turned to Owen. "I'll be taking my wheel back. The mate's not on watch for a while yet." His hands again on the helm, he asked, "So tell me, my friends, we've a two day sail to Cork City, then what?"

Grace saw Owen hesitate. "While in Cork, my wife would like to buy some shoes. We had no chance to shop for them in Galway. After that, we'll stay aboard if we may and go on with you to Dublin. In a city that size, a smith can find honest work, I warrant."

That they hoped the great ships crossing the Atlantic left from Dublin, he didn't mention. So he didn't want the captain to know the extent of their dreaming, Grace realized. He was right. It would be better for all if they kept their secret locked safe in their hearts.

CHAPTER TWO

"FASTER. *FASTER*. MOVE ALONG, YOU DRAB."

Ross Rushmount cursed and flipped the reins over the mare's back, but flogging her yet again would do no good. He'd bought her for Anne because of her gentle nature, and that wouldn't change no matter how wild he might be to overtake O'Donnell and the girl.

And overtake them he would. But how he missed the chestnut's fire, his front hooves pawing the ground eager for a run. Given free rein, he'd fairly fly, leaping over low walls and hedges, every ride the ride of a lifetime. Chances were strong his like would never be seen again. Rage pounded through Rushmount's gut, flooding up like gall into his throat. Yet he didn't dare waste time searching for the steed. O'Donnell was his prey. Once he had him in his grasp, he'd find the chestnut as well.

That scow he'd shot at was headed for Cork City. Or so he'd been told, though his bribes had failed to persuade even one of the sorry-looking tars to give chase. His English speech and clothes, and mayhap something in his bearing had caused them to refuse. Even the gold coin shimmering in his palm hadn't sufficed to move them. He could only surmise they'd had a glimpse of Grace and disliked his weapon raised in her direction. Fools. What good would she be to him dead? It was the blacksmith he'd aimed at.

He'd wasted little time on the docks arguing with the louts, instead quickly deciding to ride the mare southeast, taking a path or lane when he found one, turning to the open fields when he did not. In the darkest hours, he'd dismounted and rested by a stream while the mare cropped at the grass, but from here on, their stops would be brief. He estimated he had a good chance of reaching Cork first. The trader would be dependent upon the sea breeze and would set a slow, steady course. Still he had no time to lose. From Cork, O'Donnell could head elsewhere. Dublin perhaps, and in a city that size, the trail might well be lost for good. To make up for the mare's plodding gait, he'd keep their rest stops brief. She had a strong heart and a broad back. She'd last the distance.

The docile creature performed as best she could, somewhat like Anne, as cooperative as her nature allowed, but dull, dull as ditch water. The girl, now, was another tale. A woman in full she was, holding him at knife point when he'd tried to take her. The recollection excited him still. But the blacksmith had interfered before she'd been put to the test. He should kill him for that alone.

By late afternoon, the mare grew tired and still no sight of city walls. He dug his heels into her flanks, urging her to hurry, but to little avail. Once he had the chestnut, he'd fly like the wind and pay a hireling to plod back to Rushmount Manor on the mare.

At the thought, he settled comfortably into the saddle and tried to put worry from his mind. Should the trading vessel arrive in Cork before he did, it would not leave again in a hurry. First it would have to be unloaded, the cargo sold, the crew paid, the deck swabbed. Rushmount allowed himself a smile. Perhaps not the latter.

Evening drew nigh. He halted the mare, raised a hand to his eyes and peered into the distance. Unmistakable, even in the fading light, were the rising towers of Shandon Castle. The time had come to decide what to do next—whether to go immediately to the docks and seek out his prey or go to the authorities? Get English law and lawmen to aid him? His hands fisted on the reins. He would turn to the law—solid English law.

The full darkness of night had nearly clamped down before he drew close to the city walls. He braced himself for what lay inside the enclosure. The rank odor of feces and urine and unwashed bodies and rotting food and smoke from a thousand fires would be almost beyond endurance. Worse than London, and Cork City only a fraction of the size. Strange that despite the filth and squalor, plague hadn't visited the town in nearly a century, yet poor London had been brought to her knees the summer last with a third of her people dead.

He rode through the north gate, straight into the city's hubbub. Without dismounting, he blocked the way of an elderly man scurrying to get out of his path.

"You there," he called. "Who is lord mayor here?"

The man looked up, startled into speech by Rushmount's arrogant English voice. "Sir Thomas Barry, 'tis his name."

"Where does he reside?"

"Straight ahead, in the inner city. Everyone knows his house."

Rushmount touched a finger to his hat brim and rode on. If the mayor couldn't help him, he'd seek out the sheriff, but he'd rather begin by inquiring of a gentleman.

After several false turns down squalid alleys and byways, he spurred his mount onto a main thoroughfare lit with torchlight and lined with large stone houses, at its apex a mansion with a barred gate at the street, and within, a cobbled courtyard. The lord mayor's manse, he presumed. No need to ask. He grasped a leather bell cord dangling by the gate and gave it several savage pulls. The clamor brought a corpulent man in green livery running to the gate.

"I implore you, sir, stop," he exclaimed. "The lord mayor is dining."

"Is that so? Then my visit is well timed. Tell your master Lord Rushmount of Rushmount Manor, Ballybanree, requires a word with him."

To his fury, the man turned on his heels without answering and hurried back through the courtyard and out of sight. Rushmount waited with growing impatience for several long, tedious minutes before he again heard shoes clattering on the cobbles. The gatekeeper selected a large key from the metal ring hanging on his belt, unlocked the gate, and opened it wide.

"Enter, sir. Mayor Barry bids you welcome. If you follow me, I'll show you the way."

"See to my horse, as well," Rushmount ordered, tossing the reins carelessly over a hitching post.

The man's face clouded for an instant—*was he not used to authority?*—but he nodded and, with a well-trained flourish, ushered him indoors.

For an Irish household, this one was passing fair, Rushmount noted. The thick stone walls blocked the city's noise and most of its odors, and the candles glowing against paneled walls presented a pleasant scene. As he entered a small inner room, the sight of the lord mayor seated at a laden table reminded him he hadn't eaten all day.

The mayor, a tall man well past middle age, his white hair clubbed back at the nape, English style, rose from his chair, favoring him with a curt bow and nothing more by way of greeting. Clearly, the Irish here were a different breed from those in Ballybanree. Interesting. Cities, despite their obvious defects, did offer entertaining diversions.

Rushmount bowed correctly, deeply. "Lord Rushmount . . . ah . . . Lord Barry."

"Rushmount is it?" the mayor asked, his voice coolly polite.

Ross nodded briefly, determined to have his air of hauteur exceed Sir Barry's.

His host seemed not to notice. "Do sit, man, and sup with me. I'm delighted to have you . . . ah . . . surprise me this way." He sat, filled a goblet with claret and handed it to Ross. "My lady has retired for the night, but the kitchen lass will bring you a plate of food. Simple stewed lamb. I trust that will satisfy the weary traveler."

"Indeed. But I have no time to waste on dining."

The mayor leaned back in his chair and regarded Rushmount with somber curiosity. "Oh? What brings you to Cork in such haste?"

"A horse."

"Pray, explain." The mayor bent to his meal and, with great delicacy, pierced a morsel of lamb with the tip of his knife.

To hide his growing annoyance, Rushmount sipped his wine. *An inferior vintage.* "I seek your help, lord mayor, in reclaiming my property, an outstanding steed, a chestnut stallion of Arabian breed. He was stolen from me a few nights ago. And the thief . . . an Irishman . . ." —he paused to clear his throat—"and his woman are here in Cork. On a packet boat from Galway. Or so I believe."

"Or so you believe."

The man dared to mock him?

The lord mayor picked up his goblet and drained it then leaning forward, pushed his pewter plate out of the way and rested his elbows on the table. "Can you describe this . . . ah . . . Irish thief?"

"Yes, a blacksmith with a powerful body despite a damaged leg."

"You have witnesses to the theft?"

Frustrated, Rushmount spat out, "My bailiff. His wife. Another man, a visitor."

"So a man with a crippled leg stole your horse. And you did nothing to prevent him?"

The mayor twirled the stem of his goblet as if they were merely engaged in polite conversation.

Rushmount took a gulp of the wine and grimaced. It tasted like piss. "He had me tied up, held at knife point."

"I see." The trace of amusement playing about Sir Barry's lips infuriated Ross. "But surely you'd not risk the docks at this late hour, even for the sake of a prized steed?"

"Of course I'll risk it."

"But I will not," Lord Barry said lounging back at his ease in the arm chair. "Nor will I rouse my sheriff and his guard to search our docks in the middle of the night for a man you *believe* is in Cork. On a trader you *believe* headed our way. No, we will wait until the morning light. Your quarrel with this blacksmith will, I daresay, keep till then."

"He may be gone by morning." Rushmount slammed his goblet onto the table top, what was left of the remainder of its sorry contents slopping over onto the damask cloth. He stood and stared down at the pompous man. "I am a peer of the realm. You cannot refuse me."

The lord mayor arched an eyebrow. "Though Irish I may be, I govern Cork City at the pleasure of His Majesty, King Charles II. My will, not yours, prevails here."

Blast the man. He was enjoying Ross's discomfiture, enjoying the besting of an English lord. More than words, the smile signaled he would not be swayed or intimidated. Outside of killing him where he sat, Rushmount had no choice but to capitulate. The risk of bringing the king's wrath down upon his own head was too great, even for the chestnut that, oddly enough, he loved.

The one whose blood he longed to spill was O'Donnell's. A feverish desire to put his hands on the blacksmith seized him. If it were the last thing he did in this life, he would have him. Keeping his resolve to himself, he bowed deeply, ostentatiously, from the waist, allowing nothing in his face or demeanor to reveal his rage. "As you wish, milord. You know best in these matters."

CHAPTER THREE

"YOU CAN'T GO INTO CORK CITY ALONE, GRACE," Owen said the next morning. "You might get lost. Or hurt. Anything could happen."

"Anything? That's what I love about cities."

"All the more reason for a fine sailor like Tim to go with you."

Tim grinned, displaying brown stumps of teeth. "'Twill be an honor to promenade through Cork with a beauty like yourself by my side."

"Thank you kindly, Tim," Grace began, "but—"

"For my sake, Grace," Owen said. "We leave on the morrow's high tide. If I can get to a smith early today, I can repair the mast before sundown. We owe the captain that much at least."

"Aye," she agreed, "we do." She turned to the grizzled sailor with a dazzling smile. "Well then, Tim, shall we stroll about Cork City?"

"Take care of her, Tim," Owen charged.

"I'll never take my eyes from her and neither will anyone else, I wager." Tim chuckled at his own humor and nimbly leaped ashore.

On tiptoes, Grace arched up to kiss Owen's cheek. Before she could move away, he clasped her to him. "I'm starved for my wife," he murmured in her ear. "Since the night we were wed, we've not loved each other."

Her face grew hot. "How could we, wrapped in canvas on the deck all night? Besides, we've no bed. No pillow. No sheet."

His white teeth gleamed amid a four-day stubble of dark beard. "True, I said I wanted a proper bed for our wedding night, but that wish may have to be abandoned." Uncaring who might see, he held her tighter.

"Perhaps not." She smiled up at him, every imp in the world in her glance. "Captain Dean is giving us a wonderful gift for our wedding."

Owen's brows knit together. "What do you mean?"

"The news will keep till I return. 'Tis worth waiting for. At least I think so." Twisting free of his embrace, she leaped ashore before he could stop her. "You'll like it," she called over her shoulder, and with a wink flipped the hem of her skirt at him before holding out an arm to Tim. "Shall we, sir?"

Tim crooked his elbow in hers and, to Grace's great delight, they headed off the wharf into the excitement of Cork City. Like Galway, the streets twisted and turned, helter-skelter, willy-nilly, a bewildering jumble of houses and shops and animal pens all crowded together along the hills sloping down to the waterfront.

"A giant maze, it is," she told Tim as they crossed a river bridge and started into town.

It was filthy and exciting. The houses crowded against each other inside the city's high stone walls with little or no space between them, so unlike the few huts of Ballybanree village where a plot of earth surrounded each one. No tall trees pierced the sky, only church spires and the turrets of a great castle. Larger than Rushmount Manor it was.

Streets and alleyways teemed with throngs of people all busily going about their business, the likes of which she could only guess. The noise was beyond belief, what with passersby chatting with each other, merchants hawking goods from their stalls, and carts rattling over stones.

As they walked along, she spied marvelous wares: cloth of every color, household goods, shiny, unused pots, trinkets of glass and metal . . . and food. Her mouth watered at the sight of plump sausage rings suspended from a stall roof, piles of fresh baked breads, and heaped-up mounds of turnip and cabbage, and entire rounds of cheese. How different it all was from the sleepy lanes of home.

The jostling, the movement, the voices, the crowding all thrilled her, but the odors assailed her nose. Looking about for the source of the foul smell, she spied sewage running through a ditch in the center of the lane, the stench from it filling the air. But it was a sensible way to remove the waste of so many people. What else could one do with it? Still, Ballybanree for all its poverty had never stunk like this.

Nor had it ever been so exhilarating.

"I love city life, Tim," she said over her shoulder.

Tim sniffed the air as he hurried along. "It stinks to high heaven," he said. "Always did."

"No matter. It's alive."

"Ha! You think so, young mistress? Then what's your pleasure? Old Tim can take you to it with nary a false turn."

She stopped, taking care to keep her brogues well away from the noisome contents of a ditch. Were all cities the same? Their offal a price one paid for the thrill of being there. Well, everything in life had a price. Even shoes.

"I need a cobbler. One who sells women's shoes."

"I know just the one. Come."

Tim led the way up a steep hill, its slope crammed with open stalls. Though weather worn and thin as a twig, he led a fast pace. Grace hurried to match him, hardly daring to stop and peek at the fascinating goods spread out on either side. At the top of the lane, he lurched to a stop in front of a stall hung with shoes and boots of all sizes and types—men's women's, children's. The stall keeper, a fat man with greasy locks, halted his loud hawking when Grace approached.

"Shoes, my lovely lady?" he asked softly, his voice as insinuating as a leer. "I have them, as you can see. All kinds, with hardly any wear, just a few scuffs here and there. Nothing you'd notice. Like new, they are. Take these. Worn by our lord mayor's wife once or twice only." He leaned forward to better continue the lie. "To her son's wedding and a funeral. Her mother-in-law's," he guffawed. He held out the shoes in his dirty hands, their leather cracked and broken.

"No buckles?" Grace asked.

"For buckles, you need a metal smith. I deal in leather only." He thrust the shoes at her. "Try them." Leaning over the board that served as a counter, he looked down at her feet. "Those brogues won't last any time on these cobbles."

Grace looked at what he'd pushed into her hands. Were these the shoes of her dreams? Surely not. She returned them. "Do you have any the lord mayor's wife wore to the wedding only?"

The vendor threw back his head, the roar of his laugh louder even than his hawking. "Ah, a beauty with a bite. No, mistress, you're looking for a brand new pair. I deal in the slightly used. For what you ask, you need a shop and a shoemaker."

"Where would I find such?"

Tim tugged on her sleeve. "I know. Come. We'll go where the gentry shop."

"Sorry, sir," Grace said, yielding to Tim's urging.

"So I'm not good enough for the likes of you?" the barker yelled, already holding out another pair of broken-down shoes for her to inspect.

No one paid the slightest attention to his ranting, Grace noted. Did cities leave you alone then, to act as you wished, with not every word and movement recorded and held up for reckoning? A good thing if true, she thought. It left one free.

Following Tim's quick lead, she hurried after him through more twists and turns, up one hill and down another, until the houses became larger, the streets wider, the passersby more richly dressed and far quieter as they strolled the broad thoroughfare.

"We're here." Tim finally halted beneath a carved wooden boot suspended over their heads by heavy metal chains that creaked and swayed with every breeze. In the bowed window curving out to the street, she spied a man with a hammer in his hand seated before an upturned shoe. On display near him, for all to admire through the glass, stood polished new shoes for both women and men, with fine heels on some and buckles as well. One pair, tucked closest to the window so they wouldn't be missed, was fashioned of breathtaking red leather. She had never seen the like and gasped at the sight of them.

The cobbler dipped his head when they entered without stopping his tap, tap, tapping at a shoe in the making. He couldn't speak for the mouthful of tacks he spat out to attach the sole.

The tacks used up, he offered a greeting. "Good day, mistress. Is it shoes you're after?"

Grace inhaled the shop's rich aroma of newly cured leather and nodded. "With buckles. I've wanted them as long as I can remember."

"Well, you've come to the best place in Cork City for that." The old man, sans teeth and hair, pulled himself erect and, leaning over the shop counter, peered down at Grace's feet. "You're from the country?"

"'Tis nothing to be ashamed of," Grace retorted with a lift of her chin.

"A mere observation, dear lady. Shoes tell tales of the wearer." His thin-lidded eyes narrowed as he lifted his gaze to her face. "But you already know that." His voice gentled. "Your longing has told you so."

At the truth in what he said, Grace nodded. "Shoes are a vain desire, no doubt."

"Also practical." The cobbler's mouth lifted to show an expanse of bare gums. "That moleskin won't last long against the cobbles." On slippered feet, he hobbled out from behind his counter holding a piece of oak-tanned hide and a stick of charcoal. "Stand on this, and I'll trace your foot. Then you can choose your leather. I have various kinds, thick to thin, black for the most part, but a few dyed bright for the whims of fashion." He lowered himself to a stool in front of her and contemplated her shabby brogues. "I require half paid in advance and the rest when the shoes are finished. One week from now."

"A week? But?" Grace's hand flew to her mouth, capping it closed. She had nearly blurted out that she couldn't wait; they'd be leaving the next day at high tide and none too soon even then. For who knew if Rushmount might still be in pursuit of them? The wound at her temple throbbed at the thought. "I hoped I could have shoes today. I had no notion they would be made to fit me alone."

"For a fine pair of shoes there's no other way." The cobbler sniffed slightly. "Unless you frequent the stalls. Many of my shoes are hanging there. They won't fit precisely . . ." his gaze wandered back to her feet ". . . but they'll be better than—"

"Thank you, sir." She stepped away from his stool. The sudden heat flaming on her cheeks told her they were scarlet. "So sorry I mistook what needed doing. Come, Tim," she said. She fled the shop hardly hearing its bell tinkling as she shut the door and raced down the hilly street.

For the first time since they left the wharf, Tim hurried to catch up to her. "Stay a moment," he said, halting her with a hand to her sleeve.

At his touch, she stopped and whirled around to face him. "Oh, Tim, I'm ignorant beyond belief. I should have known shoes such as I've dreamed of don't appear at the snap of the fingers."

"With or without shoes, you're the most beautiful woman I've ever seen. Him"—his head jerked toward the shop—"and that other *skiboureen* are the only two men in Cork City who'd waste time studying your feet." He squared his shoulders until they looked almost wide. "And I'm true to my word. Not known for lying is Tim O'Toole."

He's trying to comfort me, and he has, the darling man. Leaning forward, she kissed his lined cheek. "Those were lovely words."

"And deserving every one, you are." He cleared his throat. "Is there more shopping you have in mind?"

"Indeed! Can you take me to a linen monger? I need a pillow and a sheet."

"I MET THE GREAT MAN HIMSELF," Jeremy Dean said to Owen. "While you were off to the blacksmith's. He stepped onto the *Moira McGee* like he owned her. A more arrogant pup I've seldom seen. It gladdens my heart that you took his horse."

"Rushmount?" Owen dropped the metal strips he carried onto the deck planking. "He's here?"

"Aye. Himself and the sheriff. They boarded every vessel on the shore. Searched them all. Looking for a horse thief, they said. And his woman."

Owen peered at Jeremy through narrowed eyes, a muscle flickering angrily at his jaw. "What did you tell him?"

"Nothing."

"He must have seen the mast. Suspected something."

"I told him a crate crashed into it, and as soon as I had the wherewithal, I planned to replace it."

"That satisfied him?"

"I can't be certain. It satisfied the sheriff." Jeremy looked toward the city. "Let us hope Tim and your Grace come aboard soon. That she'll attract attention in the town, I have no doubt. Though she's as safe as can be with Tim," he added quickly. "He knows the city like a man knows his woman."

"Be that as it may, I'm going after her." Owen dropped his tools on the deck next to the metal strips.

"No lad. That would be adding fuel to the fire." Jeremy's glance swept over Owen's injured leg. "You'd be noticed, too."

The accursed leg. It set him apart.

"You'll only increase her chances of being caught. Let Tim look after her. 'Tis the safest course to set."

He shook his head. "I cannot."

"You must. For her sake."

Owen sighed and slowly nodded. No doubt Jeremy spoke wisely. He'd stay put and finish the task he'd begun, but if Grace and Tim had not returned by then, he'd go after them—or go mad.

Earlier, at a blacksmith's forge he found with the aid of Jeremy's mate, he fashioned two half round iron strips with matching flanges. With the metal hot and malleable, he had pierced the flanges with several holes. Wrapped around the mast like a collar on a man's neck and then bolted into place, they would form a strong binding around the mast's splintered wood.

Jeremy clapped Owen on the back. "I wish for your sake we could leave today, but the cargo must be tended to, and my own wife awaits me." He laughed. "As a married man, you know of such things."

Let him have a moment's jest, Owen thought forcing a smile onto his face. Jeremy Dean was a good man.

With the mast repaired, its new metal collar gripping the wounded wood like a vise, Owen stripped to his smallclothes and dove in off the bow to wash the sweat from his body. Naked is how he preferred to swim but not in so public a place. Was he becoming modest of a sudden? Afraid that what was overtaking his mind would show for all to jeer at?

Perhaps. His longing was something to be shared with Grace alone. Despite the rare warmth of the hot sun, the water was cold. It's what he needed most. No, not most. Most of all, he needed Grace. Still, the cold should help. But Christ, he groaned aloud, they had to have a room to themselves and a bed. He plunged under the surface. Clean now, he'd get dressed and go looking for her despite Jeremy's warning. He cursed himself for letting her face the dangers in the city without him to—

He surfaced to the sound of his name floating toward him. Suspended in the water, he glanced toward the *Moira McGee*. Grace stood at the bow, her hair in the late afternoon sunshine glowing like a beacon, shining for him alone, drawing him close, keeping him alive.

He swam back to her, his eager arms slicing through the water.

"Owen," she called again. "Look!"

He tossed the wet hair out of his eyes hardly able to believe what she was holding up for him to see.

CHAPTER FOUR

OF ALL THE GIFTS JEREMY DEAN MIGHT HAVE GIVEN THEM, this was the very best on earth. A bed to themselves for a whole night, Owen exulted, and no one about to disturb them. Earlier, when he carried Grace's bundle below, he'd eyed the narrow bunk with a wry smile. It would do. Aye, very well, indeed.

After stowing the bundle, he joined Grace by the rail on the upper deck while the captain gave the crew final orders.

"You two, then," Jeremy said to Sean and Colin, the lads on watch, "you're not to go below deck all night. Not even if a squall blows up. Only if you see the guard sniffing about the docks again. Then you act fast to warn our passengers." He shook an index finger in Colin's face. "Go below for that one reason only. I trust you take my meaning."

Putting a fine touch on the situation Jeremy was. So let the lads grin, Owen thought. He was too happy to care.

The last of a mackerel catch had been rolled ashore and carted off for sale in the city. As soon as the hull was reloaded with cheese and butter for transport to Dublin, they'd be left alone with only the watch above decks.

When at last Jeremy made ready to leave for his home in the city, Owen threw an arm around his shoulder and clasped his hand. "We've only just met, yet you're my friend for life."

Jeremy sighed and gripped Owen's outstretched hand. "A sad day 'twill be when one Irishman can't help another. Besides, that lass of yours, she's a treasure for certain . . . in more ways than one . . . defying the *senasech* as she did with no care for her own safety." His thoughtful look left him as he grinned of a sudden. "I stowed the jug below. Help yourself to it and any food on the shelf."

"My thanks to you." Owen doubted he'd want either food or drink. Grace would be his food, his drink, she alone a banquet from heaven.

With a smile for Owen and a touch of his hand to his cap for Grace, Jeremy said, "I'll be back at dawn. Till then fare well."

Till then I'll be in paradise.

Before stepping away, Jeremy paused, lowering his voice so Owen alone could hear. "I doubt the great man and the sheriff will return, but if they should, the alleys hereabouts are dark enough for—"

"Hiding?" Owen finished. "There'll be no hiding, Jeremy. Not for me. Grace, now, that's a different matter. She cannot fall into Rushmount's hands. The man has evil intent toward her."

Jeremy nodded. "I can well imagine."

"So if he should come round again, the lads can spirit Grace away, but I'll stay and confront him." At the cloud that passed over Jeremy's face, Owen added, "I'll not make you a party to our troubles. I'll meet him out on the wharf."

"I'll pray that won't be necessary."

"Aye. That's not how I intend to pass the night."

Yet as the long summer gloaming streaked the sky with purple, then slowly faded into dark, Owen didn't rush with Grace down the stairs to their snug cubby. A strange reluctance stayed him, a desire to have the anticipation singing within him go on forever. And a thread of fear that the glorious reality opening before him would disappear unrealized, unfulfilled, for he still couldn't believe Grace was his. *His.* Owen O'Donnell's, a dour man with a withered calf.

Ah. He shook himself out of the black thoughts. No more goings on about the leg. What was done was done and no helping the fact. Grace understood. She always understood. So when he caressed her palm with the tip of one finger, she dipped her head in agreement. *Yes!*

They left the sunset and went below. With his heart pounding in his chest, he struck the flint and from its spark lit the single candle in their tiny room. Then he closed the door and the porthole covers facing the wharf, leaving one on the ocean side open to the moonlight and the water, and the salt air. No one would interfere with their peace from there.

To his utter delight, Grace spread the new sheet over the bunk's thin mattress and plumped up the pillow at its head. "My wife," he said and opened his arms.

She didn't run to him, but stood gravely beside the tidied bunk. "I must wash before I come to you," she said. "You're clean from the ocean, but I've done little since yesterday except wipe away the blood. Tim brought me a bucket of fresh water. Let me use it first, love."

"No." He crossed the room in two paces and pulled her to him, pressing his need against her thigh, letting her know what power she possessed. "Let me."

"But . . ." She glanced down in confusion, her lowered lashes fanning out on her cheeks.

"You don't want me to?" he whispered.

Her glance still lowered, she said. "No one ever has except my Mam when I was a wee babe."

"Your body was one with hers, and in Ballybanree it was twice one with mine. 'Tis much the same thing."

"Ha!" Her whoop of a laugh lit up her eyes and revealed her white, even teeth.

God, she's perfect.

He bent to kiss her. When she caught her breath again, she asked, "Where do you wish to begin?"

"Here." He reached out a hand and began a soft caressing of her breasts, then tiring, in a moment, of the linen waist between his fingers and her flesh, he tugged the garment over her head, flung it on the bunk, and slid her shift off her shoulders.

"I have a bit of soap," she said, and before he could touch her, she went over to her bundle on the table and removed the sliver with its scent of lavender. She walked back to where he stood with a wet cloth in his hands . . . waiting.

"I love watching you move," he said. "You sway. That alone would drive a saint to worship new gods. Always, always walk like that before me. I love it so."

With a smiling face, she held out the soap. He rubbed it on the cloth. His hands alive to the very tips of his fingers, he reached out and gently ran the cloth over her skin. "Raise your hands over your head." Even to his own ears, his voice sounded hoarse. As she did his bidding, his hands moved under each rounded globe and then up under her arms wiping at the small furze of hair, then back to linger on her breasts. "I won't kiss them yet," he murmured. "Or I'll not be able to continue my lovely task."

As he stooped to the bucket to rewet the cloth, he heard her sigh, in contentment or disappointment at losing his touch, he didn't know, but the sound echoed in the small room like music.

He stood. "Turn, love." She did, grasping her tumbled hair in one hand, lifting it off her neck, leaving her back free for him to clean and caress. He ran the cloth down the shallow indentation of her spine as far as her waist. She shivered. "Are you cold, then?" he asked.

"No." Her voice no more than a feather in the air.

"Take off your skirt." She nodded and let go of her hair. It fell in a curtain to her breasts. With fingers gone clumsy, she fumbled at the tie letting the skirt drop to the floor and the shift along with it. She kicked them aside.

His voice thick in his throat, he said, "A goddess I have for a wife."

"Half washed and chill into the bargain," she said, trying to laugh but unable to. She bit her lip as Owen bent over the bucket, wrung out the bit of cloth and said. "I'll finish your back now."

As obedient as a child, she turned again and soon felt water drip down her buttocks to her thighs. He dried her, easing a piece of rough cloth over her skin. "Turn to me," he said.

She obeyed, welcoming the cool damp, welcoming the guiding fingers. "Owen," she murmured tormented as never before. "I cannot stand here any longer. I need to lie down. Please. No more."

"I could do this forever."

"You have such powerful control then?" Without waiting for an answer, she moved away from his touch, and with an impish grin, like a mischievous child, plunked her feet in the bucket for a moment splashing water over the floorboards. "There!" she said stepping out. "Done. Now, husband come—"

A noise overhead startled them both into silence.

"Wait," Owen said, his body gone tense. "Listen." Loud thumps interspersed with muffled shouts filtered through the decking. They stood transfixed by the bunk hoping for a return to silence, but the noise increased, the thumps growing louder, the shouts stronger. "There's trouble overhead," Owen said. "I'd better take a look. Dress yourself, love, and bolt the door." He caught her to him in a quick kiss. "I'll be back in a trice."

She dressed quickly and tied her hair back with a scrap of ribbon. She had no intention of staying below while her husband placed himself in harm's way. That could be Rushmount up there.

At the door, she glanced back feverishly. Surely there must be something here she could use as a weapon? Her searching glance revealed nothing except . . . ah, of course. Picking up the bucket of bath water, she stole up the stairs on bare feet.

He had his back to her, not Rushmount after all, just a wee urchin, not yet a man but already a mighty fighter. The stick in his fist held Colin at bay, as he circled him, daring him to come into range. A quick glance aft showed Owen grappling hand to hand with a man nearer his own size. She knew Owen's strength. He'd not need her help. But a hapless Colin did.

"Boyo," she called to the urchin.

He swiveled. The bath water caught him full in the face. At his howled outcry, Colin pounced, knocking him to the deck, pinning him in place.

Grace picked up the stick and stood over him looking down at the lad's crop of curly black hair wet now and dripping into his eyes and onto his ragged clothes. She had seen such rags plenty on the children of Ballybanree. So he'd had a desperate need to be thieving then. "If he releases you, be still. No running, you hear?"

No response.

"The bucket's empty now, but I can swing it," she threatened. "Hard."

"You're naught but a lass," he retorted.

"Aye, but I soaked you well enough, didn't I? And will again if need be."

He gave her a filthy look, but didn't answer.

"Let go," she urged Colin.

As fast as a wild animal, the ragged urchin shot to his feet, but Colin's big paw caught him by the nape of the neck and flung him face down on the deck, securing him with one hefty foot on his back.

Their prisoner held fast, Grace looked to Owen. The sounds of his scuffle had abated. Was he harmed, after all? In answer, he came around the wheel house with a tall stripling whose arm he had in a tight lock behind his back. Without releasing him from his grip, Owen stared at the urchin who lay in a puddle and then at Grace with an empty bucket in one hand and a stout stick in the other. He laughed at the sight.

"Where's Sean?" Colin asked.

"Out cold," Owen said. "They must have surprised him with that stick Grace is holding. He's a knot on his head the size of an egg." He peered at Colin. "Were you two alert?"

Colin looked down at his feet. "Sean was asleep. 'Twas my watch. These two crept up silent as cats. They were on me before I knew—"

"Never mind. I trust Sean will awaken in a while." Owen's lips curled up at the corners. "Maybe a bit of a wash would arouse him, Grace."

No one would take his meaning, but she blushed, nevertheless. Toying with her, he was, humoring himself. Well, let him. It was wonderful to see him happy and so at ease with her that nothing could dismay him … besides, she would toy with him later … in a way he would love.

She filled the bucket from the rain barrel on deck and carried it aft to where Sean slept on his back like a well-fed babe. With a sigh of regret and a stab of misgiving, she tossed the water on him in one fell swoop.

Shocked awake, Sean jumped to his feet, sputtering and blowing and cursing his head off. "Now that you're up," Grace said mildly, "would you come forward? Colin's worried about you."

When they returned to the bow, Owen released his grip on the stripling. "Sit down beside your friend," he ordered.

Without a word, the lad slumped down and sat fingering his swollen lip.

"Now let the wee tiger sit up, Colin. He's not going anywhere. Are you?"

No response. Colin lifted his foot. The urchin sat glowering at the circle of faces peering down at him but made no attempt to move.

"What's your name, son?" Grace asked.

No response.

Colin prodded him with the toe of his boot. "Answer the lady."

Nothing.

Grace squatted before him, eyes level with his. She asked again, her voice soft, "Your name?"

"I have no name."

"He speaks. A good thing in an Irishman." She leaned in closer. "Sir No Name, why did you climb aboard us tonight?"

Silence.

"We must have an answer for the captain."

The older thief, a lad, too, for all his gangly length, spoke up. "I'm Reid. He's my brother, Matt. We saw no lights. We thought no one was aboard and—"

"Are you hungry?" Owen asked.

"We were born hungry," he retorted.

Grace met Owen's eyes. *More of the same.* Like the villagers of home, Cork City's people suffered, too. The lust for profits had Ireland bled white. Yet Ballybanree produced enough for all, and the hull of the trader burgeoned with food.

Damn.

Grace pounded her right fist into the open palm of the left. She couldn't save the world, but she'd do what she could tonight.

"Owen, did Captain Dean say we could eat what's in the cubby?"

"He did."

"Well, why don't I go below and bring it up? We can all sit down and have a feast with our guests here." She paused, looking directly at Colin, Sean and Owen. "Before we let them go."

Later, after the lads had eaten their fill and leaped ashore to disappear down a dark, quayside alley, Owen followed Grace below. Once in the cubby, he took her in his arms. "I love you entirely," he said. "I love what you say. I love what you do. I love you dressed. I love you undressed." He ran his hands down her back, feeling her spine, and her hips, and the buttocks he had so recently bathed and caressed. "The sight of you earlier in the candlelight is scalding my memory."

"There are more memories waiting to be made," she murmured.

"You know I want to stay, love, but that could have been Rushmount who crept up on the lads. I can't leave them to watch alone while we take our pleasure." He pointed to the bunk. "My Irish conscience would be in the bed there with us."

She sighed. "I expected you to say so." She reached up to brush back a strand of hair that had fallen into his eyes. "Our love is a beautiful dream, Owen, but I want the reality of it."

"I, too, Grace, and soon. Imagine how we'll ignite when we're finally free to be together."

"'Twill be a bonfire we'll cause."

"Aye. A bonfire of the O'Malleys and O'Donnells."

With that promise and a kiss, he left her to spend the night alone on Jeremy Dean's narrow bunk.

Chapter Five

"ARE ALL CITIES BUILT NEAR THE SEA?" Grace asked. "Galway is, and Cork, and here's Dublin the same."

"Most, I warrant," Owen replied. "Or by a great river. 'Tis the easiest way to ply trade or travel to and fro."

Fascinated, they watched at the railing as Jeremy Dean guided his slim craft into the wide arc of Dublin Bay, past the headlands of Dalkey to the south, and then by the rocky crags of Howth on the bay's north side. "Trim the sails, lads," he called out as they approached the mouth of the River Liffey. "With the traffic ahead, we'd best ease our way to the quay. No need to rush it."

Bisected by the river, the city sprawled on both sides of the broad valley. Larger than either Galway or Cork, the bustling waterfront would surely have a ship large enough to brave the Atlantic, one not afraid to plunge into that watery vastness and lose sight of land for weeks at a time. The idea made Grace shiver, whether in fear or anticipation, she couldn't be sure. But of a certainty, adventure with all its excitement and danger awaited them.

She took Owen's arm, nestling close to him as they floated up the Liffey, the buildings surrounding the river slipping by one after the other seemingly without end. She concentrated on the boats lining the wharf, studying them for size and sea worthiness. Were any large enough? Owen had said she'd know the minute she saw a sea-going vessel. So far, out of scores of moored ships, she saw none much larger than Jeremy's trader.

Owen stroked her hand. "Don't worry, love. We'll find a way."

She smiled up at him. He could read the very thoughts as they unfolded in her mind. "You know me full well, Owen."

His fingers tightened. "Not well enough."

"You would put duty first last night," she said, the merest hint of chastisement in her voice.

He laughed, the sound warm and rich to her ears. "You would have wanted it no other way."

"Are you always right?"

"Always."

"I'll remember that." She enjoyed their banter, the sense of freedom and peace that flooded her being. Surely Rushmount would never menace their lives again. He was an evil memory and no more. The breeze blew up and she shivered, pulling her shawl tight about her.

When Jeremy had his vessel securely moored, Owen slung Grace's bundle over his shoulder, and they went to take their leave. "You'll find work in Dublin," Jeremy assured them. "Plenty of need here for a good blacksmith, and after what you did with my mast, I know you're one of the best." He held out his hand. "'Till we meet again, my friend."

But we will never meet again Grace realized, as Owen grasped Jeremy's hand. She wished with all her heart she could tell him so and bid him a true farewell. But for his safety, as well as their own, it would be better not to. Instead, when he turned to her, she kissed his cheek. "A rare, good man you are, Jeremy Dean." She hugged him close.

"Now, now, lass, you'll be swelling my head for me." He cleared his throat. "I sail to Dublin once or twice a twelve month. Look for me in the spring."

Not wanting to speak the lie it would be, Grace nodded and, taking Owen's free hand, leaped ashore beside him.

"We'll cross the river at that bridge ahead," Owen said. "Jeremy told me it's new built and even has a name. Can you believe that? As if it were human."

He was trying to distract her from the leave taking, and, loving him for it, Grace pretended an interest she didn't really feel. "What name did they give it?"

"'The Queen Maeve Bridge.'"

She stopped mid-step. "Queen Maeve? Sure and it's well named. For an Irish warrior woman, not some English knave." Her chin lifted a bit. "Granuaile would have been a fine name for it, too."

"Ah, the bride of my heart has the mind of a . . ."

"Patriot," she finished frozen in place by a disturbing thought. "What kind of patriot flees her own country?"

Owen dropped the bundle on the stones beside his feet. Ignoring the passersby, he pulled Grace to him, brushing a brief kiss near the small wound at her temple. "A country is not a place only. The spirit within you, the thirst you have for justice and decency—Ireland spawned those desires. She'll be with you no matter where you dwell."

Held warmly against him, she looked over his shoulder at the span crossing the Liffey, their bridge to freedom. "I married a wise man," she said.

He laughed again and picked up the bundle. "Glad I am you think so. Now let's see about our passage." Half-way across the bridge, he halted. "Look!"

A fat seaman, his breeches riding under the moon of his belly, lumbered down the gangplank of the largest ship at berth. He shouted a final order to a crewman on board before making his way across the cobbles to one of the stone houses facing the river. Without a pause, he stepped down to the house's lower level and disappeared inside.

"Ever been in a pub, love?" Owen asked.

"Sure and you know the answer."

"Today the veils will be torn from your eyes. Come, we're off to the . . ."—he glanced up at the sign, a painted tankard flopping in the breeze—". . . Ale House." He grinned. "Judging from the name, it's run by an Irishman without imagination."

"Is that possible?"

"Hard to believe, I know." He grasped her hand. "Stay close."

He won't have to say it twice, Grace thought, as he opened the scarred door of the Ale House and the stale odor of sour brew and smoke and old sweat struck her in the face like a blow.

At the sight of Grace in the doorway, the raucous laughter rising up from the revelers at the crowded tables came to a momentary hush. Owen's grip on her hand tightened. "Don't be afraid," he said in her ear. "They'll be looking only."

"I'm not," she lied as the noise rose up again. *It never paid to honor your own fear.* She held her head high while they made their way through the throng to where the fat seaman sat, a tankard already half empty before him, a runted, scurvy-ridden man across from him and an empty stool by his side.

"My lady would like a seat," Owen said.

His elbows never leaving the table, the seaman looked up. Before he could snarl a refusal, his glance fell on Grace. "Help yourself, mate. There's room for your beauty at Malachy's table. For you, too, there being no stopping you," he added, chortling at his own humor. "Give it over," he ordered his runted crony who scrambled to his feet and shuffled away without protest.

Owen rested the bundle on the hard-packed floor. The fat man ogled Grace when they sat, but to her relief, his huge belly prevented him from leaning in close to her.

"Ale?" he asked. Without waiting for a reply, he shot a fist the size of a ham into the air. "Annabelle! Two more."

The barmaid hurried to their table with two mugs of ale. A lass, hardly out of childhood, she was pretty enough despite tired eyes and dark, unkempt locks. Large, pale breasts rose above her low-cut bodice for all the world to see.

The seaman pawed her buttocks.

Why isn't she pulling away or slapping his hand? She can't. Or won't. Dear God.

Grace's mind flashed back to Ballybanree's mean excuse for a pub with its single rough board balanced on two barrels, and Bessie, the jaded village slattern doling out the ale. Had Bessie allowed such liberties? No doubt. But never having been in the hovel, only taking peeks on occasion through its open door, she hadn't been aware. She'd been an innocent child then. Well, no more. She was a married woman now and knew the world for what it was: a place filled with evil and—God help her—with excitement.

Malachy tossed down a few coins. Annabelle swept them into her apron pocket and walked off. "Malachy pays, he does, for the lady's ale. Yours, too," he said to Owen, "for bringing her here." He leaned as far forward as his belly allowed, his foul breath wafting across the table. "But Maly's not a fool. You didn't bring this beauty into the Ale House for no reason." He emptied his tankard in one long swallow. "Annabelle!" he bellowed. He thumped the empty on the boards and upped his chin at Owen. "Men always have reasons for a taste of Maly's company. So tell me, boyo, what's yours?"

"We're seeking passage," Owen said evenly.

"Ah, of course you are." Malachy tried to bend closer. "Any smuggled goods to be shipped as well?"

"Not at all. What an idea." Grace said.

He guffawed at her shock. "Maly must have his jest. No harm intended. So where are you destined?"

Grace felt Owen's hand gripping her knee, signaling that he would do the probing for information. "Where do you sail?" he asked.

"You've no particular place in mind?"

Owen shrugged and waited while Maly shifted on his bench, searching for the barmaid. After he caught her eye, he turned back to them. "Well, since you're asking, I've sailed the Irish coastline the whole of my life. I know it like the curves of a woman's body." He leered at Grace, and she gazed back at him, her eyes flat with disinterest. "I've voyaged to France betimes. Spain, too. "

"Do you cross the Atlantic?"

"The Atlantic? In that tub? Mother of Christ." Malachy guffawed and wiped his streaming eyes with the back of a hand, so caught up in his own jest he didn't stop to pinch Annabelle when she hurried over to refill his tankard. After taking a minute to catch his breath, he slipped a dirk from inside his shirt and began picking his teeth with the edge of the blade.

Grace watched his eyes narrow into slits of suspicion. Was he threatening them with his weapon while pretending otherwise? "You sought me out particular like. Why?"

"You came off a good-sized boat," Owen said.

"You thought I'd cross the ocean in the wee *Sea Devil*?"

Owen shook his head. "I doubted it, but you might know someone who does."

"Humph." He tucked the knife back inside his shirt. Grace wondered if he'd slash the lard in his belly as he bent forward again, but he seemed not to care that the point of a blade pressed against his flesh.

"For what you seek, Liverpool's the answer. Not London this year. I hear tell it's been raided by the Dutch, and the English fleet destroyed. Lying in shambles 'tis, blocking the Thames. Aye, Liverpool's what you'll be needing."

"You mean Liverpool, *England*?" Grace asked.

"There's only one Liverpool I know of, and she's in England, for certain."

"England is the last place on earth I want to go."

"Most Irishmen feel the same. But there's no help for it. Not for an Atlantic crossing." Malachy cocked a thumb in the direction of the harbor. "The *Devil* out there can ply the Irish Sea. She's sizable enough for that, but for the Atlantic you need a galleon, or a square-rigged frigate at the least." He sneered. "From the country look of you both, I doubt you've ever seen one."

"True," Grace said, chin hiked, "but we've seen pigs aplenty."

Before Malachy could retort, Annabelle thumped a wooden bowl of kidney stew in front of him and handed him a spoon. He ignored the bit that slopped over onto the table and began shoveling the food into his maw. Grace's mouth began to water. They hadn't broken their fast since last night.

"Owen?" she began.

"You're hungry, lass. We have enough for—"

"Keep your coin. For the beauty, here, Maly provides. Part of the service. For special passengers only."

"No," Owen said. "We'll not take passage after all."

"Suit yourself." Malarchy slurped up the last of his stew and drained his tankard before lurching to his feet. He hiked up his breeches as far as they would go then flung a few more coppers onto the tabletop. Before turning to leave, he ran his gaze back over Grace's face and form. "If you change your mind, come aboard before next high tide. We're heading for the English coast. I'm a fair man," he added. "I'll settle for whatever you can pay."

"Why should you?" Owen said with an irritated frown.

Beads of sweat trickled down Malachy's forehead. He flicked them away with a blunt finger. "Since you're asking, 'twould honor the *Sea Devil* to have a beauty like yours on board."

They watched his unsteady progress as he wove his way between tables like a big ungainly beast. When he opened the door, the pub's stale odors immediately swallowed up the brief burst of fresh, salt-laden air.

"Dear God, Owen," Grace said. "He's a wicked man. Jeremy was a gift from heaven. How will we ever find his like again?"

"Ireland is filled with good men. We'll find another. It's just a question of time, love."

Drunken shouts from a nearby table had Annabelle scurrying over with the ale pitcher in her hand. As she poured out the dark brew, she ignored the hands reaching for her buttocks and thighs, even the one groping at her breast until a nipple burst free.

Coarse howls rose up at the sight. All giggles, Annabelle joined in the laughter, wriggled herself back into her soiled linen waist and hurried to another table.

What else must the lass engage in? Grace wondered, shuddering at the only possible answer. As she followed the girl's twistings and turnings about the room, a thought struck her. "Owen, Annabelle will know."

His brows drew together. "Know what?"

"Who the good men are. The ones who come in for a mug or two of ale and a dish of hot food. Not for . . . for . . ."

"I understand your meaning, Grace. No need to explain." Owen took a swallow of his brew. "You may well be right. Let's call her over."

"Aye." Grace grinned at him. "Why not? Everyone else is doing so." She sat on the edge of the bench, her back straight, hands gripping her untouched tankard, her eyes sparkling as she looked about the noisy, crowded pub filled with seadogs and thieves and the riff-raff of the docks.

"Are you enjoying this, love?" Owen asked.

"Of course not."

"Is that so?" The corners of Owen's mouth quirked up. "You little fraud. You're loving it."

She swiveled to look him full in the face. "I never lie about anything serious. Only in jest. For the humor in it," she added stoutly.

"Well, I'm happy my wife's enjoying one of Dublin's worst stewpots."

"How can you be sure it's one of the worst? 'Tis the only one you've ever been in."

He laughed. "True. God, you're going to give me a run for my money."

"Now *that's* no word of a lie," she said, raising a hand to catch Annabelle's attention.

The girl came to them without a pitcher of ale in her hands for once, wiping her palms on the front of her apron.

"My wife would like a dish of hot food," Owen said. "And so would I. What is your fee?"

"Tuppence each."

"That's fine. And bread if you have it." He lowered his voice. "We'll have a word with you as well."

The girl glanced over her shoulder, but at the moment, no one sought her out.

Grace beckoned her closer. "You must know the good seamen. The ones who can be trusted to deliver passengers safely. Not like the man we sat with earlier."

Again the girl looked about with the fast, nervous glance of a rabbit caught in an open field. "There are a few." She put a hand in her apron pocket, clinking her coins together as they rolled between her fingers.

Owen took a pence from his breeches pocket and pressed it into her free hand.

"Is there such a man here now?" Grace asked. "One who doesn't paw you, who speaks with kindness?"

The girl hesitated.

"One who treats you as if you were a lady born? That sort of man?"

"There's one. Over near the door. The one with the baldy head. Master Casey. He captains the *Dublin Lily* and he never—"

"Annabelle!" The same hoarse cry rose up from a second table and then a third.

"The baldy man. They say he's fair in business dealings as well." She went to scurry off, but on an impulse, Grace held her back with a touch to her wrist.

"We're going on a sea voyage. Will you leave this place and join us?"

The girl's eyes opened wide. "Leave this place? Whatever for? I love it here." She pulled her arm free. "I'll bring your food as soon as I can."

"Bring it to Master Casey's table," Owen said to Annabelle's retreating back. "We'll be joining him there."

Chapter Six

"THERE'S BOUND TO BE RATS." Grace shuddered at the *Dublin Lily's* cluttered, greasy deck. "Must we go below?"

"We'll stay out in the air as long as we can," Owen said. "I'm sorry it's slovenly, love. But Master Casey is an honest seaman, and the only one about the docks leaving for Liverpool with the tide. He'll get us there swiftly. And safely," he added after a quick glance at her dubious expression.

Lest he think her complaining, Grace nodded. "We were right not to wait for another ship. The more miles between Rushmount and us, the better. Besides, the sovereign we kept aside for spending must be nearly gone by now."

"No need to worry. Captain Casey was more than fair about his price. We have the value of a few more meals left."

They stood by the sloop's railing, watching the calm expanse of the Liffey slowly rise as the tide found its way upriver. At the high water mark, the crew hoisted anchor and unfurled the sails. With a sharp snap, the canvas billowed in the breeze, and the ill-kept, ill-named *Dublin Lily* headed toward open water.

Grace had vowed she wouldn't weep at her last sight of Ireland, but that promise was severed as they rode the swells into the Irish Sea, and the outline of Dublin slipped away forever. When her straining eyes could see nothing more than roiling, gray water, she slumped down onto the slippery deck and covered her face with her hands.

A second later, she felt Owen crouch beside her. "Cry it out," he whispered, "until your heart's emptied altogether. Then you'll have space in it for our new country where we'll be free to live in peace on our own land. Tenants to no one." He spat out the word 'tenants' like a curse.

Grace raised her head to find his dark eyes mere inches from her own. "I always knew you hated your life in Ballybanree, but never more than at this minute." She wiped the shed tears on her sleeve and managed a smile. "Sure and I'm over my sorrowing, but my heart will never be empty. It has you filling it."

"You have me, all right. But on the other hand, married woman, you've had me not. At least not since our vows." He grinned before planting a kiss on her wet cheek. "But your day—

or night. . ."—his grin grew wider—"is coming."

She kissed him back. "By all that's holy, I hope so."

Contented, they sat side by side, hand in hand, on the open deck, breathing in the last of Erin's salt air. The *Lily* rode the waves sturdily. She was a short, stubby craft, broad of beam, her hull well able to accommodate its cargo of cheese and salt beef and ham destined for English tables.

On occasion, they'd learned, she carried travelers like themselves, but not often. Few Irish sailed to England—straight into the Lion's mouth— unless they were on the king's business. And unless there was no help for it, anyone so employed would not take passage on such a dirty scow. So they were alone with the crew who, after initial, spellbound glances at Grace, ignored them while they worked the rigging.

As the *Lily* made her way east, she plowed into the waters of St. George's Channel. The sea, placid till now, turned savage. The channel current ran swift and hard, and the heavily laden sloop, riding low to begin with, dipped deeper into the first of the big rollers blowing over her bow, then up she rose, thrusting into the crest. A hesitation, a shudder from her planking, and down she went again, the torrent raging like flood water the full length of her, threatening to soak Grace and Owen to the skin.

Grasping their bundle in one hand, Owen struggled to his feet and reached down to help Grace stand against the wind. But she pulled free of his hand and, shoulders heaving, bent over the rail. At once, the contents of her stomach shot into the sea. Still the spasms took her, one after the other, seemingly without end. Disgusted with herself, she could no more stop the retching than the *Lily* could stop sea foam from spewing over her bow.

Finally, when the spasms produced nothing more, Owen lifted her hands from their grip on the rail and, holding her tight to his side, helped her down the ladder to the main cabin.

He led her to a bench by a table smeared with the leavings of former meals and went looking for a mug of fresh water. Her stomach turned over at the sight of the slimy boards, but willing herself calm, she felt the urge to retch drop away. In its place, a roaring started up in her head pounding through her skull in rhythm with each throb of her pulse.

Owen returned with a damp cloth and a filled mug. Taking one look at the mug, she waved it away. "I can't, Owen. Not now. I need to lie down. And die." She groaned as her stomach lurched awake, the spasms starting up stronger than ever. She bent over the bench, well away from her skirt and brogues, but despite her straining torso, nothing spewed out. Drained and dry in the mouth, she sat up. Was Owen trying not to smile? He had the suspicious hint of one playing about his lips.

"This isn't water." He held out the mug. "'Tis a tot of rum from one of the crew. A sip will settle you. Like magic, he vowed. Try it. Wet your lips."

The *Lily* dove into a trough and lumbered out, every board groaning with the effort of fighting the channel's fury.

"The sea's gone mad," she said, taking the cup. She sipped the rum letting its fire work southward down to her belly soothing it, warming it.

"We're riding the channel for speed," Owen said. "The mate claimed we're doing four knots. At that rate, we'll see the coast of England before dark."

Grace sighed. "Maybe we're the ones gone mad, not the sea. Rushing toward England when we need to escape her entirely."

"Once in the New World, we will. There'll be a whole ocean between the past and us and unclaimed land without end in any direction you can name. We'll be free there, I swear to you."

The sloop, heavy bottomed though she was, lifted her weight yet again to meet another roller. She cut through it, dropped back, and readied herself for the next forward plunge—and the next.

Grace held the mug tight. In the lull between waves, she took a hefty swallow. "This is good medicine. Do you know that?"

"I've heard tell," Owen said wryly.

"Here, you finish the last drops. I'm going to sleep on this bench for a bit."

"A wise decision."

She peered up at him. Had his hint of a smile grown broader? She decided she didn't care and stretched out. Dear God in heaven, if this short sea voyage was so awful, how would she ever survive an Atlantic crossing of weeks on end? She wasn't certain of the answer to that at all, at all, or aware of Owen taking the mug from her hand and helping her lay down on the hard bench that felt, suddenly, like a bed of the softest feathers.

———————

"I never knew you snored," Owen said.

"How could you? I don't," Grace retorted.

"Oh, but you do. Loudly." This time, she had not the slightest doubt about his smile.

"Pish. 'Twas the poison you fed me that did it."

"Either that or you were snorting your distaste for Mother England. Don't you want to have a look at her?"

The violent movement of the sloop had slowed to a gentle cradling. Gone, too, were the wild surges that had sickened her. "We're here?" Without waiting for an answer, she leaped to her feet.

She shook her hair back over her shoulders and tidied her skirt, ignoring the slight damp that still clung to it. *England. Liverpool. What would it be like?*

With Owen leading the way, they went up on deck, and what lay spread before her eyes caused Grace's jaw to drop open. Ocean-going vessels, at last. And so many. Owen had been right; the look of the giant ships was unmistakable even to a farm lass who had never before seen the sight of them.

"They're like a forest without leaves," she marveled.

Dozens of behemoths, of varying shapes and outlines, swayed on their moorings in the deep bay water, all bearing tall, thick masts. Some had two only, but most had three mainmasts and what Owen said were bowsprits and mizzenmasts as well. Though at rest, with their sails furled, the ships still reached for the sky. *Like us*, Grace mused, thrilled with the idea. *Aye, like us, they're reaching for the stars.* On one of these gorgeous giants, she'd welcome the ocean crossing and ride the waves with ease, just as Granuaile must have done. Thrilling it would be.

She squeezed Owen's hand. "Do they all go to the New World?"

He shrugged. "I heard tell there's a shipping office on the quay that books passage. With luck it may still be open. We'll inquire. Come."

———————

The clerk, his long thin nose bent over his ledger, forgot to mask his surprise when he looked up and caught sight of them—a beautiful girl with a cloud of red-gold hair making a glory out of her shoulders and a handsome, dark-featured man with, pity, a crippled leg, his gait an awkward mockery of what a man's stride should be. How, he wondered, staring at the girl, had this cripple snagged such a prize?

The day was late for inquiries, and the clerk was impatient to be snug in his favorite pub. But the man looked menacing despite his deformed leg. He'd best hear him out.

"We've a question for you," the man said.

Bloody hell. They're Irish. He could well afford to be curt. "Ask it."

"We want to book passage to the New World. To a place called Providence."

"So?"

"Are you daft and didn't understand my request? " A darkness came into the Irishman's eyes and a tension in the big hands at his sides. "I don't believe in saying twice what should be said once only."

"I can't help you."

"What is the meaning of that? The harbor's fair bristling with ships. All of ocean-going size."

"None of them are bound for the New World."

"None?"

"You heard."

He went to move the board across his cage window, a signal his day had ended. As he did, the Irishman's fist shot out, stopping the board before it could slam shut. "I'll be wanting a fuller answer," his voice flat with purpose, "and a civil tone."

"Take care. You're not in your own country here."

"But I soon will be. Now give me the answer I require."

The clerk released an exasperated breath. That fist was close to his face. "There'll be no Atlantic crossing until spring. April at the earliest."

"Why not?"

"You missed the last crossing of the season. The *King James* left two days ago for Plymouth Colony."

The man waved an arm in the direction of the harbor. "Not one out of all those ships?"

"Read their names. They're painted plain enough on their sides. If you can read," he added, his courage returning a bit. "Most are ships of the line, warships being outfitted for service against the Dutch. You need a merchant ship. That'll be the *Seafarer.* She's due back mid winter or early spring. If she holds to schedule, she'll ship out in April. Come back in March. You can book passage then."

Keeping a hand on the edge of the closing board, the clerk rose from his stool. Standing, he had a clearer picture of the two, their worn clothing, the fellow's high boot, the bundle on the floor by his side. All their worldly possessions, no doubt. Clearly the price of passage would be beyond them. "The fee will be two gold sovereigns. Each." He sniffed noisily rubbing a finger across the moisture dripping from his nose. "No exceptions made."

"Just when I'm thinking you're a true shit of a man, you show a heart of . . ." the Irishman cocked his head as if considering all possible comparisons ". . . of gold, shall we say? I'm in a generous mood today."

To his amazement, the beauty clung to the Irishman's arm and looked up at him adoringly. When had such a woman looked at him like that? Never, he realized with a pang, as he hastily slammed the window shut. Through it, he heard a deep voice say, "We'll be back to call on you the first day of March."

Chapter Seven

"You were entirely right, Owen." Grace upped her chin at the closed shipping office door. "That man in there, he *is* a low turd."

"Such language, and you a proper, married woman."

"Am I married? Why is that hard to believe somehow?"

He stopped walking. "That's my fault, love. You've not been cherished as you should. As you deserve."

He dropped the bundle to the stones of the pier and took her in his arms. "I adore you. Please say you know that."

"I do." She sighed. "The trouble is we Irish are in love with our words."

"Ah, but we love more than words, and there's a remedy for what ails us. Lodgings. What say you?"

She nodded, delight springing into her eyes. "True."

He picked up their bundle. "And we need a resting place for all our earthly possessions. 'Tis bored, I am, toting them about from city to city."

She laughed, the sound floating as high as the masts on the galleons in the harbor.

The Liverpool seafront was crowded with pubs and inns, its walkways thronged with men elbowing their way from door to door. Wooden signs, most weather-worn but a few in garish colors or picked out with gilt, swung in the stiff, onshore breezes. Grace spied a carved mermaid dancing in the wind, beyond it a shield of lions rampart, farther away a pair of crossed swords, and best of all, a soaring eagle she nearly mistook for a bird in flight.

Engrossed in the signs, she let out a cry of surprise when Owen's fist clamped onto her upper arm.

"Let's duck into this alley, love. I don't like the look of what's ahead."

"But—"

Over her startled protest, he ushered her into a dark alley rank with the stench of rotting offal. A rat the size of a cat scurried away as Owen pulled her into the shadow of a mean doorway.

"What on earth?"

He clamped a hand over her mouth. A moment later, a motley crew of six or seven rough-clad men marched past the alley's opening and in silent menace continued along the waterfront.

Only after they had passed by did Owen take his hand away. "Sorry, love. My Irish gut told me that bunch was up to no good."

"They were just walking along quiet as can be."

"Aye. Their silence made me wary. That and the stout sticks they carried. Each one thick enough to crack open a skull."

He dropped a quick kiss on the mouth he'd just uncovered, his gaze raking her face as if searching out her thoughts. "You know I'd never step aside for any man. I feared for you." As he ran a hand over her hair smoothing it, loving it, he grinned of a sudden. "I'm a mighty warrior in truth, so a half dozen ruffians with stout sticks would be even odds. But still . . ."

"No need to remind me that you're a man among men," Grace assured him. "I know so already. Besides, war's not what we're after."

Owen nodded, his head lifting to cock an ear at the distant sounds of a scuffle. "My Irish instinct also tells me we should leave the waterfront entirely. If you can brave the stink, let's go down the length of this alley. I think it ends in another main road."

"If we run, the smell won't last long. Oh," she uttered, aghast at what she'd said.

"Not to worry, love," he said, taking up the bundle yet again. "You run ahead. I'll catch up."

She shook her head. "We'll walk together. We're married. That means we act as one in all ways."

He smiled wryly. "Aren't we having the very devil of a time with one special act?"

"Aye. That's why we need to find a room. Come." She tugged on his hand, hurrying eagerly down the noisome alley. At its end, where the air blew clean, Owen stopped to stamp his injured leg on the pavement.

"Has the feeling gone from it?" Grace asked.

He nodded, annoyed as always at the mention of his mangled calf. She'd have to remember how much he hated the crippled limb and cursed the childhood accident that caused it. A sad happening for sure, but in every other way he was the strongest man she'd ever known.

From this day forward, she wouldn't mention his damaged leg again. Never. Even if it killed her not to. Let him do the telling when it came to the bane of his life . . . but even that thought couldn't mar the beauty of this day, nor her longing to be alone with him. Ignoring his frown, she took him by the arm and murmured, "Husband."

"Wife." His scowl turned into a delighted smile. "I agree, 'tis hard to believe we're really wed."

"I've been your wife since that first time in the cave when we—"

"No need to remind me, love . . . ever. I'll remember that afternoon till I die."

"And not the morning I surprised you there?" She grinned up at him. "Wasn't it even more magical that time?"

He matched her grin with one of his own. "Aye, after I learned a little more?"

Her face must have flushed pink as a dawn. She could feel the heat rise up to her scalp. "There has to be even more to learn. We've only made love—"

"Twice," he finished. "And you want to again?"

She met his eyes and nodded. "I do."

Eyes smoldering, he threw back his head and burst out laughing. "Let's go on. For some reason, the feeling has come back to my leg."

They walked hand in hand for several long, stone blocks but saw no likely lodging place. The rows of sullen-faced stone houses with their shut doors and narrow windows beside and above them, gave no hint of what might lie within.

"We'll have to inquire of someone," Owen said, stealing a glance at Grace from the edge of his eyes. Radiant she was, flushed with excitement at the new sights surrounding them. She had the profile of a goddess, he thought, her nose straight and short, her chin smooth and firm. The recent hunger and sorrow combined had sculpted hollows beneath her cheek bones, the paring away causing her eyes to appear larger than ever. Green pools they were that a man could lose himself in . . .

Her voice brought him back to the moment and the cobblestone walk. "You've been stealing looks at me, Owen, for the past two blocks."

"You're a lovely sight. No wonder."

She shook her head. "Not at all. You're troubled, I can tell."

He put a reassuring arm around her waist. "You read minds now?"

"Aye," she said decisively.

"Well, we do have to find lodgings. Gloaming is setting in, and dark will be on us soon. If we have no luck, we'll go to an inn for the night and try again in the morning."

He sounded more confident than he felt. The inns might be infested with press gang ruffians like the ones they had just given the slip. What landlord could be trusted not to betray him, despite his leg, for a paltry fee? And if anything happened to him, what of Grace's fate? His arm tightened its hold on her. Had he been wrong to bring her so far from everything she had known and loved?

If in Ballybanree she went to her bed hungry, at least she had a familiar face and a kindly word for her supper. Alone in this alien place, not knowing a soul, and with only the four sovereigns knotted in her clothing between herself and the world, what would become of her? He stole a glance at her once more. What a woman he had taken to wife. With night descending and without a place to lay their heads, she looked completely untroubled.

The street they walked along gave way to an open square with a well, a dripping pump in its center, and a swarm of lads pummeling a rolled-up piece of leather, sending it flying with each kick of their feet.

Without warning, the ball came zooming through the air, hitting Owen square in the chest before landing on the cobbles. In a twinkling, Grace stooped over and swiped it up. A second later, a circle of shouting lads surrounded her.

"Give it over, miss."

"It's mine."

"C'mon."

"Whaddya want it for?"

"You gonna steal it or somethin'?" one asked.

"Have you lost your manners entirely?" Grace asked her grubby accuser. "Why would I steal from you?"

"You sound Irish, that's why."

His left hand still holding the bundle, Owen's right hand shot out and lifted the boy off his feet by his shirt front. "Apologize to the lady."

Scared-eyed but sullen, the boy muttered, "Sorry, miss."

Owen lowered him to the ground. Safely planted on his feet once more, he became brave again. "Now hand over my ball."

Grace examined what she held. It was a poor excuse for a play thing. "I will," she said gently, "if in return, you'll tell us where we can find a room to let. We only require a small room. A clean one," she added looking at the dirty, little faces glaring at them.

A hand went up from the smallest of the boys. "My mammy has a room to let. But she's never let to any Irish." He brightened. "She might, though, you're pretty."

"I thank you for that, Master . . ."

"John."

"Well, John," Owen said. "Take us to your mammy. Once there, the lady will return your ball."

A groan went up. Owen laughed. "We're Irish, indeed. But we're not thieves. And we're not stupid, either. Now lead the way, John."

Swift as a deer in flight, with Grace and the boys in hot pursuit, John raced across the square and down a narrow lane. Without slowing his pace, he looked back to see if his friends were following. Though fleet, he was heedless. Like he himself had been, Owen thought, the day he had run so carelessly over the rocks and changed his life forever. But there were no cliffs or shifting boulders here to ensnare a happy, running boy. And then, "Watch out!" Owen shouted a second too late. Still glancing over his shoulder, John had caught his bare foot on a loose paver. It shifted under his weight, catapulting him, spread-eagled, onto the stones.

The boys swirled around him. One nudged him with a foot. "You gonna lay there all day, John? Get up. The game needs finishin.'"

Grace dropped to her knees beside John's limp form. "He's not moving, Owen," she said when he caught up to them.

Owen knelt as well and gently turned the boy onto his back. A good-size lump had already started up on his forehead. "And look at his leg," Owen whispered. "Christ, he's injured his leg."

From the ripped knee of John's breeches, blood trickled along his calf and onto the cobbles. Grace took a linen square from her pocket and dabbed at the wound. "Sure and it's not deep, Owen. He's scraped the skin badly, that's all." Keeping the handkerchief pressed on the wound, she stroked Owen's cheek with her free hand. "He won't be crippled from this, don't fear."

Owen grunted deep in his throat. "Aye. Forgive me. The memory of my own fall on the rocks is bitter. I wouldn't want this wee lad to endure the same."

"Nor will he," Grace said, marveling that Owen could take on Lord Rushmount's threats without a second's hesitation, but the thought of little John limping his way through life turned him pale. Ah, what a fine man she had for a husband.

She looked up at the circle of urchin faces. "We must carry John home. Can you direct us? Here's the ball." She held it out. "It's yours if you do."

"Come on, let's show them," someone shouted, and the whole troupe led them noisily to a bright blue door fronting a narrow row house. "This is it," a lad said, holding out his hand for the ball.

"You know his mammy?" Owen asked.

"We all do."

"Then knock on the door, son. Call out for her."

In a few moments, a plump woman of middle years, a tidy house-wife's cap atop her brown hair and a neat gray frock covering her ample frame, opened the door, the glorious odor of baking bread wafting out the opening with her. At the sight of John limp in Owen's outthrust arms, she let out a scream that echoed down the lane and sent the urchins skittering away like frightened chickens.

"Your boy's had a fall," Owen said. "But he's coming to," he added as John stirred and began to moan.

"Oh, my Johnny! My Johnny!" While Owen held him, the woman ran her hands over the boy's body, feeling him for damage, finally brushing the hair from his eyes, and gasping at the lump rising on his forehead.

Owen cleared his throat. "His leg, too."

"Mam?" John murmured.

"Yes, dearest, yes. I'm here. Mam's here."

The boy raised his arms to his mother, and she took him to her, nestling him against her breast. "What happened?" she asked Owen, and in the next breath, "Who are you to be carrying my son?"

"Owen O'Donnell, at your service, ma'am. This is my wife, Grace. Your son struck his head. Tripped over a paver directing us to you."

"To me? Whatever for?"

"My wife and I require several months' lodging. John here told us you have such."

Her eyes gone wary, the woman didn't answer at once. "You're Irish."

"They gave back the ball," John whispered from her arms.

"You're a fine lad," Grace said to him. "We're that sorry for what happened. Some day I hope to have a son I can be proud of as your mam is of you."

John wriggled out of his mother's grasp and stood up. Despite a knob on his head the size of a goose egg, and a knee covered with drying blood, his face lit up with a grin.

"She's pretty, Mam. She talks pretty, too."

The woman glanced down at Johnny, hugging him tight to her side. "Thank you for bringing the boy home safe. He's a good one, my Johnny." She paused, but only long enough to smile. "My name's Martha. I charge tuppence a week for a room. More for meals."

Grace grinned at Owen. "Could we have a look at the room?"

They followed Martha up the stairs, up and up. In all her life, Grace had never been so high off God's earth. When they finally reached a small room cozied under the rafters, she felt like the soaring eagle she had spied on the pub sign, ready to take flight and wing into the clouds hovering above the window. A glass window it was, with diamond-shaped panes that would let in the light when closed but none of the chill.

Tucked under the slanted ceiling stood a bed wide enough for two. The little space the bed left held a table and two chairs. With backs to them, Grace noted with satisfaction. A peg board for hanging clothes ran the length of one wall, and in a corner a chipped china bowl for washing rested atop a small wooden chest.

It was heaven.

And in England, of all places.

Grace clapped her hands and whirled around. "I love it, I love it!"

"I'm glad you're so well pleased, young missus." Martha righted her cap and picked up the end of her apron, a habit Grace would soon come to recognize. "And you, young mister, are you pleased as well?"

"Indeed. We were hoping for a room just like this. And for someone like you as well."

Martha beamed and rubbed the apron hem even harder. "You're hungry?"

"We are." Owen winked at Grace. "My wife here is especially empty."

"Come downstairs when you're ready. I'll fix something for you," Martha said.

Later, after bowls of Martha's vegetable stew and bread topped with soft cheese they spooned from a crockery pot, she served them tea. When she left them sipping it in the snug kitchen that had Grace fascinated, being half below ground and half above with two small, high windows up near its ceiling, Grace leaned across to Owen. "The leaves are new."

He picked up his cup decorated with tiny blue flowers, the finest china he had ever held in his hands. "But don't you desire more than new tea leaves?" He lowered the cup to the saucer. "Or have you forgotten?"

"Never. How could I when I've longed for you since the night we first spoke? The night I asked you to bury Da." Her eyes threatened tears. "After Rushmount hanged him for taking the deer. But I didn't have to ask. You already had Da safe in the earth. 'Twas then I knew I'd love you forever."

With a finger soft against her skin, he flicked away a tear escaping down her cheek. "No more sorrow for the past, *mavourneen*. We're on our way to a grand new life."

"And starting it in England. How unbelievable."

"Starting it tonight."

He stood, leaving the dregs in his cup, and reached for her hand. She rose to meet him. Together they mounted the stairs to their room and closed the door on the entire world.

Chapter Eight

At high noon, the sun poured through their window, sending shafts of gold onto the bed and into Grace's eyes. She sensed the rays but kept her lids closed. The night had been so perfect, how could the day, even a sun-drenched day, compare?

Owen rolled to his side. Propping his head on an elbow, he gazed down at her. "Do you feel married now?"

Her eyes flared open, straight into his. "How could I not? You were . . ."—she searched for the perfect word—". . . relentless."

He lay back, hands behind his head, elbows out, a smile lifting his lips. "Relentless," he repeated, sounding as if he liked the idea.

Satisfied he looks, Grace thought, like a cat with a bowl of cream. The sight made her happy. Now it was her turn to rest on one elbow and gaze down at her husband's face, its contentment flooding her heart. "No doubt I've you completely worn out."

"Ha!" He seized her, and drawing her under him, kissed her breath away. "A challenge is it, to my manhood?"

"Precisely."

Leaning over her, his dark hair falling into his eyes, his beard stubble rasping at her shoulder, he said, "I'm rested now from all my labor in the night hours."

"I can tell."

"Oh, is that right, married woman. How? Exactly."

Her hand reached down and grasped him. As her fingers encircled him, he drew in a quick breath and moaned aloud.

"That's how," she said.

"You've your facts entirely straight."

She laughed. "So do you."

He joined in her laughter and tossing off the linen sheet, he took her in the sunlight.

———

"Do you think she heard us?" Grace asked him later. She sat on the edge of the bed wrapped in the sheet, brushing the tangles out of her hair.

"Certainly. The woman's not deaf. And your cries reached the heavens."

She dropped the brush to her lap. "No. Surely not. I'll never be able to face her."

"Wee Johnny lad's her son. She must have done the same. She'll understand."

Grace laid the brush down on the rumpled bed. "No one's ever done the same, Owen. Only you. Only me."

He pulled on his breeches and sat next to her, running his fingers through the richness of her hair, watching enthralled as the sheet slipped to her waist. "I suppose all lovers think the same way. That they alone discovered the glory, the excitement." He cupped her breast. "That may be what keeps the world new. Each pair of lovers rediscovering its wonders. Over and over again."

"Over and over?" She raised her arms to her hair.

Undone by the sight, he dropped to his knees in front of her and began to kiss her body as eagerly as if he had not spent the night making love to her. And she to him.

"Forget my words," he said, his voice no more than a hoarse whisper. "You have the right of it. There's only you in the whole world. Only you. Only you."

He unwound the sheet from around her waist. "Sit there like the goddess you are and let me worship you."

———

The long, blue shadows of late afternoon filtered through the diamond panes by the time they were dressed and ready to seek out the company of others. Before they left their room, Owen hid six of the gold sovereigns in a small chink he cut in the wall.

"They'll be safe behind the wash stand until March. That leaves us a few pence and a full sovereign for spending. We'll ask Martha how much extra we'll owe her for our food each week and where you can find those shoes of your heart."

Grace sat tying on her brogues. One already showed a small hole in the sole. "Can we spare the coin for shoes?"

"We can and must. I'm already overdue in keeping my promise to you. And I intend to find work as a blacksmith."

Grace jumped to her feet. "Work for pay? I've never done so before. But I'll do the same. I'm strong. There must be much I can do. Let's go and ask Martha."

"So you can't wait to descend from heaven to the drab realities?"

"Pish. There's nothing drab about our life. Come. Let's ask." She wrinkled her nose. "And find out where to empty the chamber pot."

He laughed. "Even heaven has its reality."

"But that doesn't make it less magical."

"Thank you for saying so, love. Now let's see if the good woman has food for us. I'm starving."

As Grace had discovered yesterday, going down the stairs, narrow and steep as they were, was more difficult than climbing them. No cottage in Ballybanree could boast of stairs, just a ladder, perhaps, for those who had lofts, and one climbed down a ladder backwards holding onto a rung each step of the way. Stairs were different, but with more practice, she'd soon be running up and down like Johnny did last night. For now, she clung to the wall and made her way slowly. Besides, she ached between her legs, and every move rubbed and chaffed. She'd practice on the stairs another time. Once would be more than enough for today.

At the bottom, Martha awaited them. "Well glory be. At last. I was about to send John to see if all was well with you."

Grace felt the heat rise in her face.

At the sight of her blush, Martha peered closer. "How long, may I ask, have the young O'Donnells been married?"

"Four nights," Owen replied, a grin splitting his face wide open.

"Oh, so that's the way of it." Martha lifted her apron and plucked at the hem. "Now you're ready for food. Fair famished, I warrant," she said, her grin nearly matching Owen's.

"We'd welcome some food and a bit of a talk if you can spare the time."

IN HER KITCHEN FILLED WITH THE AROMA of stewed apples, Martha put eggs on to boil and sliced a rye loaf and a thick wedge of cheddar cheese.

Grace sniffed the air. "There's something smelling glorious in here, Martha. Apples and something else. What is it? Sure and it's making my mouth water."

Bent over the boiling pot, Martha looked up in disbelief. "Cinnamon in the apples. You've never smelled cinnamon before?"

Grace shook her head.

"It's a spice like cloves or nutmeg." At Grace's puzzled expression, she said, "You've not had those, either, I suppose."

"Neither one."

"A shame. They give a lovely flavor to food." Martha spooned eggs out of the water, put them in two bowls and placed them on the table. "What else have you done without on that island of yours?"

"Freedom," Owen said taking his place at the table. "That's why we're here. We're seeking it."

Martha sank onto a stool across from him and rested her plump arms on the tabletop. "No one's ever free. Not in this life."

"Not in our country, for certain. But we'll be free in the New World. We'll think and worship as we wish there and live on land of our own."

"The New World. I like the sound of it," Martha said. "So you'll voyage out in the spring, then?"

Owen nodded. "That's our intent. But until a ship leaves, we need to pay you for our food and lodging, and find shoes for Grace and work for me. I'm a blacksmith by trade."

"And work for me, too," Grace said. "Can you help us find such?"

Martha waved a hand at the food. "Eat now and let me think for a while."

They needed no second urging.

She watched their enjoyment without talking, her broad forehead creased in thought. Only when egg shells and cheese rinds and rye crumbs littered the table, did she heave herself to her feet. "Good glory, I forgot to give you a drink to wash down your meal." From an ironstone jug in the scullery, she poured ale into two pewter tankards and hurried them to the table.

She settled back on her stool, her ample buttocks overlapping it on either side. "There's something about you both I trust. Don't ask me why, but I do. So before we speak of business, let me tell you a little about myself. I'm a widow. Johnny's my younger son. I have an older boy, my Billy." Her chin quivered. "He's been gone a twelvemonth now. Fifteen years old he was when I saw him last. Tall and strapping, even then. That must have been his downfall."

"I don't understand," Grace said. "Has something happened to him?"

"He was seized by a press gang."

"A what?"

Martha's face clouded. "Ruffians that roam the docks. Those ships from London clogging the harbor . . . those man o' wars . . . each one carries two, three, four hundred men, maybe more."

"So many?" Grace asked, stunned by the sheer number.

"Aye. Both to sail them and to man the guns in battle. It's a harsh life aboard ship. Men die or desert, God help them, and the captains go mad looking for replacements. I should know. That's how I lost my Billy."

Overcome, she laid her head on her arms and began to sob, her shoulders heaving, her breath shuddering in and out.

"Surely he's not lost to you, Martha," Grace said. "He'll be back one day, pounding on the door when you least expect him."

Martha raised a mottled, tear-stained face and wiped herself dry on her sleeves. "He may, but my William, my husband, died two years ago on board the *Intrepid*. One of the best bosuns who ever set sail, he was. Captain Stanley told me so when he came with William's share from the voyage. An honorable man, Captain Stanley." She spread her arms wide. "That's how I've kept this house for my lads. What with boarders like yourselves, and my baking, and Billy's earnings on the docks." With a stifled sob, she leaned across the table capturing Owen's hand in her own.

"Stay clear of the waterfront. The shipmasters are desperate for fresh crews to fight the Dutch. Until they leave Liverpool, no able-bodied man will be safe." She stopped. "Oh, dear. I didn't mean—"

"No reason to fret, Martha. I injured my leg as a lad. You speak the truth. I'm not able bodied"

"You certainly are," Grace retorted.

Martha drew in a breath and darted a quick glance over at Owen. When their eyes met, they both burst out laughing. After a mortified second, Grace joined in, and soon tears of a different sort began rolling down Martha's face. She wiped them away with the back of a hand. "This calls for a celebration," she said, getting to her feet. "We'll share an ale together, and I'll answer your questions as best I'm able. Though I can tell you now, I know nothing of blacksmithing."

"My first question, Martha, is what will you charge us for food as well as lodging?" Owen asked.

"Now that depends. Can Grace help me with the baking and the delivery of the loaves?"

"Indeed, I can."

"Good. I have two ovens, one in the garden for large orders and this smaller one here in the kitchen. Sometimes I have both fired up at once and could use a helping hand." Martha's eyes narrowed a bit while she calculated. "Let's say a shilling a week—if you can manage it."

"We can," Owen said.

"That will do nicely. Clean bed linen once a month and two full meals a day." She walked to the rear door. "Now come outside and I'll show you where to empty your chamber pot."

Chapter Nine

"**Y**ou're capturing eyes wherever you go, dearie," Martha said one morning a week later. "I've been watching it happen for days now. And it won't do. It won't do at all. We have to make you less conspicuous, so you'll be safer delivering my breads about town."

"Safer?" Grace asked.

"Yes." A forefinger on her chin, Martha surveyed Grace from head to foot. "We'll start with your hair. It must go."

Grace's hands flew up to the tresses cascading over her shoulders. "You mean cut it off?"

"Not at all. But people stare at you. Surely you've noticed."

"I've been aware of glances. But I paid them no mind. I thought it the way of city folk."

"All eyes are drawn to beauty. That's dangerous in a town like Liverpool with men from all over the world walking its streets."

Like the ruffians she and Owen had ducked into the alley to avoid. "Mother of God, every single strand is attached to my head. What's to be done about that?"

"First we'll make plaits and coil them at your nape with bone pins. Then we'll cover your hair with a linen cap."

"But I'll look like an English housewife." The thought appalled her. She'd hate being mistaken for English.

If Martha guessed, she didn't let on. "It's a good thing when a woman walking on English soil looks English," she said firmly. "And your hair's not all that needs changing. Come with me. Come."

She hustled Grace out of the kitchen and, chatting all the way, led her up the stairs to the cramped bedchamber she shared with Johnny. "Since my William and my Billy boy have been gone, the hunger's always on me. I'm so fleshy that when Billy returns, he'll not recognize his mother."

"Oh, indeed, he will. You're the same you. Only there's more of you, perhaps, than there used to be."

A little breathless from her climb, Martha chuckled and flung open the lid of an iron-bound chest at the foot of her bed. Lifting out some neatly folded garments, she laid them on the coverlet, and after a little more lifting and sorting said, "Ah, here it is." She took out a blue linen frock. Though creased from its stay in the chest, it was clean and only slightly faded. "Can you believe I once wore this and only two years past? The cloth is sound, so I thought some day I might fit into it again." She sighed. "But I know better. That day will never come."

She held the frock out to Grace. "It looks to be a good fit for you. Here. Take it, dearie, as a gift."

"A gown?" Grace marveled, holding it up to herself. "I've never had a gown—"

"It's hardly that."

"—with the waist and the skirt attached to each other. Sewn together into one piece. Oh, I love it! And the color, too. Shall I put it on?"

"By all means."

Grace shrugged off her heavy, black woolen skirt and her well-worn waist, its ivory linen overdue for washing, and slipped the blue linen frock over her shift. "It has buttons," she exclaimed, fastening the top, "and a wee pocket hidden in the skirt."

Her face wreathed in smiles, Martha said, "A fine fit, just as I suspected. A bit loose in the waist, but when we tie an apron around you, it'll fit like a tanner's glove."

Grace kissed Martha's cheek then whirled around, setting the light-weight skirt floating about her legs. "It feels wonderful on. Like I'm naked."

"Well, you're not. You're properly dressed. Or you soon will be," her tone leaving no room for doubt. "I'll plait your hair for you, and there's a little cap in here you may have as well. That leaves only shoes and stockings."

Grace glanced down at her scruffy, homemade brogues, their skins soiled and stretched and worn to a nub. "There's a wee hole in one of them."

"I'm not surprised, what with you walking over rough cobbles for days. You need leather soles and heels to take the wear."

"Heels and buckles." Grace's eyes shone then quickly dimmed. "But a cobbler needs days to make a pair. I tried in Cork City, and—"

"I know a place we can go to where I wager you'll find a pair this very morning. But first, if you'll sit on this chest, I'll show you how to dress your hair English style."

———————

GRACE COULD HARDLY WAIT FOR OWEN to return from seeking work. What would he think of her transformation? He had never seen her in shoes and thin, white stockings and a blue frock. With all that and her hair tidied under the cap, chances were he'd hardly recognize her.

She kept raising her skirt out of the way so she could stare at her shiny, black shoes with their gleaming pewter buckles. They were exactly the shoes of her dreams, hardly worn and fitting perfectly, with heels that made her taller than God intended her to be, and above them her ankles neat in their city hose. Two pair she had and garters holding them snug just below her knees.

Martha had been right about the clothes making her less conspicuous. With the cap covering her hair and proper English garb, she had attracted far less notice as they walked about delivering Martha's bread. Occasionally, she felt the eyes of a man lingering on her face or her snug frock, but the blatant stares of yesterday were gone. I fit in, she thought, not entirely comfortable with the idea, but Martha had lived in Liverpool her whole life long and her judgment could be trusted.

To think that kind and wonderful Martha belonged to the hated English race. So good people, as well as bedeviling ones, lived everywhere. A sobering realization.

At dusk, before gloaming melted into darkness, she heard Owen's unmistakable step on the cobbles. She ran to open the door. At the sight of him, all thought of her new clothes fled her mind. He looked exhausted, with shadows ringing his eyes, and his uneven gait more pronounced than usual.

"*Mavourneen*," she whispered.

Startled by the Gaelic, he stopped in the middle of the lane. "Grace?"

She nodded. "None other."

His glance swept over her. Head cocked to the side, he described a circle with one finger. "Turn around."

She did so, letting the skirt whirl about her calves. "Well, what do you think?"

"I love the frock. I love the shoes and stockings. And I love you, but . . ."

"But what?"

"The cap. I have no love for that."

"Nor I, but Martha said the cap will be better for walking about the town."

"Ah, I understand. She's correct. But while in the house will you take it off?" He paused. "And never wear it in bed."

"You have my promise." To make her word come true, she untied the thin strap under her chin and tucked the cap in her skirt pocket. "Better?"

"Nearly," he said, drawing her inside and closing the door. His hands fumbled at her hair. "The plaits. Can you undo them?"

"I'll just uncoil them. Martha worked so hard at making me over I can't offend her." She loosened the hairpins and put them in her pocket with the cap. The freed plaits, their ends curling defiantly, fell across her breast.

He touched the end curls with a single finger. "'Twill do until later when we're alone."

Telling herself a hot meal would repair the fatigue on his face and in his step, she said, "We've a stew tonight, and the best wheat bread you've ever tasted. Come, Johnny's at table already."

He resisted the tug of her hand. "Last night, I spied a rain barrel out back. 'Tis nearly dark now. No one will see if I strip bare and have a good wash before supper. But I'll need a scrap of—"

"—cloth to dry with. I'll run up to the room and get it for you and bring clean smallclothes and your other shirt."

"How very wifely you're being."

"You don't like that?" In mock challenge, she rested her hands on her hips and swayed them a bit from left to right.

"I adore it, as you know full well. Now start up the stairs so I can look at your high heels and your ankles as you climb. 'Twill be a whole new experience for me."

"Humph," she said, relieved that he felt inclined to jest. Surely the wash and the meal would wipe away the wear from his face. She paused halfway up. Was it simple fatigue she was seeing in him or something more? On an impulse, she glanced back over her shoulder and caught him unaware, looking as if the entire world rested on his shoulders.

"No," she said, the short, English word crisp and definite. "I won't allow it."

Owen had stripped to his smallclothes and folded his breeches over a chair. Their single candle threw his silhouette against the opposite wall, exaggerating his form into a looming shadow. At Grace's "No" he froze in place, then snuffed out the candle with his thumb and forefinger and dropped his smallclothes to the floor.

He didn't go to Grace, but stood still and naked in the darkness at the foot of the bed. His voice alone came to her. "Understand this, for I will never repeat it again. I am your husband, crippled leg or no."

"I—"

"I'm not through. As such, I will do everything in my power to please you. But . . ." he let out a ragged breath ". . . there will be times when I cannot please you, when I must do what has to be done. This is one of those times. Do you understand me?"

She didn't answer.

"Do you?" Stubborn as ever, he wasn't about to give up his train of thought.

"No, as God's in His heaven, I do not."

"Then understand this. There *is* something I will repeat till you tire of hearing it. I love you, Grace, more than life. If you love me in return, you'll not ask me to do less than a man must do."

"But we've always done without money. I don't care about money, just about you. The thought of being separated for months and months . . ."

"If you'd been with me these past days, you'd know that traveling with this tinsmith is the best work I'm likely to find."

"But—"

"No one wants an Irishman. The minute I open my mouth, I'm damned by it. And as much as it pains me to say so, my leg is no help to me either. This tinsmith, now, this Roger Preston, had me shoe his horse for him. When he saw my skill, he agreed to pay me six pence a day and my food. Lodgings, too, when we can find them. He seems an honest soul."

"*Seems.*"

"Aye. The harsh life in Ballybanree may have cost us much, but it sharpened our wits. I trust the man. We'll take his team and cart and make his yearly rounds about the countryside. He says he has people awaiting him in villages to the east and south of here. They save broken pots and plows, even their weapons for him to repair. And there'll be horses and oxen in need of shoeing."

Grace tossed off the sheet and knelt in the center of the bed facing his shadow. "I'll come, too. I'll cook for you and the tinsmith. I'll wash our clothes in the streams. I'll forage for kindling. We'll be together as we intended. Day and night. Not you gone to only God knows where, leaving me here alone."

"No." His voice came out of the dark, hard and unyielding as flint. "No. You will not come with me."

"How can you refuse me? I'm your *wife*. Not some baggage you can dump like . . . like a bundle dropped on the cobbles."

"You're sputtering."

"Don't you jest. I'll not have it. To be left alone is not what I bargained for."

"Is it not, little wife?"

"No."

"There's that English word again. I fear we're becoming overly fond of it."

She ignored his weak attempt at humor. "I bargained for a *whole* New World, Owen. With you. Not life alone in an English port city." Without the moon lending light, it was impossible to see his face clearly, but his deep sigh told her a scowl was upon him.

"The last thing on this earth I want to do is leave you, Grace. You must know that. But I'll not have you endure the hazards of the road. Two men alone in a tinsmith's cart can fend for themselves, but the life would be harsh for a woman. You'll be safer here with Martha and more comfortable through the winter months."

"Safe?" She clenched her fists by her sides. "Everybody wants to keep me safe. It was not the need for safety that brought me here. As you well know."

"Grace."

"Don't speak my name. I will not answer to it. Never did I think we'd part. Except for the death of one of us. Only for that."

"Grace."

"Stop." She clapped her hands over her ears to block out his voice. The bed settled as he sat on the edge by her side. His hand reached out and found her shoulder. She shrugged it off. "Now I'll say the words *you* don't wish to hear. Don't touch any part of me. I will not have you."

"There's no need to—"

"You want to go from me then go. Now. Why wait for morning? Go now."

"This is not the way for us to part."

"Is there a good way? I don't know of one."

"Grace, you cannot spend the winter in an open cart."

"What of your welfare through the winter months? Am I not as strong as you?"

He blew out an exasperated breath. "In this moment you are stronger by far. But I must do this, Grace," he declared, his voice softening. "We'll need my wages, or we'll arrive at our new home empty-handed. In the meantime, you'll fare well here with Martha. And I'll be back in time to book our passage. Robert Preston has a plot of land to put to the plow, so we'll return by February at the latest. While I'm gone, take one of the sovereigns from the hiding place, buy a traveling chest and fill it for us. Linens, bedding, kitchen tools, and some warm clothing. I've heard winters in the New World are fierce." He stroked her hair, his hand trembling. "Let's use the next few months wisely. And this night. We can use it wisely as well."

Hurt to the quick by his resolve, she turned her heart into stone, willing away tenderness, forcing her mind to resist the reason in his words and the necessity of his purpose, filling herself, brain, body and spirit with a cold despair she knew she'd come to hate, but God help her, she was powerless to resist it.

"This room holds nothing more for you tonight, Owen O'Donnell. Nothing."

Chapter Ten

FOR THE THOUSANDTH TIME, GRACE FLAILED HERSELF with the same question: *How could you let him go the way you did? With bitterness spewing from your mouth. Without a kind word of farewell. Without a Godspeed. Without an I love you.*

The hell she'd been in ever since was her punishment and well deserved, for certain. Worse, in the small hours, before the morning sun lit her room, she would give herself over to the bleakest thought of all. What if Owen never returned? What if she never knew whether he lived or had died? Then this hell of unknowing would last until her own death, and that punishment she would deserve as well.

She shivered into her clothes. The rays of light fingering the window this Christmas morning showed she'd slept later than she should have. But for once, the solitary bed had been a welcome haven after an endless week of running about town delivering Martha's breads and pasties to the inns and alehouses surrounding the docks.

In celebration of Christmas, she'd had a warm bath last night. After Johnny went to bed, she'd tugged the big wooden tub out of the scullery close to the kitchen fire and filled it with buckets of steaming water. By tenting her knees, she had just enough room to sit and let the steam surround her and take away the aches and stiffness, but nothing could take away her longing—Christmas and no Owen in it.

She had to hurry dressing for church service, a Protestant church service. But did it matter where she prayed? Back in Ballybanree, Father Joyce had said only one God ruled the heavens. A noble concept, though she would never know a heaven unless Owen returned to her safe and sound.

In the freezing air of the unheated garret, the black wool skirt and the thick stockings she'd knitted for herself warmed her legs and feet. She donned the new waist she'd sewn and hurried into her lined doublet, its gray sleeves cunningly slashed and pieced with black inserts. With unerring accuracy, Martha had steered her to a used clothes stall and haggled with the vendor until the price of the garment fit Grace's slim pocketbook. A good thing she had. Liverpool's winter blew cold and bitter damp, far worse even than the winds off Connaught's rocky coast.

The tips of her fingers had lost their feeling in the icy room. At this rate, she'd never get her hair tamed and neat in time for church service. She collected her brush, hairpins, and the cap. Martha's fire would be ablaze. She'd tidy her hair there and wash her face and hands on a scrap of wet cloth.

The moment she opened her chamber door, a sweet, spicy aroma greeted her. The house almost always smelled of good cooking, but this morning the odor wafting through the air was more enticing than usual. She hurried down the stairs into the kitchen.

"What is that—?"

"Happy Christmas," Martha and John called out in unison.

"Happy Christmas."

Their smiles came close to splitting their faces, and then she saw the oranges—three of them—one at each place. And at her seat, a small package wrapped in clean cloth and tied with a green ribbon.

"Open it, Grace," Johnny said, his excitement barely contained. "It's a present."

"She can see that, son," Martha said, keeping busy by the fire.

Grace sat and picked up her orange. Holding it to her nose, she inhaled deeply, delighting in its perfume.

"They're from Spain," Johnny said.

"I know. But I don't know how they taste."

"Delicious. I've had one before. Try it."

"I will, indeed, and thank you. 'Tis a rare treat. But first, shall I open my present?"

"Yes!"

She untied the ribbon and unfolded the cloth. At her quick gasp of pleased surprise, Johnny exclaimed, "She likes it, Mam."

"I love it." She held up the white linen collar with its edging of pointed lace. 'Tis the most beautiful gift I've ever received."

"It's for that new gray frock you've been sewing on," Martha said. "It will set it off nicely and your pretty face as well."

Grace stood to kiss Martha's cheek and catch Johnny in a quick hug. "My friends. My *English* friends," she marveled. "I love you both." She never thought she'd say such a thing, but her words rang true. She loved these English people.

If God could create that miracle, surely he would create another and bring Owen back to her soon. Heartened, she said, "I have something for you as well. I'll just be a minute." More buoyant than she'd felt in weeks, she ran up the stairs and returned with two pair of knitted mittens. She held them out shyly. "For you. I had nothing to wrap them in."

"We don't need wrapping, do we, Mam?" Johnny slipped a small hand into one.

"Not at all. They'll keep our fingers warm all the way to church."

"And back," Johnny added. "We're having plum pudding with dinner today."

"Is that what's causing the heavenly aroma?"

"It is. Have you never had plum pudding before?"

"Never."

"And not an orange, either. What kind of country is your Ireland?"

"A beautiful country."

"Then why have you and Owen left it?"

"We seek a new country where we'll be free. Where we can claim a plot of land as our own. God willing, Owen and I will spend our lives there together. We beg the Almighty for that, and I pray He will return Owen to me very, very soon."

Johnny's face turned solemn, as if he understood.

She bent to kiss the boy's cheek. *Dear God, I've already said my Christmas prayers. The visit to the Protestant church will be an outing only. A lonely one without my beloved.*

TWO WEEKS LATER, REED'S ALEHOUSE DOORS had just opened for the day when Grace walked in with her basket of bread. No customers were about, just the tapster, a new man she hadn't met before.

"I'm the bread girl," she said. "I've three loaves for you."

"Five, I'm thinking," he said, and leaning across the rough-hewn bar, he put both heavy hands on her breasts.

Not moving an inch, she looked down at the red knuckles and dirt-rimmed nails resting on the front of her doublet. Then slowly and deliberately, she looked up into the tapster's leering face. "If my husband saw your hands there, he'd chop them off. And likely not stop at your hands." With her eyes never leaving him, she watched his fingers slide away and his mouth twist into a sneer. "You owe me twelve pence," she said before he could voice a retort.

"No, six for three loaves."

"And six more for the insult."

"Bloody likely. Who do you think you are, the queen of the realm?"

"I'm someone who'll never be back with another loaf of the best bread in town. Explain that to your Master Reed."

The sneer slid from his face as quickly as his hands had slid from her breasts. Reaching into the till under the bar, he took out six pence and whacked them onto the bar top. "That's all you'll get from me, you Irish tart."

She picked up the coins. "That's enough. You've paid for the insult to my person. Since you don't want the bread, good day to you."

As she turned to go, her back as straight as her outrage could make it, he shouted, "Wait up." He reached into his pocket and whacked down another six pence. "Hand over the loaves."

She picked up these coins as well. "Gladly." Folding back the cloth covering the basket, she removed three crusty loaves and placed them in front of him. "And here's your insult money." She flipped the six coins back onto the bar where they rolled about before rattling to a stop. "Keep them. And keep your hands off me in future."

She went to walk away, the bakery basket over her arm, but thought better of it. This was not Lord Rushmount with the power of life and death over her and the ones she loved. The tapster was not her enemy. Why make him one?

She retraced her steps and held out a hand. "Shall we shake and forget?"

He wiped a hand on his stained breeches and stuck it out. "Why not? You bested me fair and square, the prettiest girl who ever did so." He roared, his guffaws greeting the first customers of the day as Grace ducked out the open door and made her escape.

So that was the way of it? Take no abuse from any man. Stand your ground and then make the peace. But while she trudged the Liverpool lanes on her rounds, the basket becoming lighter, the purse hidden in the pocket of her skirt becoming heavier, her triumph gradually faded away.

Owen, too, was making rounds about the countryside. What abuses was he enduring, what with the Irish lilt to his speech and his leg always the butt of ridicule from lesser men?

With her heart heavier than the purse jouncing against her thigh, she sold the last of the loaves. On the way back to Martha's, a flurry of activity near the quay caught her attention. In the midst of the usual dockside hubbub with its welter of humanity, its carts and drays and piled up crates and barrels, a handsome carriage drawn by a matched pair of high-stepping blacks splashed over the cobbles, coming to a stop in front of a moored sloop.

The ship, sleek and black as the horses, looked somewhat like the sloop she and Owen had taken from Dublin. But this one flaunted sails white as the cloud puffs above; its brass fittings gleamed in the thin January sun, and its decks, as she could see even from the quayside, had been scrubbed to a shine.

She watched the crew lower a gangplank to the dock. At that, the footman jumped down from his high seat to open the carriage door, and like a soldier facing his commander, stood at attention in his smart green livery piped with orange.

Grace drew closer. Someone important must be aboard the sloop. Empty basket forgotten on her arm, she waited to see. After several minutes, a plainly dressed, elderly woman came out on deck carrying an infant swathed in lacy shawls, a girl child by the look of the frills enveloping her.

Holding the child close, the woman stepped carefully along the planking. The footman came forward to take her arm and help her into the carriage. Could this woman be the cause for all this fuss? It didn't seem likely. And then Grace saw the reason: A beautiful, fair-haired lady dressed in light blue silk, the quilted doublet topping her gown fashioned of the same sky blue, and a bonnet in blue as well, its long, white feather trailing over the brim before coming to rest on one slender shoulder.

Grace drew in a breath at the sheer wonder of such clothes. In the next second, that same breath rushed out of her body as a tall man, straight of back, arrogant of stride, emerged on deck and, taking the lady's arm, assisted her down the planking and into the waiting carriage.

Dear God. Lord Rushmount. Bewigged and arrayed as never in Ireland, but Rushmount all the same.

After a few clipped words to the footman, he climbed into the carriage with the two women and the infant. The servant leaped up next to the driver, and with a quick flick of the reins, the horses sprang into motion, and the carriage and its occupants drove off.

Although her heart had begun a wild beating, Grace was sure Rushmount hadn't spied her in the crowd thronging the dock. In her English clothes and cap, he wouldn't have recognized her in any case. Yet the sense of safety she had begun to build like a wall around herself evaporated. Nothing had changed. Like a fool, she had allowed Martha's kindness to lull her into a false security. She should have known England held no safety for two Irish runaways.

Pulse pounding, she walked off the quay, mindless of the jostling crowd, or the noise, or the sea breeze plucking at her clothes. Slowly, she made her way up Church Street to Martha's lane. She could tell no one what she had seen. No connection, however trivial must be made between herself and his lordship.

Still, he *had* driven off. But where had he gone? And what if he returned and recognized her as she walked about the city? What protection would she have against his accusations? This was his land and these were his people, not hers. At his slightest word, she and Owen both would be in mortal danger.

Without knowing Rushmount's whereabouts, she'd not have a peaceful day between now and the time the *Seafarer* left for the New World. With a weary step, she continued trudging toward home. No, not home. Martha was not her mother, after all, nor young Johnny her brother.

Only Owen was family. He alone. And God alone knew where he was and how much she longed for him.

CHAPTER ELEVEN

JANUARY SLOWLY SLIPPED AWAY, each of its endless, dark days blurred by tension and longing. Late one afternoon, walking up Martha's lane, the empty bread basket over her arm, her purse filled with coins, Grace noticed the sun still shone, its light dim and gray but not totally gone. *The days were growing longer.*

She burst into the kitchen with more energy than she'd felt in weeks and dropped the basket and the purse on the table. "Do you know if February is here? The days are brighter. I'm sure they are."

Martha looked up, pink-faced from the oven's heat. "I'm glad you're back, Grace."

"Aye, but—"

"I'm not certain of the month, dearie. Johnny might know, but he's off with those urchins somewhere just when I need him."

Grace removed her doublet and cap. She pocketed the hairpins and began releasing the plaits, letting her hair fall around her shoulders and down her back the way Owen loved it. For surely, with the days growing longer, he'd soon be home.

"I'll make us some tea," Martha said, "and a bite to eat." She hesitated. "I hate to ask, dearie, but there's another delivery to make."

Grace shook her hair free. "So late?"

"Aye. To the Binnacle Inn near the wharf. They've a houseful of travelers and running out of wherewithal to feed them. I promised their boy I'd send six loaves before dark." She opened the oven, slid in a wooden paddle, pulled out the loaves, and poked one with a straw.

"Done. As soon as they're cool enough to handle, will you make the trip?"

Weary though she was, at the sight of Martha's worried face, Grace said, "I've nothing to do for the rest of the evening except wait for Owen." She laughed, but there was little humor in the sound.

"Don't worry, dearie. It's almost planting season. He said the tinsmith puts in a crop. They'll be back any day now." Martha cut a thick slice off yesterday's rye loaf and slathered it with butter. "Will you eat this before you leave? You've a long walk ahead of you."

"I'll wait till I come back. Then we can enjoy our tea together." Grace slipped the loaves of still warm bread into her basket. With only one stop to make, she wouldn't bother to replait her hair. No need. If she hurried, she'd be back before dark.

"See if the innkeeper will pay a little extra for the inconvenience," Martha said as Grace shrugged into her doublet. "If so, it's yours to keep."

With a quick kiss for Martha's cheek, Grace left on her errand. The salty air had turned chill, its raw breeze lifting her hair and whipping at her skirt. She hurried down the slope toward the waterfront, clutching the basket close, grateful for the bread's warmth against her side. The sunlight was fading fast as she wended her way, anxious to make the delivery and get back to Martha's kitchen and tea. Was Owen as chilled at this moment as she? Was he huddled somewhere in the tinsmith's wagon, thinking of her, longing for the day when—

"Watch it, miss," a man warned, looking not at all displeased that she had nearly bumped into him on the narrow walkway. She'd better keep her mind on her task and not be dreaming, but how hard it was to put Owen from her thoughts.

Owen, my love.

The alley they had darted into their first day in Liverpool loomed ahead. She peered down it. The stench hadn't diminished, but it looked deserted and led to the main road by the quay. The alley had kept them safe once before. She'd risk dashing down it, cutting off the long, round-about route to the inn, the better to get back before dark.

Halfway down the alley, she spied a pile of rags in a doorway. It stirred, and a dirty, bare foot jutted out. She ran faster, the breads jostling each other, the basket banging against her hip.

At first, in her haste, she didn't hear the horse coming up behind her until the sound of hooves striking the cobbles caught her alarmed attention. She glanced back over her shoulder. A black stallion was bearing down, racing along as swift as if the alley were a highway.

Where to go? No doorway ahead, no niche, no depression in a wall. She'd be crushed under those powerful legs. Could the rider not see her?

She pressed against a soot-smeared wall, the basket swaying on her arm. If the horse caught at the basket in passing, she'd be pulled into harm's way, but before she could stoop to place it at her feet, the stallion was upon her, so close that even in the dim light she could see the whites of its eyes and the flecks of sweat beading its coat. Dear Mother, she could die under those hooves. But of a sudden, the horse careened to a halt, the savage hand of the rider sending its forelegs flailing the air before it skidded to a stop.

Grace raised terrified eyes. "Rushmount!"

In his aristocrat's formal wig and clothing, he sat his saddle with ease, on his face the look of a sleek cat that had cornered its mouse.

She dropped the basket and began to run. In an instant, the stallion blocked the alley. Ross Rushmount leaned down, and with a single arm, pulled her up onto the saddle in front of him where he held her like a carving in a vise. "Don't struggle. You're not going anywhere without me."

She pulled in a deep breath, ready to expel it in a scream. His arm hardened. "If you cry out, I'll kill you."

"Kill me, then."

He laughed. "You don't want to die, Grace."

Holding her tight enough to crush her ribs, he switched the reins to his left hand. With his right, he reached into his high boot top and grasped the handle of a dirk. He pressed it to her throat. "One scream and I cut. I won't be thwarted this time."

Frantic in his grip, she struggled to break free.

"Stop it, you little fool." The tip of the dagger pricked her earlobe. "You want me to go deeper?"

Was she ready to prove his bluff? To die? To be sliced in the ribs and tossed to the ground while he rode away before anyone knew what he'd done? To all of the hasty, barely formed questions, the answer was the same. *No.*

They had reached the end of the alley. He cantered out into the quayside sending passersby scurrying away as the horse took the center of the road. Reining the stallion to the right, he moved away from the bustling dock with its moored trading vessels, inns, pubs and bawdy houses, into an area Grace had not traversed on foot.

With every clop of the stallion's hooves, they rode farther away from the sights she knew. Despite the knife's steely presence against her side, she had to free herself. She had to. But how? Then an idea struck her, causing her heartbeat to quicken. If she pretended to faint, he might loosen his grip, and she could wrench free before he could stop her. It was worth a try.

She slumped back against him, closed her eyes, and let her hands flutter down, limp to her sides.

"Ah, that's much better," he said. "Why fight when you've no hope of winning?"

He cradled her to his chest, wrapping both arms securely about her, holding the reins, the accursed knife in front of him in plain sight. She could have sworn he dropped a kiss on her hair. Good God in heaven, the man thought she was giving in to him. Either he had never attended a fainting woman before or her play acting wasn't convincing. Whatever the reason, her ruse had failed. From beneath lowered lids, she glanced out over the horse's bobbing mane. A procession of stately houses stretched ahead, their stone faces broad and high with fan lit doorways looking out to sea. As long as she could see water to the left, she'd find her way back, no matter how far they traveled. But what if Owen came home this very night and found her missing? Believing that in her anger, she had deserted him? The thought was not to be borne. Aye, she had to get away, and soon.

Rushmount slowed their pace and loosened his grip on her. Had he dropped his guard? She could only hope. Breathing deep and full, she concentrated on strength for one powerful sudden lunge. She would yank herself forward in the saddle then leap to the ground the instant his arms slackened their hold. Her pulse quickened. She might escape yet. But as her muscles tensed for flight, his grasp tightened, and the knife again found her throat.

"I knew you hadn't fainted," he hissed in her ear. "Not you. Now sit still or you'll come to harm. We're almost there."

She fell back against him, overcome for a moment. She was his prisoner. Nothing could save her, only her own wits.

At the next curve in the road, he reined to a stop in front of a grand row house with a glossy door sheltered under an arched portico. Tucking the knife back into his boot, he slid from the saddle taking her with him, his iron hand clutching her upper arm. She glanced frantically about but saw no passersby, no men on horseback, only one carriage off in the distance. It was now or never, but no one, she realized, with a sinking heart, would hear a cry for help.

"Don't bother to scream," Rushmount said, as if divining her thoughts. "There's no one to hear."

Never loosening his hold, he pulled her with him to the top of the wide, shallow stairs and lifted the brass knocker, banging it with all his might against the heavy door.

"Damn the man," he muttered as they waited in the gathering dark, the fishy odor of low tide filling their nostrils.

Through the narrow side windows, a candle flickered, the bolt slid back, and the door opened a tentative crack. Rushmount shoved it wide, nearly knocking the candle out of his footman's hand. "See to the horse," he barked to Thomas who, after a startled glance at Grace, placed the candle on its stand and hurried to obey. "Sleep in the stable tonight. I don't want to be disturbed," Rushmount ordered.

Grace tried to catch the man's eye, but he scurried down the steps without another glance in her direction. With his free hand, Rushmount banged the door shut and shot the bolt, the sound echoing through the silent rooms. "If I release you, don't do anything stupid."

"Release me?" A spurt of hope pulsed for an instant then died stillborn. He would let go of her arm, that's all.

"Walk ahead, into the room on the right." He stayed close behind her, carrying the candlestick into a cavernous chamber so strange in the flickering light she forgot her fears for a moment. *The room was filled with ghosts.*

She looked around, startled. Everywhere, white sheeting shrouded the furnishings, turning them into mysterious, hidden objects. She could only guess at what wondrous things they concealed. Using the single flame, Rushmount ignited several candles on a gleaming, many-branched candelabrum. In this brighter light, she could make out the lofty ceiling crisscrossed with intricate beaming such as she had never seen the like of, and walls embellished with elaborate paneling also draped, here and there, in white. The coverings might be hiding canvas oil paintings. She had heard tell of them.

She turned to Rushmount. "What manner of place is this?"

"Oh, you wish to converse? Excellent."

"I merely wondered what sort of prison I'm in."

He smiled slightly. "A prison? Hardly. It's the seldom-used house of a friend . . . you needn't know his name. He allows me the use of it when

I'm in town on business." He pointed to one of the shrouds. "Sit. I can assure you there's a seat underneath."

She took a step backward, perching gingerly on the edge of a padded chair. He moved the light closer, to a shrouded tabletop. "Now that I've answered your question, do the same for me. What brings you to Liverpool?"

She glared at him. She'd tell him nothing.

He didn't sit, but stood over her, a fragile film of patience on his face. From it, she knew he wouldn't wait overly long for a reply. Her mind raced through possible tales, anything but the truth. He must never know where she and Owen were headed. That was their precious secret, not for his ears, not for his thwarting.

"You're taking your time answering," he said. "Preparing a lie for me, are you?"

She tossed her hair back. "Not at all. Why should I lie to the likes of you?"

"The likes of me, is it?" He stepped closer. "What are you doing here, in England of all places?" His lip curled. "The nation that stole your ancestral lands."

"Aye, the very one."

He laughed. "We both know differently, but go on, I'm waiting."

"Owen and I are married. We're here on a job of work. He's a fine blacksmith . . . the pay is far better than in Ballybanree."

"You're married?"

"Aye."

"That doesn't matter."

"It does to me. And to my husband who is looking for me at this very minute."

"He'll never find you." Rushmount seized the candelabrum. "Walk out to the hall ahead of me. Go up the stairs."

"I will not."

"You will, or I'll summon Thomas to rouse the constable. I'll claim I found a burglar in my house."

She hesitated, weighing her options. In the hands of the authorities, she wouldn't have a chance against a lord of the realm. He could accuse her of anything, theft for certain, even witchcraft, and be believed. He could have her hanged like her Da before her.

With the burning candles held high, he came closer to her, the tapers creating a pool of light that revealed a tall, hard-muscled man determined to have what he wanted. Her eyes flickered over his face. From its hint of a smile, she doubted he would call the constable. His revenge would be of a different sort. Upstairs. Her thoughts beat in her skull like caged birds. She *must* escape.

"Upstairs," he repeated, his expression void of humor.

What lay ahead she could well imagine. For now, she would have to do as he demanded, but with every step she would look for a way to escape.

When they had climbed the broad staircase to the first floor, he said, "Down the corridor. The last door on the left." The moving light spread uneven shadows along the way. It was like walking through an alley without stench but with its own terrible menace.

At the last door, she stopped. "Go in," he ordered.

She turned the handle. *Dear God, help me.*

The door swung open on noiseless hinges. What lay inside took her breath away.

The shrouds were gone, no ghosts in here, only a demon of a bed. Bigger than any she had ever seen, it dominated the chamber with its hangings and coverlets and heaped pillows. A fire burned in the grate taking the chill from the air. The window shutters were closed against the night.

The same lustrous blue cloth draping the bedstead had been fitted to the walls. On them hung uncovered paintings, one of a beautiful young woman, others of country scenes, their meadows and trees as real as life.

Rushmount set the blazing candelabrum on a table by the bed. The sound of its heavy metal base striking wood pulled her back to the present. As beautiful as the chamber might be, it was her prison, nothing more.

He walked away from the bed. Yanking the elaborate wig off his head, he tossed it over a high-backed chair, uncovering his own short-cropped, dark hair. He unbuttoned his black doublet, pitched it at the chair then loosened the linen stock at his throat. "Do the same," he said.

She stood unmoving in the center of the room.

"Take off your doublet. No need for it in here. My man Thomas has laid a good fire." He unfastened the wrists of his white sleeves and rolled them up to his elbows.

She continued to stare at him without moving.

"Take off your doublet. Or I will."

Under his watchful eyes, Grace began fumbling at the buttons, twisting them open slowly. He followed every move of her fingers. "Now your waist, or whatever you call that upper garment."

"No."

"And then your skirt and shoes and stockings."

"I'll do no such thing."

"Fine. I'll be happy to oblige." But instead of making good his threat, he crossed to a brightly painted clothes press at the foot of the bed, and flinging open the lid, bent down to search through its contents.

Was this her chance? She crept toward the door, stealing but a few paces away before he straightened and turned, holding a green frock in his hands. "I knew I had seen Lady Carolyn in a green gown."

She froze.

He shot her a disapproving glance. "What are you waiting for? Strip."

She shook her head.

He walked toward her, the gown draped over one shoulder. "I'll tear off every stitch if you don't begin immediately." He smiled. "I'd enjoy that, but I'm not sure you would, and I want your pleasure above everything." His smile deepened. "Even my own."

Was his smile meant to disarm her? What kind of idiot did he take her for?

"Start."

He stood mere inches in front of her with no intention, Grace knew, of moving until she did his bidding. What chance did she have against him? Over six feet tall, and though not as powerfully built through the arms and shoulders as Owen, he'd lifted her effortlessly into the saddle, his grip merciless. As he watched her, a frown replaced the smile on his lean face. For a sliver of a second, she wondered if other women might admire that face with its hawk nose and sharp cheeks angling down to a wide slit of a mouth. The eyes, dark like Owen's, glittered with nervous irritation in a way her husband's never did, penetrating what they observed, violating its essence, possessing it with every heated glance. He was a greedy man, and God help her, she was his next feast.

She began to remove her clothes.

When she stood shivering in her shift despite the fire, he said, "Enough. Any more and I'll forget about my little game. Here, go behind the screen in the corner, take off that sorry excuse for an undergarment and put on this gown."

Without touching him, she took the gown from his outstretched hands, the fabric marvelously soft against her fingers. Velvet, Martha had declared such to be when she saw its like in the stalls. She went behind the screen, grateful for its shelter, and removing her shift, quickly dropped the gown over her head. The lady it belonged to must be slighter than herself. The sleeves and waist clung tightly, or perhaps such a fit was intentional, but surely not that of the bodice. Cut low in a deep round curve, it barely covered her breasts. They rose above the rich cloth, white as rising moons. How could she face Rushmount's gaze so exposed?

You fool, she chided herself. He's only begun. Would he let her go . . . at the end . . . or kill her? If he did, no one would be the wiser. Thomas, his footman, would never betray him. Should she die here, Owen would live his life in anguish, wondering all his days if she had met with foul play or had left him on purpose, each possibility worse than the other, each one tearing him in two.

Whatever evil Rushmount had in mind, whatever happened this night, getting back to Owen was all that mattered, nothing else—not her virtue, not her pride, not any humiliation Rushmount could devise.

Armed with that intent, she came out from behind the screen, her back straight, her pale breasts curving above the velvet neckline, her hair cascading unbound over her shoulders.

He had turned to stir the fire. The velvet rustled as she moved and he swiveled about, poker in hand, his eyes raking over her, a whisper of a sigh escaping from his mouth. "You are what I thought you would be. Magnificent. My barefoot queen." He dropped the poker to the hearth and came forward.

"I'm not yours. Never think that. Never. I'm only your prisoner. And a mighty coward you are for seizing a helpless woman."

"*Ha. Helpless?* You're the most powerful woman I've ever known."

"Sure and you lie. I have no power. If I did, I'd leave at once."

"No." He shook his head. "I will have you. I've wanted you since the first night I ever saw you. On that sorry excuse for a road outside of Ballybanree. When you found my overturned carriage and came to my rescue. Do you remember that night?"

"Aye. The night you named me thief."

He took her in his arms, his lips close to hers, his eyes intent on her alone. "I was right. You are a thief."

She struggled to pull free. "I am no such thing."

"Grace." The reverent way in which he spoke her name gave her pause. She met his glittering eyes. "You have stolen me."

Though startled by his sudden tenderness, she retorted, "You've the truth all twisted. I'm the prisoner here, not you."

"You're not the least bit afraid, are you?"

"Not at all," she lied.

He grinned. "Then come and sit by the fire for a while. I want to admire you in that gown. I've dreamed of you in green velvet. With shoes on your feet, I will admit, and your hair dressed high and jewels at your throat." His grin broadened while his heated gaze played over her. "But I prefer this version."

When she didn't move, he beckoned. With a sigh, she came forward and sat by the fire.

"Good. Have you ever tasted a fine Madeira wine?" She didn't answer, only stared at the flames. "A foolish question," he said, moving to a chest topped with decanters. He filled two goblets and offered her one. She shook her head. "Take it and drink every drop, or I'll force it down your throat."

"You're an evil man."

"Remember that." He thrust the goblet into her hand, watching as she drank. Despite her reluctance, the wine's ruby red warmth flowed sweetly, loosening the tightness around her heart, filling her empty belly with its heat. Finished, she dropped the goblet to the floor, not caring when it rolled across the room. Rushmount drained his own goblet and refilled it from the decanter. He held it out to her. "For you."

She shook her head. "No more."

"You heard me."

She kept her lips closed, head erect, shoulders back. This time he *would* have to force her. Let him try.

He took a sip from the goblet. "I agree," he said.

She looked at him, puzzled. "Agree?"

"Yes, the vintage is poor. Not among the best years. What a remarkably discerning palate you possess." He reached into his boot and removed the dirk. Holding the goblet in one hand, the knife in the other, he stood in front of her, smiling calmly. "Your choice. Usually I don't have to drug a woman to get her to my bed. But you, of course, are different from the others." His smile fled. "Decide. Quickly."

The silent vow she had made earlier flooded into her mind. *Owen. I must get back to Owen.*

She reached for the goblet and raised it to her lips.

"Good girl. Finish it."

She did, then dropped the empty goblet, and watched it roll across the carpet to meet the first one.

He bent forward, his hands on the chair's arms, enclosing her in the seat, his mouth only inches from her own. "Do you know how I found you?"

She shook her head, forcing down her mounting terror.

"Your hair. It drew me like a beacon. And if I had any doubt it was you walking along that shabby street, the way you moved convinced me . . . every inch of you alive and alert—"

"Alert? Dear God, I was daydreaming. Or you never would have caught me."

"But I did." His lips touched hers. His mouth wasn't a mere slit after all, but fuller than she had imagined and warm like the warmth spreading now from her belly throughout her whole being. As Rushmount's hand came down on her breast, she felt a spark ignite. The sensation lasted no more than an instant before she willed it away, but when he lifted her against him, she knew she would regret that instant for the rest of her life.

But it would only be that single instant and nothing more. She belonged to Owen. She would die belonging to Owen. Gently, she moved back in Rushmount's embrace. Holding him at arm's length, letting her hands roam his shoulders, she gazed in his eyes, forcing an affection she didn't feel onto her face, deceiving him, beguiling him. "Ross," she whispered as soft as if she were uttering a love word. "Ross."

"You've never spoken my name before. The sound of it on your lips is most pleasing. Most pleasing." He bent forward to kiss her mouth. "Say it again. Say my name. It's like music."

"Ross . . . Ross."

He tangled his long fingers in the hair tumbling over her shoulders. "Now," he murmured. "You're ready now."

"Aye."

She moved to the bedside, her hands below her bosom as if to release the gown's clasps. Modesty caused her to turn from his eager eyes and fumble with the hooks.

"Let me," he said with a hoarse laugh. "I know these garments well."

Before he got close enough to touch her, she reached out and, grasping the flaming candelabrum in both hands, flung it on the bed where it fell onto the welter of pillows. Instantly, as if they had been waiting for just this moment, flames leapt high, licking at the hangings, the coverlet, the sheeting, the yards and yards of rich fabric draping the bedstead.

A howl erupted from Rushmount's throat. "Are you insane? You'll burn the house down!" He cuffed her out of the way. Yanking his doublet off the chair, he beat the flames, but the fire's appetite was too strong to be sated so easily. "Water," he roared. "I need water. Where's the wash jug?"

Some questions don't deserve answers.

Grace spied her doublet on the floor near the chair. She seized it, ran out of the chamber, and down the broad stairway to the heavy front door. Shooting the bolt took all her strength, but after a brief struggle, it slid back with a steely click that sounded like thunder to her ears.

She stepped outside, slamming the door behind her. She'd left the rest of her clothes and her precious shoes in the bed chamber. She regretted losing the shoes, but she'd move faster without them. Not wasting a second, she ran into the dark night, her doublet unbuttoned, her breasts jouncing free until the cold air warned her of her condition, and with trembling fingers, she buttoned herself decently and pressed on.

She had to disappear before Rushmount came after her. But dear God, there would be no help for her along this grand boulevard of solid stone fronts. How could she pound on one of these magnificent houses and ask for aid against a lord of the realm? No one would believe a strange, disheveled woman with wild hair when he accused her of setting his house afire. She'd best keep moving and hope the deserted streets would remain empty until she reached Martha's kitchen.

How long it took her she never knew, but, finally, under a high midnight moon, she pushed open Martha's back door and collapsed inside on the floor.

"Praise the Lord, you're back," Martha cried out, jumping up from a stool by the hearth. "I've been sick with worry the whole night long. Not knowing, thinking all manner of thoughts." She hurried over to where Grace slumped against the door, too weary to move, and peered down at her, her eyes widening at the sight of the green velvet gown. "What happened?" her voice filled with a kind of knowing.

"I was taken." Unable to go on, Grace covered her face with her hands and burst into tears.

"Taken?" Martha crouched down and brushed Grace's tousled hair back from her forehead. "Who took you, dearie?"

Grace shook her head.

"You don't know who it was? Some man?"

"Aye, a man."

"He had his way with you." Martha stated the fact baldly with no question in her voice.

"No. I had my way with him." Before Martha could ask another question, Johnny wandered into the kitchen, roused from sleep by the sound of their voices. "What's the matter?" he asked at the sight of Grace on the floor in tears. "Why are you sitting there in your doublet?"

"Remember, last evening I told you she was feeling poorly. She still is, a little." Martha went over to Johnny, kissed his cheek and turned him around toward the stairs. "Now back to bed with you. Go on."

"But Mam, what—"

"She has a chill, that's all, Johnny. A posset will put her to rights."

He nodded and staggered sleepily back to bed. Martha hurried over to Grace, still huddled where she had collapsed, too listless to move. In the safety of Martha's kitchen, the enormity of what had happened overwhelmed her. Rushmount had tried to soil her, body and soul, and had nearly succeeded. For a certainty, the fire she started was a hanging offense, and what if Rushmount had perished in the blaze?

If he had, she'd killed a man and risked burning in the fires of hell forever. Dear God, would she ever feel clean and whole again?

"Dearie, you can't just lie here like this," Martha said. "Come sit on the stool by the fire, and I'll make you some tea." She managed a smile. "We never did have our tea yesterday."

When Grace didn't respond, Martha tugged at her arms to pull her to her feet.

Grace looked up, hollow eyed. "No tea, Martha, thank you kindly. A bath is what I long for. I feel soiled in every pore."

"Aye. The fire's aroaring. It won't take long to heat the water. If you move from the doorway a bit, I'll fetch some from the rain barrel."

Grace slid along the floor on her bottom so Martha could get out to the barrel, then sat with her back to the wall and waited as unmoving as a block of wood. From the scullery, Martha dragged the wash tub near the hearth. As soon as the water heated, she filled the tub, mixing kettles of hot water with buckets of cool before hurrying off for a piece of soap and some cloths for drying.

Grace shrugged out of the green gown, grateful to be rid of it. On a sigh, she stood and slipped into the warm bath, welcoming the way it eased the tension and fatigue from her aching muscles, even welcoming its heated sting on the soles of her feet. After months of being protected by shoes, her skin had become too soft to withstand running barefoot on icy, rough cobbles.

Let them hurt.

She deserved the pain. For she could not deny that one fraction of time when she'd responded to Rushmount's caresses—a moment of terrifying fascination. She shuddered, remembering. She'd enjoyed the pressure of his wide, insistent mouth, his hand on her breast. What might have happened had she not made her escape? Her body had betrayed her in that single hot moment . . . there might have been more, many more such moments . . .

Martha bustled back into the kitchen, spreading the drying cloths before the fire to heat. When she glanced down at the tub, she saw the water near Grace's feet turning faintly pink. "You're bleeding."

"Aye, but in my heart most of all."

"Oh, dearie." Martha dropped onto a stool. "I'm so sorry. This is all my fault. I should never have sent you out so late."

Grace sat straighter, sending water splashing over the rim onto the stone floor. "In no way are you at fault. Please don't think that." She grasped at Martha's skirt with a wet hand. "But you must promise me you'll saying nothing of this to anyone. For safety's sake, no one must know. No one. Not Johnny, and above all, not Owen. Promise me, Martha, that you'll never tell Owen. Never."

Martha nodded solemnly. "I promise, but I think perhaps you should."

"No. Never. 'Twould be the end of us."

Looking as if she too could weep, Martha said, "I'll do whatever you wish."

Grace wiped a hand across her eyes. "Thank you." She looked from Martha's troubled face down at the water. The pink tinge had deepened. "I have to change my prayer this day."

"How so, dearie?"

"I must pray that God not let Owen return until my feet heal. And until I can find another pair of shoes."

Chapter Twelve

"WAKE UP, LOVE."

A dream, it was, the most delightful one Grace had ever had. She could hear Owen's voice in her ear and his breath on her cheek. So real they were, they caused her to moan aloud in longing for him.

"Wake up, love. I've come home to you."

No dream.

Her eyes flared open. In the starlight shining through the open window, he stood as tall and strong, as real as a man could be. She sat bolt upright. "Tell me it's true. Tell me I'm not imagining you."

He laughed. "Not at all. For proof, here's this." He bent over her and kissed her lips, but the kiss felt strange, not like the kisses she remembered with aching clarity. She reached out to touch him, fearful that her fingers would meet nothing but air. "You've a beard." she said. "No wonder I didn't know your kiss."

In the half dark, he stripped off his clothes and slid in beside her. "You've more to remember than a kiss." His hands, warm under the coverlet, caressed her. They started at her shoulders and moved slowly down until he had apprised all of her. "God has been good to me," he murmured into her hair. "Now let me be good to you."

———

"HOW COULD YOU STEAL IN HERE WITHOUT A SOUND?" she asked the next morning. "Martha bolts the doors when she goes to her bed."

"I saw a candle gleam, so I tapped on the shutter. I surprised her at the table having a bit of a feast for herself."

"In the middle of the night?"

"Aye." He grinned. "I joined her."

"Owen O'Donnell! You stopped for food before coming to me?"

His grin widened. "I did. I knew I'd put the strength it gave me to good use."

She sighed, contented. "And so you did."

"Aye."

"Did Martha tell you about our winter?" she asked, studying his face.

"She did that, filled me in nicely with all your doings."

No lines furrowed his brow, no hint of anger, nothing untoward. Martha had kept her vow of silence. Thank God for that, at least.

"I've been worried for you, Owen. Not knowing how you fared had me half crazed these past weeks."

"In your heart of hearts, you knew I'd fare well and come back to you. As I have."

"I hoped so, but as for knowing—"

"All's well that ends well, love, and I've brought a hefty purse with me."

"You have, indeed. And a beard. I like the feel of it when you kiss me. But in truth, it does make you look older."

"A good thing, that. I'll be taken more seriously by those we meet."

As she studied him in the clear morning light, his banter ended abruptly. "Have these months apart gone badly for you, love? You're thinner than I remember."

He ran his thumbs over the hollows in her cheeks. Her eyes were huge, and against her white skin, the luxuriant red-gold of her hair caught at his heart. If anything, she was more beautiful than ever, more tempered, more *aware*.

He picked up her hand, caressing the fingers one by one. "I regret the worry and the uncertainty. I promise you we'll never be apart again. Not for any reason." He squeezed the fingers he held, and drawing her close, laid her head against his chest. "I've been anxious for you. Wondering over and over if the coins I earned warranted our separation." He kissed her hair. "The answer is they did not. Nothing on earth is worth that. I ask your forgiveness."

She pulled away a little and looked straight into his eyes. "God help us, Owen. You've brought back a fortune. 'Twill make our lives easier."

"Aye." He drew her back onto the pillow. "Last night when I sat with Martha, she gave me a message for you. Johnny will help her take the bread around today. She wants you to rest."

"Rest?" Grace's laugh pealed out into the room. "Isn't she the grand woman, Owen? And to think she's English."

———————

The last of February slipped into March. On the first day of the new month, they returned to the shipping office. With only merchant vessels anchored in the bay, the harbor looked larger than Owen recalled it, but the same pinch-nosed clerk greeted them with a sniff of recognition.

"You're back. I remember you," he said to Owen. "You've sprouted a beard, but your gait's the same."

Owen merely raised an eyebrow. Why let this toad know his insult had met its mark? "Do you have anything more important to tell me?"

"You're too early. The *Seafarer*'s not arrived in port yet."

"A fact we can see for ourselves," Owen said. "When do you expect her?"

"In a few days, or a few weeks." The clerk shrugged his narrow, black-clad shoulders. "It's difficult to tell."

"Has word arrived that she's in peril?"

"No, no." The clerk glanced about the quiet office with alarmed, rabbity eyes. "She was sighted a week ago and signaled all was well aboard."

"Excellent. We're here to book passage."

"If you wish." He sniffed the higher air above his head. "Providing you have what's necessary. Two sovereigns. Two, that is, for each of you."

Owen took four gold coins from his breeches pocket and held them out in his palm. "A receipt first."

"You read?"

"In English, Gaelic and Latin. The question is, can you write?"

The clerk cleared his throat and reached for his quill. Without speaking, he scratched his way across a scrap of parchment and held it up.

"Correct," Owen said after scanning it quickly. "Here's your fee. We'll check back each day."

"Don't expect her to leave before April. She'll have to be unloaded and outfitted afresh. April first," he repeated, "at the earliest."

Owen folded the paper and put it in his pocket. "My wife and I thank you for your courtesy." He winked at Grace and took her by the arm, letting his wooden boot stomp across the office floor boards, and letting the clerk know that despite his crippled leg, the loveliest woman in Liverpool walked at his side. But he closed the office door quietly. Ah, the poor excuse for a man. He felt pity for him, two sound legs or no.

BY MID-APRIL, OCCASIONAL CROCUSES, VIOLETS AND DAFFODILS showed their bright faces in Liverpool's meager gardens. Buds appeared on the stunted city trees while birds busied themselves with their nesting, twitting and darting about, filling the spring with song.

Half dressed on the morning of their leaving, Grace opened their window to the soft air. "Ballybanree must be beautiful now."

Owen came up behind her and wrapped his arms around her waist. "If you wish it, Grace, we can return."

She twisted around to face him. "You really mean that?"

He nodded. "This very day. If that's what you want."

She left his arms. Sinking onto a chair, she propped her elbows on the table and hid her face in her hands. He knelt beside her and pried her fingers away. "What is it, love?"

She sniffed away her tears. "You know me overly well, Owen. No wonder you just spoke as you did. You know I'd never go back to being a slave on Rushmount's land." She swiped at her cheeks with the back of a hand. "Lately I'm in tears at every wee thing. A sign of weakness, I fear."

"A sign you have a heart in you. Leaving your homeland, and now Martha and John, is hard. You'd be a cold woman, indeed, if you didn't regret such losses." He wiped away a tear escaping down her cheek. "And God knows you're not cold or weak."

Comforted, she smiled and stood to finish dressing.

Their sea chest, strapped with strong iron bands Owen had wrought, waited downstairs for the carter to haul it to the docks.

Grace glanced about their room, their first home, trying to memorize each detail. Ah, there's little to see, she thought, but much to remember. Shawl in hand, she walked down the stairs for the last time. At the bottom, Martha waited by the chest, her eyes red, her hands wringing the life out of her apron hem.

Grace pulled her into a tight embrace. "I'll never forget you, Martha. Never. You'll be with me for the rest of my life."

"I wish that were true." Martha's tears streamed unchecked. "But it isn't. It's just the valiant way you Irish have with words."

"Don't be sad." Grace stepped back and smiled. "You have Johnny and a good life here, and one of these days your Billy lad will walk in and surprise you."

"Yes, I live for that." Martha managed a smile of her own. "Go now, to your New World. May you find everything there your heart desires."

Grace grinned. "You're beginning to sound Irish, Martha."

"High time you left then, before I'm corrupted entirely."

"Ah, from the sound of you, I fear 'tis too late!"

So they parted with a laugh and a tear and a hug for young John. By the time they followed the carter to the waterfront, Grace's own tears had dried. In their place, a rich excitement filled her soul, the unease of earlier in the morning disappearing completely at the sight of the *Seafarer* moored in the harbor. A galleon Owen called her, weighing nearly two hundred tons and with a keel of well over one hundred feet. Even Granuaile had never sailed on a ship so huge.

Seaworthy she was, indeed, and their home for the next two months. But as Owen helped her into the skiff for the ferry ride out to the waiting ship, the memory of their rough passage from Dublin flashed through her mind. She forced the worry aside. Caught in the galleon's huge sails, the wind would quickly drive them across the Atlantic. Or if not quickly, no matter. These coming weeks would pass whatever happened.

Pulled steadily along by the four oarsmen, the boat tossed and rolled in the choppy harbor waters. Grace ignored the pitching, refusing to let her stomach give in to it. Once aboard the galleon, they'd find her deck steady and firm. The *Seafarer* would ride the crests with no pitch to her at all, not like this wee acorn bobbing against the tide.

To her relief, they soon drew alongside the ship, halting near a rope ladder dangling down to the water's edge.

"Help your woman aboard," one of the oarsmen called out to Owen. "We'll see to the chest."

"I can manage the ladder," Grace declared. With the oars holding the skiff clear of the ship's side, she timed her leap carefully. When a wave lapped them closer to the hull, she grasped the ladder's low rung and swung up. In minutes, climbing hand over hand, she had mounted to deck level where burly deckhands seized her arms and pulled her aboard. Owen climbed up after her, his movements clumsy but dogged. In no time, he, too, stood on deck.

Now for the chest. A line flashed down from the yardarm, and one of the oarsmen secured it around their box. At his shouted signal, everything they owned in the world hovered over the sea for one breath-taking instant before the pulley went into action, and with much creaking of the straining rope, safely hoisted their chest to the deck.

Two crewmen lifted it. "Come with us," one said to Owen. "We'll show you below."

Their snickers as they carried the chest did nothing to reassure Grace that their quarters would be first-rate. As she suspected, they hauled the box down two flights of stairs and dropped it deep in the hull next to an upright beam. Near it, against the ship's side, lay a thin pallet.

"You're the first passengers aboard," explained one of the men. "You get the best spot."

The best? In the gloom, relieved only by the light filtering in from the hatch two decks above, and from a few open portholes, she could make out a large, open space strewn with sleeping pallets, but no enclosures or doors or curtains for privacy. Only the chest, jammed next to the beam, would block them from the view of all eyes. Ah, she sighed, Martha's garret room had her spoiled. She and Owen would have precious little privacy.

"We thank you," Owen said to the crewmen. "This will do very well."

Very well?

"I know what you're thinking, Grace," he said when they were left alone, "but think of this instead: the voyage is a means to an end, and there's an end in sight."

"Sure and I know that, Owen. Now what say you we go up on deck and enjoy the air and watch the sights?"

"Aye, but first, while we're alone, I must kiss you. I fear that's all I'll do for some weeks to come."

"I already know that," she said, annoyed.

He laughed before kissing her breathless.

Up on deck, activities had increased to fever pitch. Barrels and crates and slope-topped chests clogged the deck. Aided by the crew, several more passengers had struggled aboard. There were a few families, the parents looking anxious and troubled, the youngsters excited and bright eyed. But many of the passengers coming aboard were women traveling alone or with children, voyaging to join their men who had gone ahead a year ago or more to establish homes in the New World. After her winter alone, Grace shuddered at the idea of such a long separation, even for the best of all possible reasons. Though eager to meet her fellow passengers, she stayed by the rail at Owen's side. They'd all have weeks to become acquainted. Indeed, considering where they'd be quartered, they'd likely have more acquaintance than any of them desired.

For now, she'd watch the outline of Liverpool silhouetted against the shore. She might never see a city so sizeable again. Somehow, she didn't care. The exhilaration she'd felt months earlier at crowded, noisy streets had left her, though her knowledge of their dangers never would. Still, she'd fill her eyes with a city while she could.

A pair of skiffs began plying their way toward them. The first carried two male passengers, or so they appeared in the distance, and the second, a great number of boxes and trunks.

With all that luggage, the passengers wouldn't be simple voyagers. They must be gentry. The boxes piled high reminded her of the day she spied Lord Rushmount getting into his carriage with his lady wife. Grace shaded her eyes with a hand to better watch the boats draw near.

No.

Inhaling a shocked breath, she dug her fingers into Owen's arm. "Look there." She pointed at the first boat. "It's him. Dear God, Rushmount's coming aboard."

Owen looked down at the bobbing craft hovering alongside. His jaw tightened. "Aye. That's Rushmount, all right, and his man servant with him."

So he hadn't died in the fire.

Grace felt the blood drain from her face and pool around her heart, making each breath she drew as ragged as if she were running up a steep hill. Dear God, would this man follow her for the rest of her life, everywhere on earth, to its very ends?

"He mustn't see us, Owen. Not now. Not here." She must have sounded anxious, she realized, for Owen glanced at her in surprise.

"You're as pale as I've ever seen you, lass. You fear him so?"

In answer, her hand clutched his arm all the harder.

"Very well, then. Come, we'll cross to the starboard railing."

As they made their way amidships through the confused mass of people and supplies, Grace felt the moment of fearful recognition give way to bitter anger. Although the moored ship hardly moved, nausea threatened to rise again, and her throat filled with bile. She gripped the starboard rail and looked out to sea. Despite her turmoil, the beauty of the water spread out like a blue-green carpet leading straight to the future calmed her. Nothing Rushmount could say, nothing he could do, would keep them from that future. As her resolve hardened, an unholy thought swept through her mind. She should have killed Rushmount when she had the chance.

God help her, she had wanted to in Ballybanree when he'd tried to force himself on her. She'd had a knife in her hand that night, but only her wits as defense the night in the townhouse. That she had escaped unharmed both times didn't lessen the man's evil intent. She had never done anything to enflame him, only walked the earth as one of God's creatures. She raised her hand and quickly blessed herself. As one of His creatures, she had no right to take a life He had created. She sighed and stared at the water. God's rules were hard to fathom sometimes.

Intent on a task, a ship's officer hurried by. Owen stepped into his path. "I have a question to ask of you. That gentleman, the one coming aboard with all the baggage, who might he be?"

"Lord Rushmount's his name."

"And going to the New World? Unusual for a royal."

"Most unusual. He's on the king's business. I hear taxes are slow coming in from the colonies."

"Ah. He'll see to that."

"No doubt." After a quick nod and an admiring glance at Grace, the man hurried off.

"Tax collector, indeed. So there's no escape from them even in the New World." Grace couldn't keep the edge from her voice.

"Governments need money to govern. 'Tis that simple. But I'm encouraged the colonies are slow to pay. In Ireland, the reverse is true. Taxes are always paid first, and the people's needs ignored. I think we'll find a great difference in Providence. If not perfection," Owen added wryly. "But today we have a more pressing problem. I think it's best not to challenge Rushmount until we're too far out to sea to be returned to land. So what say you we stay below for a while?"

"You mean hide away? We've paid our passage in gold. Why should we hide like thieves?"

He grinned at the vehemence in her voice. Her moment of fear had disappeared. He would place odds it had gone forever.

"Two days at most, love. The last thing we want is to be put ashore. We won't risk that. Instead, we'll lie on our pallet and plan our life. We'll spend the hours dwelling on all its fine possibilities."

"Very well. If you believe it best." He knew she didn't like the idea, but she smiled at him nevertheless, melting his heart completely.

Two days below would help, Owen thought, but no telling what might happen thereafter. Once Rushmount spied them, and he would, sooner, if not later, he'd likely go to the captain with his story of horse theft, demanding they be held for trial. He had no illusions as to how such a trial would end.

He gritted his jaw. Above all, Grace could not be subjected to that fate. Killing Rushmount was the simplest solution, but was it wise? Should anyone discover they had known him in the past, his death might place Grace in even greater danger . . . the man servant had been with him in Ballybanree. He would remember them, for certain.

Think, man, *think,* he ordered himself as they stood by the railing reluctant to leave the sea breeze and the salt air for the hull's gloom.

There was only one answer. He'd have to surprise Rushmount before he spoke of them to a single soul, even before he knew who they were. In her English clothing, with her hair concealed by the cap, Grace might not catch Rushmount's eye immediately, nor would he expect to see her here. The beard changed himself somewhat, but the accursed leg and his awkward gait couldn't be disguised. Rushmount would recognize Owen O'Donnell, the crippled blacksmith, the moment he walked toward him.

The salt breeze ruffled Grace's skirt and began to blow chill. They should go below while all on deck was in confusion. Later, in the dark, they could come up for a breath of air. He touched her arm, "Come," he said, "the night is nigh."

They were nearly at the bottom of the gangway when a crate being hauled aboard slipped its rope and crashed to the deck. Startled, he looked up, right into the equally startled eyes of Ross Rushmount. Owen broke their glance instantly, but in that instant had a flicker of recognition crossed Rushmount's face?

Chapter Thirteen

*T*HERE, ANOTHER TANTALIZING GLIMPSE.

He'd not had so much Madeira at supper that he would imagine her. Yet just now again, a quick flash of bright hair, then nothing. Maybe his imagination *was* playing tricks. There were many women aboard. And Grace O'Malley wasn't the only redhead in the world.

Rushmount's hand tightened on his goblet. He leaned on the railing and tossed the wine dregs overboard. He'd had enough for the day. Enough to imagine her around every curve of the deck, but not enough to deny he'd been a fool to let down his guard that one unforgettable night. His lapse had cost him dearly. He'd had to restore the destroyed bedchamber. Luckily he'd managed to put out the fire before the entire house went up in flames. His scarred hand would be an eternal reminder of his own stupidity. And of how cleverly, how easily, Grace had eluded him.

For days afterward he'd scoured the mean dockside byways and lanes looking for her, yet none of his inquiries had borne fruit. Strange, no one on the docks recalled her. No doubt, he'd been lied to. One look at her and you'd remember her forever, but, of course, the working classes protected each another.

Only an alehouse tapster had admitted he knew of a bread girl with red hair. When questioned, the lout had claimed she was ugly as sin, her eyes so crossed a man couldn't rightly tell whether she glanced at him or the wall behind him.

Perhaps he had pressed too hard, given too large a coin as bribe.

Afterward, he was certain the man had lied. When he went back to force more out of him, he had disappeared, no one knew where.

Strange, too, how she still captivated his mind. He could have any woman he wanted . . . except this one. And to think she preferred a cripple's touch to his own. It was insufferable.

The sea breeze ruffled his hair and cooled his heated cheeks. He hated going below to his small, stuffy cabin. No matter if it adjoined the captain's and was the best accommodation on board. It had the dimensions of a coffin.

The cool, airy deck was much more enjoyable.

The last two nights, the ocean had been calm with just enough blowing wind to swell the sails and move them along at a good clip. He had no expectation the entire voyage would be so peaceful, but for now the salt air, the stars, the lapping of the water, and the isolation of the ship in the ocean's vastness, all conspired to lull him into reverie.

Or was it the Madeira?

He couldn't be certain, but whatever the cause, a peace he hadn't felt in months descended on him. Even the difficult task assigned by the king's treasurers seemed lighter tonight, and once he put foot on the colonies' shores, he resolved that King Charles would quickly receive his due. In truth, he had little choice. The chancellor's hints had been clear enough. Return with the tax monies in gold, or lacking that, in furs and timber. Or don't return.

Tonight, the thinly veiled threat hardly worried him, nor that Anne had barely been able to conceal her joy at his leaving, masking it with a specious, wifely concern. In retaliation, he'd endeavored manfully to impregnate her before he left. He hoped his efforts had succeeded. Time would tell. But even that irritation faded away under the sparkle of a sky full of stars. All he lacked to make life complete was Grace with her . . .

"Rushmount."

He stiffened. Who would dare address him in such an abrupt manner? His idyll shattered, he turned from the rail into the threatening presence of a stranger. The riffraff quartered below didn't venture onto the quarterdeck. Where was his man, Thomas? In his bed? Why wasn't he here to prevent this intrusion?

"We need to talk." The stranger moved closer.

Rushmount peered into the dark. With only starlight and the faint glow from the lantern hanging astern, he couldn't clearly see the man's face. He was bearded, that much he could tell, shoulders broad, outline powerful even in the poor light.

A sliver of fear shot through him. "I don't tarry with strangers. Get off the quarterdeck before I have you thrown off."

"Ah, so that's the way of things, is it?"

That voice. He could swear he'd heard it before. The unmistakable Irish lilt . . . but no, it couldn't be. Had there been a beard? He didn't remember a beard.

The man stepped forward, one shoulder dipping down, the other rising up as he moved. *The blacksmith.*

"Bloody hell. Is that you, O'Donnell?"

"Aye, you have the truth of it."

Despite his handicap, the cripple acted with astonishing speed. Before Rushmount could cry out for help, he felt a knife point pressed against his gut.

"I'll kill you if you make a sound. Understood?"

Rushmount froze.

The knife pricked through his doublet. "Understood?"

"Yes."

"Good. I have no heart to kill you." The Irishman blew out a noisy sigh. "Ah, sure and I'm lying now. I'd slice you in a heartbeat and count the loss of my soul as little payment, but I'm not a violent man." The knife point pricked deeper. "Most times."

"What do you want?"

"To be left in peace. My wife and I want you to forget us, yet remember one vital fact. You took her crop for the chestnut."

Rushmount guffawed. "Don't be ridiculous. That didn't begin to pay for the steed."

"Perhaps not, but you have her land as well."

"By royal decree."

"By royal thievery."

"I won't listen to this."

"An old tale, I agree, and not improved with the telling. But we, my wife and I, are willing to forget the past—"

"*You're* willing?"

"On one condition. That you do not speak of . . . shall I say our trade? . . . to a single soul."

"What's to stop me? One word and you'll be cast into the brig. Both of you."

"One word, is it? The law of the sea prevails here. 'Twill take many words, yours against mine, mine against yours. Despite your title, the captain will listen to both our stories. Would you have him hear mine? That a cripple and a slip of a lass bested you? Tied you up. Threw you over a horse's back like a sack of meal, and you helpless as a babe all the while."

"Enough!" Rushmount knew the blacksmith was gambling, trusting the captain would give equal weight to a peasant's word against that of a king's agent. The odds were strong he would not.

"My wife," O'Donnell continued, "will have her story to tell as well. Of your treatment before I arrived on the scene. How you tried to—"

"Enough, I said."

"I heard what you said. Have you heard me?" The deep voice came low and quiet out of the dark, filled with a menace Rushmount couldn't dismiss. He'd been subjected to the man's violence. He knew his capabilities. But the threat of physical harm isn't what kept him leaning on the rail, the empty goblet dangling from his fingers.

What if the story *were* bandied about? He'd be the laughing stock of the ship, and later, of the colonies. And if Grace spoke in her own defense, no man on earth would disbelieve her. His desires would rise up, and he would know her tale had to be true. Just to look at her would be proof enough.

"You're thinking," O'Donnell said, his tone now bantering, playful.

Damn the man, he was on the verge of laughing. "It's not worth the effort to contest the issue," Rushmount said evenly, refusing to give rise to the fury that assailed him. "The horse may be gone, but the land is not. I'll find another tenant to plow it. Our quarrel is over."

"Not quite." The knife bit deeper. "Your lust for my wife has been shining in your eyes far too long. Approach her in any way, and I will be forced to kill you. Regardless of what might happen to me." O'Donnell tucked the knife into his belt. "And now, a pleasant good evening to you." He turned and pounded down the short flight of stairs to the main deck making no effort to slip away silently.

Left alone in the dark, Rushmount cursed and threw the goblet he'd been clutching over the side. Yes, he'd keep his mouth closed. Once again, he'd been given little choice. But he would bide his time. At the first opportunity, he'd strike.

For he had lied. Nothing was over, not as long as O'Donnell lived. Not as long as Grace drew breath.

Chapter Fourteen

*F*OUR BELLS.
Midnight, and no Owen.

He had been gone for what seemed an age and her heart beating like a wild creature the whole time. If Rushmount made the fatal mistake of telling Owen how he'd seized her that night, anything could happen. None of it good. She could wait no longer. Tossing off the blanket, Grace reached for her shawl ready to go searching for Owen, when he returned, silent on bare feet, carrying his boots in his hands. He slid onto the pallet and took her in his arms.

"Rushmount listened," he said in a whisper so as not to disturb their fellow travelers stretched out and sleeping, or feigning it, all about them. "I had him at my mercy, but I didn't harm him. Killing him would only set off a hue and cry. You'll be safer this way. For fear of ridicule, he'll keep his lies to himself."

She let out a deep breath. "You trust him?"

"Not on your life. But I trust his pride. If he betrays us, he'll give himself away as well. That's the deterrent."

"That's the gamble, you mean." Her angry voice rose a bit above a whisper. "You're trying to comfort me, Owen, but I'm not so easily fooled. Though God may punish me for saying so, some men are better dead than alive."

"Oh, the temper on the woman."

His fingers toyed with her, gently caressing her sides, then, of a sudden, giving no warning at all, they dug in and began playing a melody on her ribs. A giggle erupted from her throat. The more she tried to stifle it, the stronger it became.

"Owen," she gasped, "please stop. For the love of God, we'll awaken the whole ship."

He kissed her cheek, and taking his hands from her sides, ran them over her body slowly, his fingers gentle once more. When his fingertips reached the soft flesh of her belly, they lingered there then went back to her breasts, cupping each one, weighing them in his hands.

A low cry escaped her lips as his thumb grazed a nipple. "Did I hurt you?" he whispered. "I did not mean—"

"'Tis all right."

Something in her voice stayed his hand.

"Grace?"

"Aye."

"Are you giving me a son, love?"

"A son or a daughter . . . a daughter, I think."

"More marvelous still!" He seized her to him, pressing her close from shoulder to hip to thigh, raining silent kisses on her face and hair. Lifting her fingers to his mouth, he caressed them one at a time, then turning her hands, he pressed his lips to her open palms. "When? When did we make our daughter?"

She stiffened. She had known he would ask and had dreaded the question though the babe in her womb was his, her lawful, wedded husband's, and belonged to no other. Yet if she had not escaped in time that evil night, it might well have been Rushmount's. The thought was unbearable. Owen must never know such a possibility had ever existed. It would destroy him.

"Do you know, love?" He spoke into her ear. "Can you tell me?"

"The night you came home to me after your journeying. That night, or the next morning, the day Martha wanted me to rest." She smiled, remembering.

"You've said naught a word to me all these weeks. Yet I should have guessed. You've not had—"

"I wanted to be certain. And I feared once you knew, everything would change between us."

He drew back slightly. "All will be better than ever between us. A child of our own, Grace, think of the wonder of it. Another beloved person on this earth. 'Tis more than I hoped for, more than I deserve."

"Not true."

"Aye, very true, indeed." He sighed. "If only we were alone. I want to prove to you how much—"

"You already have." The smile that couldn't be seen in the dark rose into her voice.

"'Twould seem so, indeed." He gave her cheek one last kiss. "Roll onto your side, love. I'll content myself with resting my hand on your belly and keeping him warm."

"*Her.*"

He chuckled. "As God wills."

———————

"You and your mister, you're great ones for talking."

Grace whirled around, half-dressed, in the act of dropping her skirt over her head. An old woman stood beside their pallet with her hands on her hips and a scowl on her face.

"In the middle of the night carrying on like at midday, and me trying to sleep on the other side of this chest here."

"I'm that sorry, ma'am. We won't be doing the same again."

"I trust not."

"A special occasion, it was."

Curiosity stirred in the wizened face, brown and seamed like an apple left overlong in the sun. "I don't take your meaning. A special occasion in the dark of night?"

"In a manner of speaking." Grace secured her skirt around her waist and picked up her brush. She'd do as Owen had requested, no longer wear the cap over her hair. Instead, she'd brush it out then tie it at her nape with a length of green ribbon to keep the sea breeze from blowing the tresses into her face.

"Well? I'm waiting."

She's a feisty one, Grace thought, warming to the little woman, so scrawny and worn and full of fire. "Well, last night my husband learned we're . . . ah . . . in the family way. We had much to discuss."

"So I gathered." The woman's eyes swept over Grace, stopping at her belly. "You're not far along."

"Almost three months, I think."

The wrinkled face softened, and she held out a hand. "I'm Sara Duxbury. Your neighbor yonder." She pointed to a pallet topped with a patchwork quilt.

"Grace O'Malley O'Donnell's my name. My husband Owen's gone up to the galley to help carry down the food. Although I find I'm not hungry at all."

"Queasy?"

Grace nodded. "In the mornings mostly."

"That will pass," Sara said briskly. "Come, you have to eat. Perhaps they'll surprise us with something other than gruel."

Near the gangway, a rough, improvised table of planks supported on barrels took up part of the hold not given over to pallets and bundles and boxes. Once the men carried down the steaming kettle of gruel, as usual, the voyagers lined up with their bowls and spoons to help themselves to the food.

"We're only a few days out. It's still fresh," one of the women declared, lobbing a good-sized lump of gruel into her bowl. She peered into it and cackled. "No weevils yet. They'll be with us soon enough, I expect."

Grace's stomach turned over. To escape the odor rising up from the kettle, she dashed past the table making for the gangway and the fresh air above decks. Owen found her there a minute later white-faced and shivering in the early morning chill.

"Are you ill, love?" He pulled her near.

"Not a bit of it. This feeling is common. 'Twill pass," she said, thankful Sara had told her so.

"Until it does, you must eat something, or you'll be ill in truth."

At the worry on his face, she reached up to stroke his cheek. "Don't fear for me, Owen. This is women's work. Though I never dreamed I'd see the day when I had no love for food."

Sara came bustling up to where they stood at the starboard railing, a red apple in one hand, a blue knitted shawl in the other. "Here, young mistress. Wrap this about you, and take a bite of this apple. I suspect it will stay down where it belongs."

Grace settled the wrap about her shoulders, took the apple happily and bit into it.

"We're grateful to you, ma'am," Owen said.

"And I'll be grateful to you for some quiet in the night."

"The same won't happen again," he apologized. "We were—"

"Celebrating a special occasion," Sara finished.

"Grace told you our news?"

"Yes, she did." Sara shook her head. "A fine time to start a family. Before a voyage like this."

"Are you after scolding me?" Amusement at this worn little vixen momentarily replaced the worry in Owen's eyes.

"It's too late for that."

"Aye. You and I should have spoken three months ago."

Her wrinkled face lit up with laughter. "As if that would have made a particle of difference."

Grace enjoyed the sound of their banter and the freshness of the air after a night below in the stuffy, crowded hold. She munched the crisp apple right down to the core and felt the better for it. She tossed the core into the water.

"Good, you ate it all," Sara declared. "Later, try a bit of hardtack and a taste of cheese. Nibble when you're inclined to. Small bites, a little at a time, will settle well."

"I'll remember that." As Sara strode off, her skirts whipping about her shanks in the stiff breeze, Grace thought this is the second Englishwoman we've met with a kind heart, but we never met one in Ireland. Why not? she wondered. Why in their own land had they been treated like ignorant savages unworthy of respect or friendship?

She pondered the questions, arriving at no answers. Thankfully, the querying took her mind from the unease, which, at least for the time being, had disappeared completely. Her hand on Owen's arm, she leaned over the rail, captivated by the great, green ocean stretching to the far horizon.

At this, the voyage's beginning, the *Seafarer* held easily to her western course, cutting through the deep water faster than a sharpened plow through a furrow. Finding no heavy resistance from a rough sea, she sailed steadily onward prodded by the surge of wind in her sails, closer each hour, each day, each week, to the eastern shore of the New World.

After a month at sea, she ran afoul of a series of spring gales, and her good fortune changed overnight. As if seized in a madman's grip, the ship pitched and rocked, battered without mercy by wild winds above her and sea swells beneath.

In the hold, chests and boxes slid about with such abandon the passengers were forced to lash them to the beams or tie them securely against the hull. That helped, but the pallets constantly shifted about, ending up in piles on the port side and, at the next violent roll, sliding to starboard.

Owen roped their chest to the beam nearby, securing the edge of their pallet under the chest so its weight would hold their bedding in place.

Captain Hopkins ordered all lanterns and the galley fires put out. Until the sea returned to a semblance of sanity, hardtack and cheese, a ration of water, and whatever provisions the passengers still carried in their baggage, would have to sustain them.

Grace didn't care. The last of Sara's cache of apples had long since been eaten, and the weevils, as predicted, had begun to wriggle through the hardtack. For the last two days, she had consumed little more than sips of water.

She knew, dimly, that Owen sat by her side for hours, watching her, stroking her hair, murmuring words of encouragement. Then late one afternoon, she heard him speak to Sara.

"She's not eating. Is there nothing I can do to help her?"

"Not in this sea, but she's young and strong. The babe will take what it needs. Just pray the storms end soon and that she sleeps away the hours."

"Aye." Through slitted eyes, Grace saw Owen pat Sara's thin shoulder before coming back to his vigil.

She must have dozed, for she awakened and lay, barely conscious, on the pallet indifferent to everything around her—the sounds of the other passengers, the confusion below decks, the noisome smells of unwashed bodies and stale food. If this is what life at sea meant, how could Granuaile have loved it and lived for it? She had even birthed a son at sea. A powerful strong woman she must have been, Grace thought, as another spasm of queasiness gripped her. Unmoving, she kept still waiting for the nausea to pass, vowing she'd be as strong as Granuaile and face whatever the sea meted out.

At least the cooking kettles were cold and gave off no odor of boiling meat. At the mere idea of salt pork stewing in its juices, another fit of retching seized her. She leaned over the pallet and tried to spew the contents of her stomach into a wooden bowl. But hard as she tried, shoulders heaving, muscles spasming, her efforts were wasted. She fell back on her pillow with an exhausted sigh. In her whole lifetime, she had never before lost all will and energy like this. Despite her vow of a moment before, desire and caring and life itself belonged to another Grace, one she barely remembered.

"You've nothing left in your stomach." Owen set the bowl aside. "Try not to move, love. Rest."

As he went to lay a cool, wet cloth on her forehead, the first pain shot through her, the sudden stab ripping through her belly like a knife. She gasped. At the sound, he rose onto his knees and bent over her, his body tense, his eyes narrowed with concern.

When he went to speak, she pressed a finger to his mouth, silencing him. As if she were listening for a bell that might strike again, her eyes wide, her face wary, she waited. *There.* This time, the pain struck deeper and sharper, followed quickly by another pang even stronger than the last. She cried out at that one, hoping against hope there would be no rhythm to the stabbings. Perhaps what she felt was her stomach protesting its emptiness. But she knew better, when after a pause, the pains started up again, as relentless as waves, gathering in strength until she groaned and clutched at Owen's hands, her nails digging into his palms.

"I feel a wetness, Owen. I need Sara."

He scrambled to his feet, praying the old woman would still be below decks. He spied her sitting by the trestle table with a group of other soiled, travel-weary women. He raced to her, his gait clumsier than ever in his haste. "Sara, something's happening. Grace needs you."

Without waiting for her response, he turned to go back. Sara caught up to him, snagging him by the arm before he could reach the pallet. "Send another woman to me, but you keep away for a while."

He did as she asked then went to the upper deck to stand by the bow. The minutes passed slowly, a single endless second at a time. He blamed himself. He had endangered the one he loved most on earth. Not even the New World was worth such a price.

All around him, an exhausted crew struggled with the rigging, trimming the sails or unfurling them yet again as the wind's erratic behavior demanded. Owen hardly noticed. Nor did he hear the groans and creaking of the canvas as it fought the lines, or the soughing of the water against the keel, all sounds he had once called the music of the sea. The poetry of words held no interest for him now, only the silent prayer he repeated over and over again.

Sara found him there, just after dark. When she tapped on his back, he started, jerked out of his thoughts by her slight touch. She grasped his arm, hardly able to keep upright in the heavy weather that had the ship pitching under their feet like a frenzied animal.

He held onto her as a wicked gust threatened to blow her across the deck. "Sara, you shouldn't be out here," he shouted over the wind. Then, at the look on her face, he felt the blood drain from his own.

"It's over," she said, swiping at her eyes.

"She's not—"

"No. She's young and strong. She'll pull through this, but not the babe. It's gone."

"Ah, dear God." He slumped against the railing. So his prayer had been answered. He had begged for Grace's life. For the nameless babe, he hadn't pleaded at all. Only for Grace. In a single stroke, God had blessed him. And punished him. "I have to go to her."

"She's asleep, worn to a nub. But maybe now she'll not feel the ship's motion so much, and the sickness will leave her."

"I'll pray for that." He drew her away from the rail. "Come below. I'm eager to see Grace, and you can't stay out here."

"If you need me in the night, call out."

He clasped her to him. "We already owe you more than we can repay."

"We're placed on this earth to help one another," she said sturdily.

Putting his arm through hers, he maneuvered them across the wind-blown deck to the gangway and down the stairs into the hold. He sat by Grace throughout the night, seeing little of her face in the dark, but hearing every breath she took, every stirring, every sigh.

Toward morning, she rolled toward him and opened her eyes. "Have you been awake all night?"

Instantly, he was on his knees beside her, holding her fingers as if they were glass that would shatter at his touch. "I'm so sorry, love."

"I'm heartsick, too, Owen. I wonder . . ." her fingers fell away from his . . . "is God punishing me?"

"Why would He do such a thing? You've harmed no one."

"For wanting so much? For longing for a New World?"

"After giving us a thirst for justice? Do we not owe it to Him to seek it out?"

She nodded, a mist of tears coming into her eyes. "He has His plans. The babe was not part of them."

"Aye." He stretched out beside her, closing his eyes so she would not guess at the guilt that assailed him.

Had his prayer of omission cost them their child?

CHAPTER FIFTEEN

"**Y**OU'VE ONLY A FEW SPOONS OF GRUEL TAKEN," Owen noted. "And the same yesterday. Your strength won't come back to you that way."

Sitting on their pallet in her shift, propped against their sea chest, Grace picked up the bowl of gruel from the decking nearby. Boiled in water without salt or milk, the porridge tasted bland enough. She let a mouthful of the thick mush slide down her throat before putting the bowl aside again.

"I don't know what's come over me, Owen. Not liking my food this way. In Ballybanree, 'twas a happy day when I didn't go to bed hungry. I should be gulping down every morsel in sight."

"You've just lost a babe and had a month of seasickness. No wonder you've no desire for food. But your hunger will return, and when it does, you'll be eating up the planking."

"What a sight that will be!"

She was trying to reassure him by sounding bright, but he wasn't deceived. She was deathly pale, more so today than yesterday. Lately, blue veins under the skin at her temples and throat had begun to appear, delicate tracery he could follow with a fingertip. The sight made him want to weep.

She was starving to death in front of his very eyes, day by day more frail and weak. Like the night she went into labor, his frustration overwhelmed him. He yearned to lash out, to pound his fists against the beams and howl in protest. But none of that would do a bit of good.

None of that would save her. "I'll leave you to finish dressing," he said. "The day is a gorgeous one, the first we've had in a fortnight. As soon as you're ready, we'll go to the upper deck. The air will do you good."

"I don't think I . . ."

"You don't have to, you have to get well. And then your thoughts can spring up like a ball of India rubber." He bent to kiss her cheek. "I'm going over to the food kettle to get my own feast, love, but I'll be back soon."

"Feast, indeed." She handed him her bowl. "Please take this and empty it in the slop pail. I'll take no more this morning."

When he returned after his breakfast, she had managed to dress in the blue frock and tie her hair up off her face with a piece of blue ribbon. For comfort, she had put on her old, soft moleskin brogues.

"Ready, love?" he asked gently. "Shall I carry you?"

"Sure and don't I have two legs of my own?"

She swayed on her feet. Owen drew her to his side and together they threaded their way through the crowded hold.

Everyone looked worn and soiled and down at the mouth, Owen noted. Only the children, bored after their weeks of confinement, still had the energy to tear around the ship playing games and fighting, finding amusement where and when they could. Their tired parents had nearly given up disciplining them, anxious only for the journey to end and land to be solid under their feet once more.

He couldn't blame them. He, too, was desperate for the voyage to end. How much longer could Grace go on choking down nothing more than a few spoonfuls of gruel and sips of water? Their daily ration of infested hardtack, dried peas, and gristly salt pork revolted her so much she wouldn't touch any of it.

Depending on the prevailing winds, two weeks, or possibly three, should bring them into Newport harbor. Two weeks. To Owen, an eternity as he studied Grace, pale and wan, in the clear, morning light. He settled her on the deck in the sunshine, propped next to one of the bulkheads. Even with the sun glowing down on her, she shivered.

"You're cold," he said. "I'll go below and find something to wrap you in."

"I'm acting like an old, old woman."

"You're nineteen and beautiful. But you're right about one thing. You're *my* old woman, and I love you. Now stay safe here. I'll soon be back."

He went below. She sat quietly where he had placed her, too listless to do otherwise. Closing her eyes, she raised her face to the sun, feeling its rays warm on her skin.

A few moments later, a shadow fell over her, blotting out the warmth. A cloud? Another storm? Dismayed, she opened her eyes and glanced up, straight into the long, arrogant face of Ross Rushmount.

"You're ill," he said, something strangely like concern flitting across his features. She looked away, angry to be stretched out at his feet while he towered above her. "I never expected to see you again. Not like this, certainly . . . so pale and thin." He frowned and bent over her. "Your eyes are still beautiful . . . and your hair . . . but where's your outrage and all that passion I remember so well? It set you apart." He lowered his voice. "After that night, I searched for you everywhere . . ."

His face a study in fury, Owen strode across the deck and gripped Rushmount's elbow.

Rushmount threw a startled glance over his shoulder and tried to wrench free. "Get your hand off me, O'Donnell."

"Aye, but first I'll have a word with you."

"We've had our words."

"There are a few more in the language we haven't yet used."

With his one hand never leaving Rushmount's elbow, Owen used the other to cover Grace with a blanket. He smiled at her. "I'll be back in a trice, love."

Again, Rushmount tried to pull away. Owen's grasp tightened. He had no intention of releasing him and knew the man's pride wouldn't allow him to cry out for help. Walking in lock step, he force marched him toward the stern. Only when they were out of Grace's sight and hearing, did he ease his hold.

"I told you to stay away from her."

Rushmount blew out a snort of distain. "Don't be ridiculous. The ship's too small for such restrictions."

"You're brave enough in the daylight with people about, but what of the night when darkness covers all?"

"I don't have to listen to your fanciful, Irish claptrap."

Owen stepped closer. "She's dying."

Rushmount's sneer fell away. "Good Lord, she's wasted, but I had no idea."

"You can save her."

"How?"

In some part of his mind, Owen recognized the shock on Rushmount's face and his question as genuine concern. He'd pursue the thought later, at his leisure. This was not the time.

"I understand we've two, maybe three, more weeks at sea. That's too long. She needs decent food. Now. Today, and every day till we make port."

"Oh, I see." The sneer returned to Rushmount's face. "You're asking me, no actually you're begging me, for food. How interesting, O'Donnell. The shoe, I take it, is on the other foot."

"Say what you will. You know damned well I'd starve before taking a mouthful from you. But you're right. For her, I beg. So shall we have your man fill a basket?" Owen couldn't resist a little smile, "with your next meal?"

"I could refuse you, but I won't. Not after seeing her. Wait here. I'll inform Thomas."

"I prefer to watch what goes into your largesse."

"You fear I'd poison her?"

"The idea occurred to me."

"That's not the revenge I seek. When my turn with her comes, I want her alive and full of fire."

"You expect me to rise to such stupid bait?"

Rushmount shrugged. "Suit yourself. In the meantime, I'll give her some food since you've begged for it."

In Rushmount's cabin, Thomas was in the act of laying out a meal. From the cage of live fowl carried on board ship for Captain Hopkins and his royal passenger, Cookie had killed and roasted a chicken. Fresh white bread scones were piled on a plate and next to them a pot of honey. Best of all, Owen spied oranges heaped high in another bowl. "I'll take all of this," he said, "and a bottle of Madeira. Lacking that, a bottle of any red wine you might have."

"Sir," Thomas began.

"Give him what he asks for," Rushmount said. "Fill a basket."

"I need a mug as well and a piece of napery. When this is gone, in a day or two, I'll be back" At the cabin door, Owen paused a moment. "Despite the differences between us Rushmount, I thank you for your generosity."

"Just leave."

Owen nodded. "For today."

He walked along the upper deck toward the bow, the laden basket over his arm. Now to tackle the main obstacle, convincing Grace to eat. Without a doubt, she'd refuse to touch Rushmount's food. His jaw tightened. The stubborn little fool. Either she would eat or they'd both die, for he had no intention of living without her.

He increased his pace, letting the wooden boot hit the deck without care for the noise it made. He'd start with the wine, convince her to sip that first.

"No." SHE SHOOK HER HEAD. "I can't swallow a bite of his food. 'Twould choke me. You were wrong to ask him, Owen. I prefer starving."

He lowered the basket onto the deck then crouched down so he could speak into her ear. "You listen to me. As your husband, I am ordering you to eat. Do you hear me?"

Her eyes blank, she stared straight ahead.

"Do you hear me?"

She continued her unseeing stare.

"You took a vow to love, honor and obey me."

"I should not have done so."

"*Ha.*" He laughed despite himself. "Too late for regrets. At the moment, you don't have to love or honor me, the obeying is what I'm after." He breathed a sigh of relief. The humor in her answer told him common sense had returned, and she'd do as he demanded. He pulled the cork from the wine bottle and filled the mug. "Here. Start with this. 'Twill warm your blood. After that, you'll have a drumstick. Then a scone with honey. And then an orange."

He sat facing her, watching her eat, watching the sea breeze lift her hair.

After a week, color began to return to her cheeks, and her form started to fill out the blue frock once again. As if to make up for all the days of denial, her appetite had returned with a ferocity that amazed her and delighted Owen.

He suspected Rushmount did without to supply him. When he approached the cabin for more food, the Englishman had whatever delicacy could be found aboard ship piled on the table and waiting. Boiled eggs, a small round of cheese intact within its red wax coating, a few bright apples, and every time, fresh-baked bread. Dipping it in the honey pot, Grace devoured every crumb.

Happily, he watched her recapture her radiance day by day. Without a doubt, he was in Rushmount's debt, a reality he accepted without the slightest regret although he knew Rushmount never gave anything away. He would exact a price for Grace's life. And it would be a heavy one.

CHAPTER SIXTEEN

Two weeks later, over the usual early morning tumult of groans and talk and scolding of children, Grace heard a sound from above. She froze in place, listening. *There it was again.*

"Land ho!"

The New World.

"We're here, at last!" She flung herself into Owen's arms, swinging him into a dance of sheer joy. In a few hours, they would be freed from this floating island with its fleas and rats and tainted food.

Eager for a glimpse of land, they hurried to the upper deck joining the other excited passengers crowding the rails. Their first sighting, a rocky coastline then the mouth of Newport harbor with its wide, white arc of sandy beach hove into view, and beyond it, on green hills by the shore, a goodly cluster of buildings. All made of wood, Grace noted with surprise. How unusual, no stone, no wattle and daub.

Sara squeezed in beside her, her beady eyes scanning the beach like those of a searching bird. Grace gave her a quick hug. Like many of the women on board, Sara was meeting her man in the colonies. Now that her husband and son had built a cabin and sown their second crop, they'd sent for her. Not a day too soon, she had announced one night at supper. "I'll see my son married before I die and my grandchildren as well."

Climbing about the rigging like squirrels in trees, the crew trimmed the sails bringing the *Seafarer* to a slow, shuddering halt. With much clanking of thick iron cables, two brawny seamen began rotating the capstan. When the anchor plunged deep into the bay securing the ship in place, the cheers of a hundred triumphant voices rose, shouting, into the air.

——————

IN HIS BUCKSKIN BREECH CLOUT AND MOCCASINS, his chest bare in the summer heat, Absalom stood hidden by the trees watching the pale-skinned people leave their giant ship in small boats and row toward land. They plied back and forth for hours until he counted over one hundred men, women and children on the beach.

For ten days, he and his men had been awaiting the ship's arrival. They had upturned their canoes and made temporary camp outside the town. This was his day to stand watch, but the news would wait until nightfall when the others returned from their hunt.

Judging from the confusion on shore, it would be the next morning or later before the ship's men unloaded the supplies Roger Williams had ordered for the Providence colony a year or more ago. Tomorrow, he would get out the copy of Roger's order he now had safe in his pack, folded inside a piece of wax-coated cloth.

As he looked on, to his amazement, many of the women ran up to men waiting on the shore, embracing them in the sight of all. No Narragansett woman would do such before others. Never once had he and his wife betrayed what passed between them in the night by so much as a raised eyebrow or a knowing smile. His jaw clenched at the memory of Naomai, her warmth turned into ice. Pneumonia, Roger had called it, a strange name not known to his people.

After her death a year ago, his mother's brother, Canonchet, urged him to take another bride. He had reached twenty-five winters; his mourning had gone on long enough; he needed sons. Each time the sachem had so instructed him, he managed to put off the day when he must choose . . . yet a man needed a woman at his side. The scene below revealed that.

He felt no need to take another mate. Since he'd lost Naomai, he'd been well served by the tribal women who had willingly sewn his moccasins and cooked his food, hoping, he supposed, that some day he would choose one among them. For it was no secret to him that his people respected his knowledge of the white man's ways.

It was good to have such knowledge held in high regard, and he took from it what he found valuable—how to speak as Roger spoke, and how to read and write in his English. Yet certain customs he would never embrace. Like this of the men and women.

Nor could he understand the loudness of their speech. A man could not walk through the forest and surprise a deer or any other creature unless he had the gift of silence.

As he waited, a red fox came close, and the birds jabbered undisturbed overhead. He hardly moved, blending with the trees, watching the panorama unfold before him until a sight so astounding caught his eye it caused his breath to catch in his throat.

————————

An hour earlier, Grace had lifted the blue frock to her knees and jumped out of the dinghy into the shallow surf. The rush of cool water against her feet and legs was heaven. Too many weeks had passed without a proper bath.

Soon now, all would change. They would find decent food and fresh water and, God willing, a home of their own. Surely in this vast territory, there would be unclaimed acres where they could live in peace. If not, their long journeying from Ballybanree had been in vain. But she wouldn't dwell on that, not on this glorious day.

She stumbled a bit in the surf. After weeks of moving to the rhythm of the sea, she would have to become accustomed to the earth under her feet once again. Owen climbed out of the skiff, splashing into the knee-high water. His wooden boot would become sodden and heavy, but she knew he'd endure that rather than expose his withered leg. She smiled over her shoulder at him, and he grinned back. The leg can go to the farthest reaches of hell he was telling her. Nothing could mar this day.

With a light heart, she raised her skirt to her knees and waded to shore. Once on dry sand, she looked about. A prudent distance from the ocean, small, sturdy houses made of whole logs—such an extravagant use of wood—formed a tight enclave. Beyond and around them, untamed forest stretched to the very edge of the water.

Two oarsmen wrestled their chest out of the boat and hoisting it on their shoulders carried it to dry land and dumped it unceremoniously onto the sand. Grace sat on the chest fanning her sodden skirt hem about her ankles. It would dry quickly in the hot sun. His breeches wet to the knees, Owen joined her. His glance combed through the throng. They would need shelter for the night and information as well. In a day or two, the *Seafarer* would take a few of the passengers north to Plymouth colony and others to Salem. Providence lay south of Newport. But how far south? And how to get there?

Grace spied Sara in the crowd, her arms around a short, slight man not much bigger than herself. "Over there, Owen. Sara's man might know something."

"Good thought, love. Wait here. I'll be back."

He hurried off, weaving his way through the tumult. Grace raised her face to the brilliant, summer sun. Her sodden skirt had half dried already. She looked down at it with distaste. Dirty and stained from weeks of wear, it felt like a soiled outer skin, one she'd love to slough off.

Ignited by the idea, she jumped off the chest and released its straps. Somewhere within lay a clean shift and waist and a gray linen skirt she'd saved for a moment like this. When she found the clean clothes, she refastened the chest then glanced through the crowd for a glimpse of Owen. No sight of him, but in the distance, she saw Lord Rushmount deep in conversation with an older man whose paunch stretched the seams of his doublet. The governor of Newport? At the very least, someone who could afford to eat heartily every day. To her relief, Rushmount clapped the portly man on the back, and still talking, the two walked away from the shore.

Ah, of course. Rushmount had no need to see to his possessions. His man Thomas would do that for him. She quelled the rising bitterness. Ross Rushmount's food had saved her life. She should be grateful, but all she wanted was to put miles between them. So far, he'd not said a word to Owen or anyone else about the night she'd set the townhouse bed afire. No doubt he wanted to keep his part in the matter hidden. Still, the sooner she and Owen departed Newport the better.

She stood on her toes peering over heads, hoping to see where Owen had gone, but he was nowhere in sight. He couldn't be far, but she wouldn't linger, she was that anxious. She turned to a man and wife standing nearby waiting for their goods to be carted off the beach to shelter. "Will you tell my husband I've gone walking along the shore?"

When they nodded in agreement, she hugged the clean clothes to her chest and hurried off. On this smooth surface, unlike the stony coast of Connaught, she had no need to carefully pick her way.

The beach followed the curve of the bay in an unblemished swath of pale sand. Here and there, high dunes studded the shore, their sandy hillocks sprouting bunches of tall sea grass. If she darted behind a dune, chances were no one at the landing place would notice. She could slip off her dirty clothes unseen and, fleet as a deer, be in that sparkling, cool water before anyone knew.

She tossed the clean clothes on a patch of dry sand behind the first sizeable dune she came to. Stripping off the soiled garments, she flung them aside. Conscious of the breeze playing against her naked skin and loving its touch, she risked a glance at the crowded landing. No one had missed her. No one looked her way. She glanced up at the trees on the rise in back of her. Nothing moved there but leaves rustling in the salt air.

Now. She took a deep breath and raced for the water. It met her eagerly, caressing her everywhere. She sank into its embrace letting it cover her to her shoulders. Then, emboldened by its sun-warmed touch, she ventured out deeper. At that, the waves began playing a rough game, knocking her to the sand, surging over her, plastering her hair to her back. She scrambled, sputtering, to her feet, feeling the sand melt between her toes as the surf surged out, then in, then out again. She must learn to swim, to go fearlessly into the deep the way Owen did, plunging in like a creature born to the sea.

"Grace!"

She tossed her wet hair away from her eyes and looked toward the voice. "Owen, 'tis glorious. Come!"

To her delight, he dropped to the sand and began removing his boots. He stripped, piling his clothes next to hers and limped into the surf. As soon as he was waist high in the water, he dove head first into the waves. An instant later, coming up alongside her, he took her in his arms.

ABSALOM HAD WATCHED THE LONE WOMAN leave the crowded landing place and walk along the shore. How unusual. A white man's woman seldom ventured out of sight of others.

Once behind a dune, she put down the bundle she carried and looked back at the busy throng, then up at the trees where he stood.

Unlike the other white women he had seen, this one had hair of a bright, extraordinary color. Nor was it bound up under a cap, or plaited like Naomai's had been. It flowed freely over her shoulders and down her back, gleaming like burnished metal in the sun.

She looked about again, then out at the ocean. Working fast, each movement quick and deliberate, she took off her garments and dropped them at her feet.

Ah. His breath left his body in a single rush. The red fox hearing it leaped away to safety. She was whiter than the sand and slender as a reed except where a woman should not be slender, and there she rounded into perfection. He had never seen a woman such as this one . . . even his beloved Naomai had been very different. Shorter. Broader of face and hips. This one

. . . there had to be words to put to her although there were none in his language. If there were any in his adopted tongue, he had never heard them.

A wave took her, tumbling her to the sand. His pulse quickened. Could she swim? Should he go to her? As he watched, torn, she righted herself and began to cavort in the water, her enjoyment clear even from where he stood.

From the corner of his eye, he saw a dark, bearded man hurry along the shore with a curious, awkward gait. Despite his labored pace, he stood tall, his upper body powerful, the muscles in his arms and shoulders obvious under his shirt.

The man called to the woman. She turned to him and waved her arm. "Come!"

The man sank to the sand to remove his boots then stripped himself of his clothes and limped, shoulders heaving, toward the water. One leg was as powerfully muscled as the rest of his body, the other shriveled below the knee to the size of a whittled stick. Had he come from his mother's womb disfigured so? Or had an accident befallen him?

Whatever the reason, once in the water, the man streaked to the woman, darting toward her like an arrow released from a bow. He came up behind her and seized her, turning her face to his. Chest deep in the water they kissed, a white man's custom Naomai had learned of and liked to practice with him. He refused to let the sigh that was forming in his chest escape. The woman pulled away from the man and splashed water at him . . . and he at her . . . playing like carefree children.

Again the man seized her in a long, lingering kiss. Had his own attempts with Naomi been so prolonged, so heedless of all but themselves? He couldn't remember.

When the kiss ended, the man took the woman by the hand and led her toward the shore. In the shallow water, she was revealed to him again, her breasts, her flat belly, her thighs, her long slim calves.

The man drew her to the dry sand behind the dune. There was no mistaking his intent.

It would be wrong to watch further. Absalom slipped away from the tree. He would return to camp and tell the others of the ship. The woman he would not mention. They would not believe such a woman would mate with a crippled man. But he had seen her obvious joy and knew the truth. She was an uncommon woman. He regretted that he would never come to know her.

Chapter Seventeen

"**I**F YOU'RE BOUND FOR PROVIDENCE, you'd best travel with the Indians. Their canoes will get you there the fastest. And safely, too, I warrant."

"Indians?" Grace's eyes widened in disbelief. "You mean the savages?"

"Aye," Sara's man, John Duxbury, replied with a suspicious hint of humor hovering at his mouth. "They'll not harm you. Not the Narragansetts. They're loyal to Roger Williams and his followers. He's the one who sent them to meet up with the *Seafarer*."

"Where are these natives?" Owen asked. "We've seen no sign of them."

"They'll be seen when they wish to be seen and not a moment sooner." John upped his chin at the stand of pines on the surrounding hills. "They'll come out of those woods so quiet like, you won't hear a twig snap or two leaves rub together. You'll look up of a sudden, and there they'll be, right in your path. It's enough to take the breath out of your body." He chuckled. "At least until you get used to their ways."

"If they move that quietly, they must be fine hunters." Grace was flooded, suddenly, with memories of the nights she'd stalked deer in the forest of Ballybanree.

"They're the best in the world, and generous to boot. Last autumn, we went hunting together and bagged three deer. They knew the colony needed meat and left all three for us. That meat saw us through the worst of the winter."

"I knew that letter you sent made life sound too easy," Sara said.

John patted her arm. "The winter's over now, Sary. I'm telling the tale so your young friends here will trust Absalom and his men."

Three deer taken without reprisals and openly shared. "Is there no law against poaching?" Grace asked.

"Poaching?" John scoffed. "The riches of the wilderness belong to all."

We truly have reached a New World, Grace thought, beaming her delight at Owen.

John cupped his eyes and squinted out to sea. After twenty-four hours at anchor, the *Seafarer* rode high in the water as her crew steadily unloaded her cargo, making room for the timber and furs they would bring back to England.

"From the way she's riding the waves, they've about emptied her." John looked up at the pines. "The Indians should be joining us soon."

Grace glanced out at the ship. Even with her sails furled, only her masts piercing the sky, she was a bold, beautiful sight. Yet Grace shuddered. She was glad to have spent the night in Sara and John's snug loft, and not on board the *Seafarer*. The voyage, a nightmare of filth and illness and violent seas, had cost the life of her child. Truly, if she were to keep her silent vow to match Granuaile's courage, it would have to be on land, not at sea. Kinswomen they were, but sent by God with different destinies.

Owen watched her frown as she stared at the *Seafarer*. "Are you glad to be free of her, love?"

Always, he knew her thoughts. She nodded. "I am that. And ashamed to say I never want to go aboard a ship again. Not for the rest of my mortal life."

"I understand. 'Twas a brutal passage. But," he added, looking over her shoulder with a twinkle in his eyes, "what is your feeling about dugout canoes?"

"What?" She whirled around. "Oh my God in heaven." Her hand, of its own accord, flew up to cover her open mouth. "The Indians!"

Twelve in all, they carried six canoes overhead, two men to each. As if they held nothing heavier than twigs, they walked effortlessly along the sand, nearly naked, only a flap of leather covering their private parts. When they came closer, she could see that though coarse, black hair fell to their shoulders, their well-muscled bodies were smooth and hairless, their copper-colored skin gleaming as if oiled.

She let out a breath. Savages, indeed. With their high-bridged noses and all-seeing glances, they had the look of hawks. Like hawks, they would be wild, efficient killers.

Near the landing place, they lowered the canoes to the sand. All but one dropped down next to their boats sitting impassive and silent. The one who remained standing reached into a pouch suspended from his shoulder by a woven leather cord. From it, he took out a piece of parchment. He unfolded it and, to Grace's growing astonishment, began to read.

At first, she thought he might be pretending, playing a game for the benefit of the onlookers. But as he read each item on his list, his dark eyes would glance up from the sheet he held and dart to a barrel or a crate. Several times, not readily seeing what his list called for, he walked over to the heaped-up pile of cargo and scanned their labels until he found what he wanted.

Seemingly satisfied at last that his list of goods was complete, he approached the ship's quartermaster.

"My men and I have come for the Providence supplies. I've checked. They're all here." He offered the list to the quartermaster who made no move to take it.

"What's your name, boyo?"

"Absalom."

"Mighty fancy. For an Indian."

The sailors standing guard over the mound of supplies guffawed.

Absalom's back stiffened, yet he replied calmly enough. "My men will gather what's ours."

"You've not asked permission, boyo."

"This is my permission."

Absalom dropped the sheet of parchment and let it flutter to the sand. He turned to his men uttering a command in his own language. In unison, they rose to their feet and, forming a tight phalanx, headed toward the supplies. Not one reached for his knife or spoke a word, or made a fast move, yet the sailors hovering nearby fell back, their laughter quickly coming to an end.

The Indians are defying them. Grace's heart leapt in her breast. What a fine thing to see. But why did she feel so? The answer came to her in an instant as clear as rain water caught in a bucket. They had been treated with contempt, like creatures not worthy of respect, as if they were Irish.

She squeezed Owen's arm. He covered her hand with his own. "I heard it, love. Good for the natives."

She glanced over at Sara's John and caught sight of a grin creasing his face. No doubt about his enjoyment at seeing the sailors bested.

With an economy of words and gestures, Absalom directed his men in separating out the cases and barrels they had come to claim. Ignoring the sailors, they piled their goods into a pyramid near the canoes.

"Now comes the clever part," John said. "Their vessels are swift, but they'll capsize easily if not packed with care. We'd best speak up if you're still of a mind to leave." His glance fell on Grace.

He believes I'm afraid, but I'm not. The realization pleased her. "I'm ready if Owen is."

"More than ready."

"Come then. Absalom knows me. Let me do the asking."

He saw them walking toward him. The little man named John, and the crippled newcomer with the powerful arms and shoulders, and the woman. Today, her hair was tied with a green ribbon, her body covered by her white woman's clothing.

They stopped a few feet away, close enough for Absalom to see her face clearly. It was as beautiful as the rest of her and burned from yesterday's sun. Tiny spots of light brown dusted across her nose. Her eyes, staring at him as if she had never seen his like before, were the color of the sea.

"These folks here," John began, "are wanting to go to Providence." He cleared his throat. "They're wondering if you can take them along."

No one could know the effect John's words had on him, for he did not allow his eyes to flicker or a muscle to move in his face. He alone knew their effect, and his own response shocked him. She was another man's woman. She had shown that plainly enough. It would be better by far not to have her near.

"We have no room for passengers," he said flatly.

"You could leave some of the supplies and send for them tomorrow." John laughed. "Take the books and the wine. Leave the rest. I'll keep it safe for you overnight."

Absalom shook his head. He found no humor in John's jest. The day was fair, the seas calm. He would pack the canoes and return with what he had been sent for and nothing else.

He turned to his men. "Begin the loading."

Her man stepped closer. "My name is Owen O'Donnell. This lady is my wife, Grace. For a year, we've been trying to reach Providence. I ask you to reconsider."

"There is no room."

"We'll leave our sea chest for another day." The man smiled easily in the way white men often did. "The lady takes up little room."

With her green eyes shining on her man, she smiled, too, revealing even, white teeth.

"No, it's not possible."

"I see."

At the sound of strident voices, Absalom looked across the sand. A tall stranger, accompanied by the fleshy one they called Governor Clark, was hurrying toward them. The tall one carried himself with arrogance. His elaborate clothes and high, polished boots spoke of wealth. More often than not, that spelled trouble in dealing with white men, but it would be wise to wait and see.

As if fearing they would load up and leave before he could reach them, the tall one called out, "O'Donnell, I'll have a word with you."

At the shouted announcement, quick anger rose up in O'Donnell's face. He masked it, Absalom saw, with another easy smile.

"Lord Rushmount. We've traveled half the world over, yet we can't escape the sight of you."

"Watch yourself, Irishman. I'm here on the king's business, not to joust with you."

"You sought me out, not the other way around. What do you want?"

"To begin with, I want to see how your lady wife fares. Last time we spoke, she was ill." The stranger's hot glance swept over the woman, lingering on her longer than a man's glance should. His mouth twisted into a sly, knowing smile. "You're better. Much better."

"State your business," O'Donnell said.

The arrogant one turned to the governor who had followed him, red-faced and out of breath. "Is this the savage I'm looking for?"

"Yes, that's Absalom."

"I have a message for your master."

"I have no master."

As if he hadn't spoken, the arrogant one said, "Tell him Lord Rushmount will visit Providence in the coming months. And tell him to be ready. He'll know what that means." His glance returned to the woman and moved slowly over her once more. "I'm glad to see you thriving."

O'Donnell tensed, his big hands fisting into clubs, but before he could lunge at the man, the woman slipped her arm through his, lightly holding him to her side. "For the food you gave me, I'm grateful, Lord

Rushmount. 'Twas a kind gesture." She swept her free arm toward Absalom. "This is Mister Absalom. I understand he, too, shares his food."

"*Mister* Absalom?" The words more a sneer than a question.

"That's correct. I've heard tell when he and his people hunt deer in the forest they give meat to all who need it. So my congratulations to you. You're nearly as generous as he is."

The tall one gasped then drew himself up to his full height. "You dare compare me to a savage, you little . . . ." He stopped, threw back his head, and laughed. "Your fire has returned to you. Excellent." Without a further word, he strode away, his heels making deep indentations in the wet sand.

His face dark with rage, O'Donnell plucked the woman's hand from his arm and went to lunge for the man.

"No, Owen, please." She grasped him by the hand. "This is no way to start our new life. Please, I beg you. Don't touch him."

O'Donnell expelled a ragged breath of anger and gave a sharp nod. "For your sake then. This time only. Never ask the same of me again."

Silently, Absalom exulted. She had defied the arrogant one using words as her weapons, and like pointed arrows carefully shot, they had hit their mark. And with another few soft words, she had kept O'Donnell from violence.

"I've reconsidered," he said. "I'll take you to Providence. Both of you and your sea chest as well."

Chapter Eighteen

HE DIDN'T HAVE TO ASK HIMSELF why he agreed to take them. He knew.

Mister Absalom. The white man's title sounded alien to his ears. He neither wanted it nor liked it. But coming from her mouth, the words rang with a warmth he found pleasing. The fire in her eyes when she spoke out to the arrogant one had pleased him as well, and her gentle touch on her man's arm, keeping him from violence. Any man would be proud to claim her, yet she had chosen a cripple, undeterred by his withered leg.

Clearly, she was a woman above other women. He could no more leave her behind on the Aquidneck shore than he could leave the supplies he had been charged with bringing to safety.

"Have you ever ridden in a canoe?" he asked her man.

"Never. Please call me Owen. My wife is Grace."

Absalom nodded. Strange names, but he would become accustomed to them if, as he suspected, they made Providence their home. "You must sit quietly. No sudden movements. No standing."

"We'll do as you advise."

"Good. Two of my men will go with you now to get your chest. We must leave while the day is still early. You will travel in the lead boat with Canonchet. Your woman, Grace, will travel in the last boat with me."

Owen hesitated, obviously not wanting to be separated from her by even the length of a few longboats. "I'd prefer to be in the same canoe as my wife."

Absalom shook his head. "Should you both need help, I might not reach the two of you in time."

"I'm a strong swimmer."

"You don't know the currents in these waters. You go with Canonchet."

"Don't worry, Owen," the woman said. "I'll be safe with Absalom."

Owen nodded, reluctance still plain on his face. "I don't like it, but you've come too far for me to stay you now."

Utilizing every available inch of storage space, the men continued packing the dugouts they had lined up in a neat row on the sand. It soon became evident, he would have to leave three cases behind with the man called John and return for them tomorrow. He made certain the box of books went aboard. Roger had been waiting a year for them. They would be the first thing he would look for.

He ignored Canonchet's scowl. His uncle understood little of the English tongue, but he knew enough to realize the two white travelers would be coming with them. *Why?* his hooded glances asked. A wise leader, he undoubtedly suspected the truth and was disturbed by it: he wanted the woman left behind.

After seeing his sea chest safely stowed, Owen helped Grace climb into the last canoe steadying its wobble until she had settled herself.

Before taking his position in the lead canoe, Canonchet came up to Absalom, his chronic frown deepening. "She's trouble."

"Trouble cannot be escaped."

"When it has hair like the sun, you should run from it."

He didn't answer. *Like the sun. Yes.*

"*Bah.*" Disgust clear on his face, Canonchet strode to his dugout.

After waving farewell to John's small, wizened wife, the woman sat motionless between the tightly packed cartons. The other boats were already afloat, cutting through the surf like sharks. When his cousin, Comise, took up his oar by the prow, Absalom shoved off. They quickly followed the others, and soon the Aquidneck shore fell away, and Conanicut, the island known to the whites as Jamestown loomed ahead. Skirting the island, they headed north straight into the bay of the Narragansetts.

Their course set, Absalom stroked easily using half his strength, half his mind. The last man in line he could stare at the woman's back without being observed. The breeze lifted her hair, tangling it about her shoulders like strands of burnished copper, sending back hints of the lavender white women liked to grow in their gardens. Her garment, in the odd manner of the whites, fit tightly to her narrow waist, revealing the indentation of her spine each time she leaned over slightly to trail her fingers in the water.

Though she sat as he'd instructed and didn't speak or turn back to glance at him, the time passed swiftly, and soon the broad slopes of Fox Point came into view, followed shortly after by the hills ringing the Providence River.

He expected Roger would be awaiting them on the shore, wondering who these two strangers might be and what they wanted. He wondered himself. *Who are they, and why had they spent a year traveling here?*

He easily understood all of their words, but their English speech sounded different from the others. Roger would know why. He knew all things regarding the colonists and much concerning the Narragansetts as well.

When Absalom was four winters old, the smallpox claimed his parents and Roger asked to raise him as his own son. Although torn between anger at what the colonists took and gratitude for what they gave, Canonchet agreed, and when Absalom grew old enough to understand, he told him it was good for one of their people to learn white customs and speech, for there was no way to stop the tall ships from crossing the great water and disgorging newcomers onto their shores. Although the sea and forests teemed with life, and grains grew in their fields, Absalom knew this steady stream of light-skinned ones disturbed Canonchet greatly. But hadn't the Great Mother Earth created all men, and didn't she nurture them equally as Her children?

While they made their way along the coast, the woman looked at the shore as though studying it carefully, one hand raised to shield her eyes against the glare. At other times, she stared into the water, following the silver trail of a fish.

She knew how to keep silent . . . a good thing . . . but he found himself wanting to hear her voice and its unusual accent once again. He grasped his oar harder. Canonchet was right as always. Trouble came in many forms. But what man worthy of the name avoided trouble simply because it threatened his peace?

In the knot of people waiting on the banks of the Providence River, he spied Roger, his mane of white hair unmistakable even from a distance. His reaction to the strangers would be interesting to watch.

At the edge of the crowd, Liliawa also stood waiting. Too modest to come forward and greet him, she let her presence on the beach speak for her. Later, she would prepare food and bring it to his wickiup, her eyes downcast, her will ready to bend to his.

Was she not everything a maiden should be? his uncle asked repeatedly, his exasperation growing stronger each time he did so. Absalom had no answer for him, or for himself, or for Liliawa. Since Naomai's voice had been stilled, he preferred the quiet of his lodge to the sound of another woman's voice.

You lie. That is no longer true.

He lifted his oar out of the water and stowed it, dripping, in the hull before leaping out to help Comise beach the canoe on the sand beside the others. Her man came running toward them, not stopping to greet anyone, hurrying to his woman in that awkward way of his. Nimbly, not needing any help, she scrambled from the canoe on bare feet, a sorry pair of what looked like moccasins in one hand.

Before running to O'Donnell, she paused to speak in that captivating voice he had been longing to hear again. "What a glorious afternoon you gave me, Absalom. Until now, the sea's been my enemy. But no more, thanks be to you." She smiled up at his face, a smile meant for him alone. Then, with a light step, she ran to her husband who caught her in his powerful arms embracing her in the sight of all.

Absalom looked away, his jaw set, chin held high. He would never become accustomed to such display. As he went to help unload the supplies, he saw Roger approach the strangers. Let the white men talk together. He had no reason to listen, merely an overwhelming interest he forced himself to deny.

"YOU'RE IRISH," ROGER WILLIAMS SAID at the lilt in Owen's first words.

If he was disappointed in what they were, Grace saw no sign of it cloud his face. His expression remained as warm and welcoming as if they had hailed from the very heart of London town. As the two men shook hands in greeting, Grace studied the person she had heard so much about. He was somewhere in his sixth decade she guessed, his body tall and lean, his face hollow-cheeked, his mouth kind. On a lesser man, his clothing might be a cause for amusement, but somehow on Roger Williams, a white linen stock worn under a fringed buckskin jacket with black breeches and buckled shoes seemed the proper garb for a clergyman. She knew she would like this man and grinned at him.

"We are Irish, indeed," Owen was saying. "And Roman Catholic into the bargain."

"Ah, the soup thickens," Roger said warmly. "Rhode Island boasts no Irish and no Catholics. We've Baptists, though, aplenty and Quakers and Antinomians and a Jewish synagogue in Newport."

"We were told a man's religion doesn't matter here," Owen said. "Nor his past."

"True," Roger said smiling. "When men seek us out with good intentions in their hearts, they're most welcome, indeed. I point out your difference only to warn you of what to expect. A welcome, of course, but no compatriots."

"Sure and everyone who lives here has left his native land," Grace said. "In that, are we not all the same?"

Roger held out his hands to Grace, taking both of hers firmly into his own. His quick smile deepened the creases fanning out from his eyes. "You strike at the core of the matter, young Mistress O'Donnell. The Indians have a saying: If you live on the land and love it, you are a native of the land."

"A grand saying, one I can truly ken, for we loved our Irish land full well. But Ireland was not allowed to love us in return. I pray life will be different here with you. And that you will call me Grace," she added softly, suddenly shy under his scrutiny.

"It will be my honor to do so, Grace," Roger replied with a courtly bow. "I suspect you have many tales to tell, and I'm anxious to hear them all." He clapped one arm around Owen's shoulder, another around Grace. "Come. We'll sup together and talk of the past. And more important, of the future." He glanced back at the boats that were being unloaded. "Absalom's men will carry whatever you brought with you up to my cottage."

"First allow me to tie on my brogues," Grace said. "Or I'll be greeting my new village in bare feet." She laughed, the sound floating on the air for all to hear. "Since this isn't Ireland, that won't do at all."

After Naomai's death, Absalom refused to abandon the summer wickiup they had fashioned together of bent sapling poles covered with woven mats and birch bark. He had repaired the winter ravages, patching the sloped walls and roof, and stayed on alone during the last growing season and this one as well, allowing neither kin nor friend to share its silence with him. Canonchet had protested, but to no avail.

In any event, this would be his last summer here. The next year, as was the tradition of his people, they would move to fresh fields that had long lain fallow. A prudent custom, it insured the continued rich harvests of maize and beans and squash they dried and put aside for the six months of winter when the earth slept.

But today the awakened land burgeoned with life, and as he pulled back the woven flap and entered his home, dimming the bird song and the sunlight, the isolation struck him like a heavy blow. Perhaps he should heed his uncle's advice to remarry, to join the clan in all fullness. Yet despite his loneliness, something he couldn't name held him back.

He slid the shaft of arrows and the bow from his shoulder and dropped his deerskin pouch on the ground beside them. He would try to sleep for a while, before Liliawa came with food, as she was sure to do, her doe eyes asking him for what he could not, or would not, give.

He had no sooner formed the thought when the entrance flap parted. Liliawa stood in the opening, a bowl of warm food in her hands. She'd wasted no time in coming to him, the food a pretext for seeking him out. He should be flattered. She had a woman's needs and had chosen him to fulfill them.

He nodded in welcome. Without that, she would turn and leave, and he had no wish to insult her gift.

She stepped in, letting the flap close behind her. "Succotash. From new beans, very small but tender, and dried corn. I sprinkle salt."

He groaned inwardly, recognizing in her few words of halting English an attempt to please him. She had dressed carefully for him, too, in a sleeveless tunic of pale kidskin that came to her knees. Her feet and legs and arms were bare, her skin, even in the half light, tawny and supple from her work in the sun. As befit the daughter of a ruling family, she wore an extravagant wampum headband, its purple and white shells woven into an intricate design of great value. Beneath the band, thick, black plaits fell forward over her shoulders.

Absalom sighed. She was beautiful, but . . . he didn't want her.

In one fluid movement, she knelt by his cold firepit and placed the bowl on the stones. He knew she expected him to tell her of his days at Aquidneck, of the colonists there, and of their cousins the Wampanaugs, and of the great ship with the word *Seafarer* painted on its bow . . . and of the strangers, the man and woman he had brought here with him.

With the lids of her eyes cast down, as if the dead ashes held a fascination for her, she waited.

"I have much to tell Liliawa of these past few days," he began. "But this is not the hour for tales. I must sleep for a while. Later, perhaps."

She rocked back on her heels and stood, again her movement fluid and effortless. Her back stiff with anger, she raised the flap, ducked through it and left him without a parting word.

So he had insulted her after all.

She was not a slave woman or a captive. If once he joined his body with hers, he would be bound to her forever. In this way his people survived, and he respected their unwritten laws too much to break them, or to uphold them for a woman he did not love.

Love. He smiled, thinking of the fury Canonchet would unleash if he were to share this thought with him. Women were created by the Great Mother to serve the needs of men, his uncle would say. Love between the sexes was a corrupt white man's concept. A man must honor the woman who bore him strong sons and planted his crops and prepared his food, but no more than that should be expected of him.

He stretched out on his pallet, his weight cushioned by the fragrant fir boughs under the buckskin covering. With his hands beneath his head, he stared up at the fading light filtering through the roof mats. In the distance, a bird twittered a final good night, but he knew sleep wouldn't come to him. Not with the sound of the white woman's voice echoing in his ears and her image troubling his mind.

CHAPTER NINETEEN

Grace and Owen followed Roger up a hill to a steep-roofed house cunningly made of overlapping boards and surrounded by a low wall of stones piled together without mortar.

Inside the wall, a sloping front yard rioted with the pinks, oranges and yellows of blooms Grace couldn't name. How grand, she thought. In Ireland, she'd only known the wildflowers that grew unattended. People there wrestled food from the earth, wasting little effort coaxing out beauty for its own sake.

In the kitchen garden by the side yard, she recognized onion sprouts and even the deep green leaves of *praities*. A strange, dangerous plant to cultivate. But what were the vines creeping like giant fingers between the onion rows and the strange greenery clinging to a series of upright stalks? Everything, the plantings she recognized and those she had never seen before, appeared to be thriving in the bright, midsummer sun. No wonder. The garden could be easily watered from the spring gurgling nearby.

From this high vantage point, the Providence River, on its way to the deeper, blue-green waters of the bay, shimmered below them in the afternoon light.

"How beautiful everything is," she said, looking about.

"Yes," Roger replied. "From the first, I felt Divine Providence had touched this place."

"'Tis well named."

"As you are, Grace," Roger said with a small bow.

"Aye," Owen readily agreed. "Both for heavenly grace and a pirate queen." He grinned. "She was the fiercest woman ever to dwell on the west coast of Ireland."

Roger's eyes lit up. "Now what would drive a woman to such extremes? That must be the first tale you tell me. Come in, come in," he invited, opening his door.

It felt good to be in a house again. Grace studied it as if it were the Bible wrapped safe inside their sea chest. In the main room, the keeping room Roger called it, the walls were smooth panels of planed wood, their solid surface pierced by two small, diamond-paned windows. To admit more light and air, he left the door wide open. In cold weather, with the tight walls keeping out drafts and a fire burning in the huge stone fireplace, the cottage would be warm and free of smoke. She'd have such a fireplace in her new home she promised herself and white-washed walls, too.

Near the chimney, she sat beside Owen on a spindle-backed settle. Across from them, Roger eased himself onto a great, wooden chair intricately carved with vines and leaves, its seat softened by a padded cushion. She'd make a crewel-work cushion like that for Owen's chair—once he had a chair.

How lovely in winter to sit gazing at the flames while supper simmered above the coals sending its aroma into the room. As soon as she had her own hearth, she'd put the spices tucked in the sea chest to good use.

Roger's big, square bed, its curtains drawn aside, took up a full corner of the room. The cottage she'd grown up in had no curtains around its pallets. She eyed them with interest. Unlike the opulent bed swags in the town house Rushmount had forced her to enter, these were simple woolen hangings. She liked the look of them. Sleeping in such a bed would be wondrously snug on a winter's night with Owen lying beside her. They could close the hangings and shut out the world . . . even this New World . . . and create a small paradise for themselves alone. As well as a fireplace and cushions, she'd surely have curtains about their bed.

The room's rough-hewn table and stools looked little different from those back in Ireland. But the books piled on the tabletop made a heart-stopping difference. Why they hardly left space for a tankard or a bowl of soup. Some day, she might be allowed to read them. All of them if she were lucky.

In the span of this single day, so many excitements had mounted one on the other, she knew they had been right to seek out Providence. With a happy sigh, she drew her attention away from the household and fastened it on Roger.

"Our daughter, Mercy, is expecting a child any day now," he was saying. "Mary, my wife, has gone to the Waterman farm to be with her. As you can see, I have little use for tidiness. But I do have an excellent supper to offer you. Goodwife Harris cooks for me while Mary's away. That's her meat pasty on the sideboard. We'll share it, but first a tankard of ale."

As he pressed his hands onto the chair arms to help lift himself from the cushion, Grace leapt up.

"Please allow me. 'Tis woman's work."

"Is that so?" Roger sank back onto his seat. "When a woman knows her duties so clearly, she knows her man's just as well. You have challenges ahead of you, young Owen," his smile taking any sting from his words.

"And don't I know it." Owen laughed.

"And don't you love it," Roger rejoined.

"Indeed, I do. I'm a fortunate man to have Grace in my life. That I know full well."

"What you are is a clever man with words, Owen O." Grace dropped a kiss on his forehead and handed them both a tankard of ale. Then she filled herself a mug from the ironstone crock standing on the sideboard amid plates and books and bits of cheese and biscuit. They had only just arrived, but already she felt at home.

Roger drank deep of the ale and wiped his mouth with the back of a hand. "Ah, that's good . . . one of God's great gifts. But not as great as womankind, of course."

"Sure and you must be Irish." Grace smiled over at him.

"I've been called many things in my lifetime, but never Irish. I like it." He laughed and took another swallow. "Now," his banter fading as quickly as it had surfaced, "tell me the story of your pirate queen. And following that, tell what you want of me."

Later, after much laughter and relating of tales, Owen said, "I'm a blacksmith by trade and . . ."

He got no further. "A blacksmith, excellent! We're desperate for a blacksmith. You've been sent by God." Roger pulled himself to his feet, seized Owen's hand and shook it vigorously. "Our present smithy, James Howard, ails. The work has become too difficult for him."

A frown creased Owen's brow. "My intention is to farm."

"And so you shall," Roger said, dropping back onto his chair. "But before you refuse my request, let me tell you about our winters. They're long and bitter, the ground frozen like stone for months at a time. That's when our blacksmith works the forge. Except for dire emergencies, we save our repairs and the like for the cold months." He leaned forward eagerly. "Will you consider it? The colony's need is great, and the work would provide you with extra income. Of course, we have little coin here. You'd be paid in barter goods for the most part. Grain or seed, most likely. Come spring, you'll be needing both."

He sat back in his chair, beaming. "A blacksmith. I can't believe it. Though I should, for the Lord makes all things possible. So what say you, blacksmith O'Donnell? Will you man our forge?"

"You've made it passing hard for me to refuse," Owen said, a quick smile replacing his frown. "So for God and Providence, I will. During the cold months only."

"Excellent." Roger clamped his hands on his bony knees. "Now let me tell you about the sachem Canonchet and how best to approach him for the land you seek."

"Aye, we do have a longing for land of our own," Grace said.

Roger nodded. "Land is worth striving for. As long as there's no evil in its acquisition."

"Ah." Owen's smile disappeared. "We have knowledge of that. All of Ireland has been seized by thieves . . . its land given over to the king's favorites . . . the people left half-starved, half-clothed, no better than slaves. We have no desire to repeat those sins here nor to . . . ." He stopped. "Forgive me, Roger. I forget myself." He leaned back on the settle and drew Grace close. "The truth is I love my country. Some part of me will miss it always. But Grace and I had to leave or die." His hand gripped her shoulder. "We have no wish to die. Or to steal land."

"No, it's our duty to live," Roger agreed, "and to pay for what we desire."

In the mercurial way Grace would come to know well, his mood changed from kindly concern to anger. "A hundred years ago, Henry Tudor used religion as a wedge to get what he wanted . . . wealth . . . land . . . power. Even in this New World, his policies continue."

Grace inhaled a breath of pure shock. "No, dear God, that can't be true. Not here."

"Ah, but it is," Roger said. "This is an English colony." He peered over at Owen. "You must have known that before you ventured forth."

Owen shrugged, his expression grim. "We did, but saw no other way. In all this vastness, we hoped there would be space for us."

"I see." Roger took another sip of his ale. "It's true there's an uncharted wilderness at our backs. An entire continent we're told. Few white men have set foot there except fur trappers and other adventurers. They've returned with wondrous accounts, some of doubtful authenticity, I fear, but not all."

Roger's eyes shone in the midst of their creases. "What the New World offers strains the imagination. And enflames the governments of England, and France, and of Spain to the south of us. But everyone forgets this is not an unclaimed wilderness. Not entirely." Grace went to protest but Roger held up a restraining hand. "It belongs to the Indian people."

As he finished the last of his ale and paused, Grace felt the summer warmth drain from her face. "Are you telling us the Indians are like the Irish? In danger of losing what is rightly their own?"

"Exactly."

"Yet here you are in a snug house. Your colony is a beacon of hope. How can that be?"

"Our royal charter differs from those of the other colonies. Here we rule with liberty of conscience." As he spoke, a note of satisfaction crept into his voice.

"What does that mean, sir?"

"We pay taxes to the king, yes, but we make our own rules of government. And the one rule we uphold above all is to buy our land from the Indians. We don't seize it. As a result, the natives live in peace with us. We respect each other as equals in the eyes of our Gods."

"Gods?" Stunned to hear Roger speak of more than one God, Grace felt her jaw drop open. If Father Joyce could hear him, he'd die of the shock.

Roger's long hands rested on the arms of his chair. "We have different gods, their Mother Earth and our Christ."

He spoke calmly enough, his expression serene, but it was his hands Grace watched. Their hold on the chair had tightened as he continued. "No one has the right to tell a man how to worship his Creator. Or to use religion as an excuse to seize his property." He bent forward, his fingers moving to his knees. "Do you know I'm an outcast from the Massachusetts colony? The church elders there banished me."

"Why?" Grace was baffled that anyone would force this kindly man from their midst.

"They feared my challenge to their authority. For them, religion is a mandate from God. Among other privileges, it gives them the right to strip the natives of their land. Much like what has happened in your

Ireland." He began massaging his knees. "So, my young friends, where does that leave us?"

"'Tis what *we* want to know," Grace said, the confusion she felt, rising into her voice.

Roger chuckled and slowly rose to his feet. "My knees stiffen, but so does my appetite. What say you we eat first and discuss your future afterward? It will seem more hopeful on a full belly." Stiff-legged, he walked to the table. "Will you serve up the meal, young Grace? And shall we have another mug of ale with our food?"

To make room on the table top, he piled the books on a stool. Grace refilled their tankards and carried three pewter dishes, wooden spoons, and the pasty to the table. Roger sat at his place, tented his hands and bowed his head in silent prayer. Owen glanced at Grace, and taking their seats, they did the same.

Roger's a man of his word, Grace thought, her spirits rising as she prayed. He's leaving us free to offer thanks in our own way. Enchanted, she poured out her heart in quiet.

As promised, the pasty proved delicious, a blend of potatoes—which is what Roger called them, not *praities*—and onion and chunks of rabbit stewed in a savory sauce, its top crust enhanced with the flavor of cheese. What a grand taste it had in the mouth. And the *praities*—potatoes— were safe to eat after all. Not poisonous as she had been taught. She had so much to learn, and unlearn, in this New World.

His meal finished and tankard empty, Roger moved from his stool back to the cushioned chair. "Now, shall we talk about that land you seek?"

WITHOUT IRELAND'S LONG GLOAMING, dark came fast on a summer's eve in the New World, and with it, bedtime. As soon as was seemly, they said good-night to Roger and went into his spare room, closing the door behind them. As Grace placed the single candle on a wall shelf, Owen leaned against the closed door, his body motionless, his expression serious.

"What have I done, love, bringing you to this wild place where most men are savages and others are filled with greed? What if the Indians won't sell us land? Or what if they do, but I lack the skill to make it thrive? At least, in Ballybanree you—"

"Shhhh." She hurried across the small room to him and stopped his worry with a kiss.

"I would be nowhere else on earth, Owen O'Donnell, except here in this wild, exciting land with you. We *will* gain our acres, and together we will make them bloom. I promise you." She flashed him a wicked grin. "Are you not happy we have a bed chamber to ourselves at last? And ours until we have a cottage built. 'Twas grand of the man to welcome us so. Shall we waste the night, then?" Her hands at the ties of her skirt, her face filled with mischief, she blew out the candle.

He crossed the room in the dark and took her in his arms. "You have no fear of what lies ahead, do you?"

"None. As long as we're together."

"I don't deserve you. I never have."

Keeping her voice silky and soft, she said, "Then I wager you don't want your just deserts."

"Ah, in that, Mistress O'Donnell, you are entirely wrong. Deserving or no, I do want them." His hands began fumbling for the ties at her waist. "Hurry. I'm too clumsy. I don't know where all the ribbons are." He gave her a quick, playful kiss before releasing her.

"Very well. If I must, I must," Grace retorted, enjoying the game she had begun and that he was so willing to play. In moments, her clothes joined his in a heap on the floor.

"Now drive me mad with kisses," Owen said. "It won't take many. One touch of your mouth will do. Come, I'm waiting."

"I'll begin slowly," she murmured.

"Begin as you like. In any way," he said, his voice hoarse.

She took his face in her hands, brushing his lips with her own, teasing him with gentleness until she sensed he had reached the point of rebellion. When she felt the muscles in his arms harden, ready to assume control, she parted her lips. He rewarded her with a groan.

She slid her hands from his face, running them across his broad, muscled shoulders then down his back, slowly, tenderly, her mouth never leaving his, her fingertips loving every inch of him as they descended to cup his bare buttocks. He pulled his mouth from hers. "The happiness you bring me, love, is beyond belief. I adore you." He drew her to the bed. "Come. It's been overlong since we've had a bed to love in."

"I've no hope of sleep at all, then?" The smile he couldn't see clear in her voice.

"Not if I can prevent it." He tugged her onto the featherbed and kissed her cheek, tasting the ocean salt still clinging to her skin. "I'm abed with a mermaid," he whispered in her ear.

"Oh, but you're not," she said as she parted her legs.

CHAPTER TWENTY

"T HE STRANGERS WANT LAND," CANONCHET SAID. "Like all the light-skinned ones. Always it is the land."

Absalom sat quietly by the firepit as he and his uncle awaited their food. The quail were nearly ready for eating, their succulent odor rising in the air, causing his mouth to water in anticipation. As soon as Riana, Canonchet's wife, slid them from their skewers and placed them on the reed mats, he would eat then seek the peace of his wickiup.

Today, at daybreak, he and Comise had canoed to Aquidneck and returned just before dark with the three missing crates of supplies. Tomorrow, at first light, he would deliver them into Roger's keeping.

"You should have listened to me," Canonchet was saying, "and left the strangers on Aquidneck with our cousins, the Wampanoags." Absalom said nothing. His uncle glared at him across the fire. "Have you no answer for me?"

"It was not possible to leave them." To his dismay, he realized he had nearly said "her."

"Bah. A man always has a choice."

"With all respect, uncle, you did not understand their words."

"I understood more than you know."

"They traveled for a year to get to Roger. Their long journey deserved its reward."

Canonchet snorted in disgust. "Their reward means nothing to me."

Riana placed a roasted quail before each of them along with a water gourd. Liliawa followed carrying maize cakes and a bowl of wild strawberries. Absalom reached for the bird. Leaning over, he ripped off a leg, avoiding Liliawa's questioning eyes. Knowing he had eaten, she would have no excuse to come to him later with food. He sighed, wondering how long it would be before his body betrayed him. His jaw tightened. Lately, his need pulsed stronger than ever, but the reason wasn't Liliawa.

Canonchet fell on his food. It occupied him for a while, stilling his complaints. But they would start up again when he had taken his fill. He was too shrewd not to suspect the white woman with the sun in her hair brought unrest along with her.

But he need not fear for his nephew. He would have nothing to do with the strangers, either of them. Although Roger had taught him as if he were an English child, the Narragansetts were his people. To them he belonged. From them he would seek a mate. But not yet.

His decision made, his body relaxed. He tore off another leg, chewing more slowly, satisfied with what he had just decided.

Canonchet belched and took a noisy gulp of water from the gourd. "Roger is bringing them to me in the morning. To deal for a tract of land."

Absalom's newly won peace drained away as he awaited his uncle's next words.

"I want you here to tell me what they say. Roger's speech is sometimes inaccurate."

"He is excellent at our language."

"Yes, for a white skin. But not always is it good enough." Canonchet rose from his blanket. "I will rest now for the night. In the morning, two hours after sunup, we meet here." He turned and stalked away, his rigid back registering his irritation.

Absalom finished his meal alone and flung the bones into the fire. He, too, would rest. He would need his wits about him in the morning.

When he stood, Liliawa flashed a quick glance in his direction. If it were not a violation of tribal practice, he would go to her and say, "Seek another, Liliawa." He regretted he couldn't do so. Despite her young loveliness, he had no desire to tie his life to hers. They had found nothing to speak of together except the routine of their days, nothing to exult in, nothing to cause the searing joy in his heart he remembered sharing with Naomai. Feeling as he did, he would not bring contentment to either one of them.

But he couldn't wound her so directly nor insult her Aunt Riana's kin in this manner. The open way white men spoke to their women had much to recommend it, but he was not white. He passed by Liliawa without speaking.

He slept fitfully. The owls hooted loudly all night, keeping him awake for hours, and at sunrise, the robins, as usual, greeted the day noisily.

He delivered the missing cartons to Roger's doorstep before returning to his wickiup to wait. True to his word, two hours after sunrise, Roger and the strangers approached the camp. Canonchet, already seated in a patch of shade on his crimson and black striped blanket, was finishing his first meal of the day. He motioned for Absalom to sit by his side.

Absalom hesitated. "It is the way of Roger's people to stand as they greet visitors."

Canonchet's thumb jerked down toward the blanket. "It is our customs we follow, not theirs." His face clouded with annoyance. "There are times when I regret sending you to Roger those years ago. You like white ways too much."

"Not all of them."

Although he preferred to stand, out of respect for the sachem's wishes, he sat, crossing his legs in front of him. On the grass facing them, Riana had spread a second blanket. Roger greeted them warmly then lowered himself onto it with difficulty, a streak of pain coming into his face. The cripple, too, had trouble easing his way to the ground, but the woman sank down with all the grace of a fawn and spread her skirts about her folded legs. Against her dark garment, her skin glowed like polished shell. Her hair, caught by the sun's rays filtering through the branches, flamed in the light. Was there another woman on the whole earth such as this one?

A pipe lay on the blanket before him. Should the trading go well, they would light it, the ceremony creating a binding contract. Should they not reach an agreement, the pipe would remain unlit. Absalom glanced at it with a torn mind. Far better for the strangers to leave the Providence colony and seek land elsewhere. Yes, that would be best by far. And the worst of all possibilities.

Roger spoke first, using the Algonquin slowly, as was his habit. "This man and wife wish to make their home among us."

The sachem sat impassive, only a slight nod of his head indicating he had heard.

"For this they need land to call their own," Roger continued.

"Mother Earth welcomes all her children. She gives herself to all men for the length of their days."

So his uncle was going to be difficult. He knew white men believed land could be possessed forever, not merely borrowed for a lifetime. But he intended to stretch out the word play and make the whites struggle. Absalom glanced over at Roger. Their eyes met. So Roger understood Canonchet's reasoning. Why should he not? They had sparred many times before.

"They can pay for a farming tract," Roger said. "Not much," he added quickly, "they do not own many coins. But a fair price."

The sachem stared straight ahead, his hooded eyes unblinking. From the trees came the caw of a jay followed by the answering call of its mate. "How much?"

"The price will vary according to the size of the land."

"I must know how much before I determine the size."

"One gold sovereign."

"Do I know of this coin?"

"You've seen one in the past. It is made of the yellow metal that never changes."

"Yes, I remember." From the glint in his eyes, Absalom knew he would agree to a trade. But his dignity must not be traded away as well, and so he pondered.

Owen, as he was called, sat as patient as stone. Most likely Roger had warned him of his people's ways. The woman, Grace, betrayed her curiosity. He watched as her glance touched on one object after another: the three eagle feathers in Canonchet's headdress, a brief flitting of her eyelids at his loincloth, and then at his own, a long glance at the summer wickiup behind them, its door flap open to the morning air, revealing Riana and Liliawa going about their tasks.

To his surprise, her gaze lay longest on the beechwood bow and the quiver of arrows hanging by the open flap. Again and again, her eyes swept over the weapons before glancing away, only to return as if she wished to weigh them in her hands, to test their balance and accuracy.

Canonchet noticed her interest. To Roger he said, "The woman studies my weapons like a warrior."

"She means no harm."

"I don't care for it."

"May I tell her of your concern?"

He gave him one abrupt nod.

Roger turned to Grace. "You're eying the sachem's bow. He wonders why you do so. Such weapons should not concern women."

"Not a woman's concern? Is that so?" Fire came into her face coloring her cheeks, and she went to rise from the blanket. Only Owen's hand on her arm and his "Easy, Grace," kept her from leaping up.

Absalom shot a glance at his uncle. He sat unmoving. Not a single muscle rippled. But the woman's spurt of anger had not gone unnoticed, of that he was certain.

He heard her speak softly to Roger in that musical way she had. "Tell the chieftain I am saddened to have left my bow and arrows in my old country. My father made my bow of yew wood. 'Twas a gift I treasured."

Canonchet heard, also. And understood. Absalom saw a question come into his eyes as she spoke. So his uncle *did* know more of the white men's speech than he let on. Pretending he hadn't noticed, he translated for him as usual and waited for his response.

"Some of our women use small bows to kill birds and rabbits. The bow she stares at is a man's bow. It is beyond her strength."

Absalom repeated his words in English.

"The bow's a beauty," Grace said. "Could I try it and see?"

Again, Owen laid a restraining hand on her arm. "My wife is a brave hunter. She has slain deer in our mother country, risking death to do so."

Canonchet's eyes flared wide. Surprise catching him unaware, he didn't hide his understanding. "Ask them how she risked death in slaying a deer. They are not marauding beasts."

Absalom asked, and Owen answered, "The law said it was wrong to hunt for food. If she had been caught, she would have been killed."

His dignity forgotten, the sachem looked across at Grace, his jaw agape. "This cannot be. The fruit of the earth is given to all men. Without it, life is not possible."

"That is why they have come to us," Roger said in his halting Algonquin. "To make a life."

Lowering his voice, Canonchet spoke only to Absalom. "Could there be truth in this tale? She is but a female, not overly robust. I have known no woman who could bring down a deer with the large bow."

"Roger never lies."

"Roger didn't tell us of her exploits. Her man did so."

Absalom glanced over at the visitors. Roger looked uncomfortable. The hard ground was causing pain to his bones. Her man's expression, to his credit, was neither anxious nor impatient, even though his future fate lay in a successful trade. The woman smiled across at them, her eyes meeting the sachem's directly without the fear most white women showed in his presence. Perhaps she did not know her glance should not meet his so boldly but be cast down in modesty before him.

Absalom's lips twitched. It would not do to smile back. To quell the urge, he averted his gaze, concentrating for a moment on a branch where a squirrel played, before turning aside to his uncle. "There is one way to prove the tale."

"How?"

"Allow her to try your bow."

"What?" Canonchet reared back on the blanket. "This has never been done."

"So?" Absalom shrugged. "If they have lied, refuse them the land." It was a chance, but one worth taking. If she performed well, she would overcome any misgivings, and he could tell from her shining eyes that what Owen claimed was true.

"Ah." Canonchet looked at him with more favor than he had of late. Without further deliberation, he stood and lifting the bow from its resting place, he held it out to Grace.

She scrambled to her feet and grasped it in both hands. She ran her fingers over the smooth beechwood, caressing every inch before holding it flat in her palms to test it for balance. Finally, she held it upright and plucked hard at the rawhide string. "The stave flexes nicely with good resistance. It has a long cast, I warrant." She stroked the bow once more before handing it back to Canonchet. "Thank you kindly. What a beautiful instrument you have."

He took it and turning to the quiver of arrows removed two. He gave one to Grace, waiting while she examined it, her face flushing with pleasure. "'Tis light to the touch and bends, but not too much, I see." She spoke in her own tongue as if he could understand every word she spoke. And he could, Absalom thought wryly. "The flint arrowhead is not too heavy for the shaft," she went on, "and tailor made for the bow. They are the finest match I've ever seen."

"Take the bow, Absalom," the sachem ordered. "Choose a target and strike."

"As you say, uncle." He walked over to Grace. "I have been ordered to choose a target. First I will shoot and then you will. Understood?"

She nodded gravely and handed him the weapons. "Aye. We'll have a competition. My father and I often competed for sport. But I think today 'twill be more than a game."

"Yes," he said, pleased that she understood.

An oak tree at the edge of the clearing bore a scar in its trunk where a storm had lopped off a limb. He would aim for its heart, a pale indentation in the wood.

He took his position, held up the bow and, aiming carefully, let fly. The arrow struck the scar dead center and held, quivering for an instant, in the trunk.

"Perfect," Grace said, her eyes aglow.

"Give the bow to the woman," Canonchet ordered. "Tell her to aim for the same target."

Absalom translated and held out the bow. She took it, her expression still grave, and sent a quick glance to her man. A look passed between them. So they both knew the stakes were high.

She stepped up cheerfully, placing her feet into the exact spot Absalom's moccasins had vacated and slowly raised her weapon. The bow was large for her, a handicap for certain, he noted with misgiving. She would be better served by one curved closer to her height. But plainly, she wasn't expecting the rules to be altered in her favor.

If the bow's size worried her, she didn't reveal it, but took a marksman's stance, one leg slightly forward, one back, and positioned the arrow. Her arms, though slim, were strong, and stretching the rawhide to its limit, she held it taut and straining. Then fast, without hesitation, she released the bow. The arrow flew to its rest coming close enough to his to shear feathers off both shafts. Together, side by side, the two missiles created a new hollow in the old scar.

As she lowered the bow, Roger and Owen clapped, the white man's way of showing praise. Ignoring their noise, Canonchet remained motionless, nothing about his posture revealing his thoughts, except, perhaps, his eyes as they focused on the arrows in the tree. After a lengthy silence, he said, "Tell the woman she shoots like a man."

"High praise, indeed," she replied with a twinkle in her eyes when Roger translated.

Absalom watched his uncle carefully for signs of male outrage, but saw none. He was a wise man. That the woman was not ordinary, he had recognized from the first.

Her husband beamed his pleasure at her prowess in a smile that split his face. For him, there was clearly no loss of honor at her mastery of the bow. Strange but good. Skill was skill after all, no matter who possessed it.

Canonchet spoke in a loud, carrying voice. "Tell her she and her man are welcome in the home of the Narragansetts. I will sell them land for their coin. Twenty-five acres southwest of the river."

Southwest. The most favored position.

"Tell her my words," he commanded.

For the second time that morning, Absalom spoke directly to her, to her face with its white skin and its sea green eyes. "My uncle bids you and your husband welcome. He has land for you."

He was rewarded by her quick, indrawn breath. Then the sachem spoke again. "There is something else."

"What, uncle?"

"She won although the bow was not fairly matched to her size. That should be corrected. Do you agree?"

Absalom nodded. "Yes, that would be good."

"The bow I made for you just before you reached manhood would fit her well. Are you willing to gift her with it?"

So she had won him over completely.

"If that is your wish, of course." With an effort, he kept his delight out of his expression.

"It is." Canonchet let his eyes go slack with disinterest as befitted his station.

Of all the people in the world, this woman called Grace was the one person he would have chosen to possess his bow, to run her hands over its surface, to press it close to her breast, to send its arrow soaring to the heart of her target. She, alone.

As he walked to his wickiup to retrieve the gift, he didn't see Liliawa standing modestly away from the visitors or her look of sorrow when she spied the smile lighting his face.

Chapter Twenty-One

THE REST OF THE SUMMER PASSED in a frenzy of activity. Owen worked daily from dawn to dusk, hurrying to ready their cabin before deep winter. In late December, hard-muscled and sun-darkened like never before, he moved their few possessions to the new cabin in a barrow he had made from scraps of unused lumber.

Their own home, on their own land, in a brand New World, he exulted, hardly believing the truth of it at last. As Grace settled their things about the room, he inhaled deeply; the pine log walls were fragrant, so fresh, sap oozed from the knot holes. He thumped an upright beam in the wall, satisfied with its solid sound and glanced up at the rafters, pleased by the sturdy look of them as well.

With the help of men in the colony, he'd laid a tight roof and built a good-sized fireplace from the fieldstones strewn about the land. To further keep out the cold, he put in a puncheon floor made from young sapling pines cut lengthwise, the half round logs facing down, the flat surface facing up for walking on. In Ireland, Grace had only known dirt floors. He resolved life would be different for her here in as many ways as possible.

Some day, when they had children running about, he would build a larger house out of planed boards like Roger's and with a private bedroom. But for now, this snug single room would do. The December chill hardly penetrated the chinks between the logs. They would be secure here throughout the worst of the weather.

In repayment for the help he'd received, he intended to offer his blacksmith services free of charge for the winter. It was the least he could do, he told Grace, for all the good that had come to them. Their debt to Roger Williams went beyond repayment. Not only had he and Mary shared their home for six months, without Roger's influence, the peace and freedom of the Rhode Island colony would not exist. Yes, they had much to be grateful for.

Happy as never before, he said, "It's been a long way home, love."

"Yes," Grace said.

At the crisp English word, and no other, Owen glanced over at her, puzzled by her terse reply.

Taking a linen sheet from their sea chest, she smoothed it over the new straw mattress. Tonight, for the first time, they would sleep in their own bed. Working quietly, she began covering the sheet with a woolen blanket.

"You have no more to say?" Owen asked as he watched her. "That's hardly Irish of you."

He came up behind her as she bent over the mattress and caught her about the waist. "Are you having regrets?" He leaned in closer to nuzzle her neck's soft velvet. "The land is wild here and colder than Ballybanree on its bitterest day."

No response. He turned her around to face him.

"Owen," she protested, "I'll never get our bed made up for the night."

"You're avoiding an answer." He held her at arm's length, the jesting gone from his voice. "I asked you a question in Liverpool. Now I'll be asking it again. Are you sorry you've come so far from everything you knew?"

"Never. I'm that glad we're here." She sank onto the half-made bed. "But I wish . . ."

He sat next to her and took her hands in own. "What? What do you wish? Tell me."

At the tenderness in his voice and eyes, she felt tears prick at her lids. "I wish just once more I could visit the oak tree where Da and Liam lie . . . and talk to Mary and see how her babe fares . . . and go to Mass at midnight on Christmas . . . and visit with Father Joyce again and . . ."

Despite her efforts to stay them, the tears slipped out and began running down her cheeks.

"Oh, love, I am so sorry. I thought you'd be happy here as I am, and as I want you to be."

"Oh, I am truly." She clung to him, her eyes weeping, her mouth laughing. "And I'm a fool, too, for being sad. We have everything—land and freedom and each other. A moment's regretting I felt, that's all."

"Nay, there's more. Tell me. You know you can."

She nodded, the tears coming faster. "Until this morning, I thought I was with child."

"Oh, I see." He stroked her back and hair, silenced by her sorrow.

"Do you? Because I don't. You love me nearly every night, yet our seed doesn't quicken."

"All in good time, love." He swept his arms in an arc around the sparsely furnished cabin. "We have a nest to feather before we bring wee fledglings into it. Isn't that enough for now?" When she didn't respond to his bantering, he said, "Let God and nature take care of our children, Grace. They will come, all in due time. I swear it." He hoped his words were true. His thoughts flew back to the night on the ship when Grace lost her babe, and he had prayed for her life alone. Surely God would not continue to punish him for that.

He lifted her chin with a finger. "Look at me." He waited until her eyes, magnified with tears, met his. "With my soul on my lips I swear to you, you will have a child one day. The day that God decides." His mouth quirked up into a smile. "Amen."

"I believe you."

"And well you should. I'm your lord and master."

"*Ha*." Swiping at her wet cheeks, she leaped up from the bed, smiling, and dropped a kiss on his hair. "I love you, Owen O'Donnell."

"And don't ever forget it," he said, rising to his feet, the better to wind his arms around her. "My life depends on it. My very life." As he lowered his head for a kiss, a rap sounded on their door.

"Oh, our first visitor," Grace exclaimed. "Who can it be?" She slipped from his embrace, ran to the door and with no hesitation flung it wide. "Absalom, what a surprise!"

Like an English gentleman, he bowed slightly from the waist. "Good morning, Grace. We've come to wish you and Owen well in your new home."

My God, he sounds like Roger Williams, Owen thought, as if he, too, had studied at Cambridge.

He had dressed for the cold, but magnificently, in beaded buckskins, the tunic and leggings elaborately embroidered with purple wampum and porcupine quills. A necklace of polished animal teeth hung about his neck. The long cloak draped over his shoulders for warmth was edged with red fox fur; his feet were clad in fur-trimmed boots.

He stood regally erect and silent, a glimmer of amusement on his face as Grace's astonished glance ran over him

For pity's sake. Sure and I've forgotten my manners entirely," she finally said, stepping back and motioning him inside. "Please, come in. Come in out of the cold."

"Aye," Owen urged. "Welcome to our home."

Absalom hesitated. "I am not alone."

"Oh?"

"My cousin, Liliawa, has also come to call."

From behind Absalom, a girl stepped forward, her eyes shyly cast down, her thick black plaits held off her forehead by a narrow strip of white wampum beads. A long, fringed skirt hung below her knees covering her leggings for warmth. Over her embroidered shirt, she, too, wore a winter cloak, its hood tossed back over her shoulders. Like her boots, her cloak was fashioned of rabbit fur, the pelts pieced together in an intricate pattern.

Tentatively, Grace stroked the cloak's softness. "How beautiful," she said.

"Liliawa has no English," Absalom said. "I will tell her for you." He spoke a few words in Algonquin and the girl smiled.

"We have a fire roaring up the chimney," Grace said. "Will you sit by it with us?"

"First, we will bring in our gifts." Again, Absalom spoke to the girl who hurried outside, setting her fringed skirt swirling about her leggings. In the space of a few heartbeats, she returned with a large bundle and placed it on the plank floor.

"The heat *was* roaring up the chimney. Now 'tis roaring out the door." Owen laughed and fastened the latch behind them. "Come close to the warmth. We've only two stools as of yet, but they're yours."

"You're our very first visitors," Grace said. "I'll make tea with honey. The water's already heated."

"My uncle will ask me of your thoughts," Absalom said. "We must show you what he sent." He took a knife from a sheath at his side and bending over the bundle, cut the strip of rawhide holding it together. Grasping one end of the loosened bundle, he pulled until it fell open spreading across the raw floor boards in a supple, black mass.

"A bearskin! Holy Mother in heaven, what a magnificent thing." Grace dropped to her knees and ran her hands through the dense fur. "'Tis thick and yet so soft to the touch. So beautiful." She gazed up at her visitors. "I'm speechless."

"That's a rarity I've seldom experienced," Owen grinned and held out his hand to Absalom. "We thank you and your uncle for such a generous gift."

"Was it caught nearby?" Grace asked, still on her knees stroking the fur.

Absalom shook his head. "A few days' journey north, in deeper wilderness. The bears don't care for us. They must be searched out. My uncle says now that you have a bearskin, you need not seek for one. They're far more dangerous to hunt than deer and vicious when wounded." He hesitated before saying, "He fears for you, I think."

"Then he must be my friend," Grace said.

Absalom turned and nodded at Liliawa who again hurried outside. She retrieved two woven baskets by the cabin door and placed them on the floor next to the bearskin.

"You missed the planting season," Absalom said. "Liliawa and her aunt, Riana, send corn for meal. With your skill at the bow, Riana says you will hunt your own meat."

"Indeed. I took down a pheasant this morning right from my doorway with the very bow you gave me. The abundance of the land is amazing."

A shadow crossed Absalom's face. "May it always be so." He pointed to the second willow basket. "What is there belonged to my wife. I've kept them, but I have no need. I thought you might."

"Your wife?"

He nodded.

Curious, Grace peered into the basket. "Oh, my God." She reached in, pulled out a pair of leather boots lined with a lustrous, dark fur and held them up. "Owen, look." She stroked their glossy surface. "I don't recognize the fur, but never before have I seen their like. They're the most beautiful I've ever seen."

"It's marten. Naomai would have beaded them, but. . ."

Absalom got no further. With a little low cry, Liliawa shrank away and inched toward the door. She fumbled with the latch until she worked it free then ran out into the cold, her cloak whirling behind her.

In the stunned silence that followed, Absalom stood rigid, his face an unreadable mask. As Owen went to secure the door once again, he glanced at the Indian, half expecting an explanation, but he offered none. No need. The girl must believe the boots should be hers. Why else would she have reacted as she did? So why had Absalom given them to Grace?

True, her English shoes *were* badly scuffed, her brogues long since discarded. In their haste to finish the cabin, they had neglected their clothing. Next to Absalom's splendor, their garments were shabby and mean, but that didn't answer the question.

And then he knew.

As Grace busied herself brewing tea by the hearth, Absalom stole a glance at her. He was discreet, his glance on her hair and her form as fleeting as an arrow in flight, but for Owen that one look said everything, and his breath caught in his throat.

He should ask Grace to return the boots, but he knew he wouldn't. Plainly thrilled, she had already tugged them onto her feet declaring the fit perfect and their warmth beyond compare. Besides, if his gift were refused, Absalom would be insulted clear down to the frozen ground.

Owen sighed. He had married an extraordinary woman and every man who met her thought the same. All the lads in Ballybanree, and Rushmount—his jaw tightened. They were not through with his lordship yet, not by a long shot, and now this strange man, half savage, half courtier. A man with noble bearing and alien ways who looked at his wife with desire in his eyes.

Another thought chilled him. Could Absalom be a threat to her safety? No, the idea was unworthy. In these past months, he had shown only the greatest of good will toward them both. A threat to his marriage, then? Although Absalom conducted himself like a gentleman, he was a man after all, a man with two strong legs . . . A sudden spurt of jealousy rose up to shame him. Despite it, he owed his guest a show of hospitality.

"Will you take a seat by our fire?"

"Do," Grace said. "Tea's ready at last."

"Thank you, no. I must see to my cousin."

Aye, Owen silently agreed, the problem with the girl needed mending. "Very well. If you would be so kind, thank Canonchet for his magnificent gift. I'm a blacksmith by trade. As soon as I get to my forge, I'll make a worthy gift for him."

"Gifts people make are the best of all," Grace declared, raising her skirt above her ankles to admire her new boots. "'Twas glorious of your wife to give me these wonderful boots."

With a curt nod, Absalom left, closing the door quietly behind him.

"We have a problem, love," Owen said when they were alone.

"The girl?"

"I fear so."

"She resented my boots, I know. But why? If Absalom's wife made them for me, why should she be angry?"

"Whenever we've been in the Indian camp, have you seen Absalom with a woman?" Grace's mouth rounded into a circle. "Oh. That's the way of it, of course. He no longer has a wife."

"My guess as well. The girl wants him."

"She should have him, then. She's comely." After a pause, she added, "And so is he."

Owen shot a quick glance at Grace, but her expression remained serene. *A jealous lover is what you are, he chided himself.*

Another knock, louder this time, sounded on the plank door.

"More callers?" Owen asked.

"I like this well," Grace said, hurrying to answer.

A gaunt, middle-aged woman stood in the doorway, her cheeks and the tip of her nose red from the cold, a black cloak clutched tightly about her bony frame.

"Emma Harris! You're just in time to take tea with us."

"I'll come in for a moment only." Emma entered, eying the bearskin with distrust, carefully keeping her skirts from brushing against it.

Owen placed a stool close to the hearth. Emma sat, untied her cloak and shrugged it off her shoulders. From the look of her, she planned to stay for more than a moment, Owen observed dryly.

"Let me catch my breath," she said. "I had such a fright."

"Whatever is wrong?" Grace asked.

The woman clutched her hand. "Those savages. I saw them walk in here as bold as brass. I feared you'd be killed in your bed."

"Did you think we'd be lying abed in the middle of the day?" Owen asked, enjoying the idea.

Emma sniffed. "One never knows what goes on behind latched doors. I came to warn you. It's my Christian duty. You're Irish and have scant knowledge of our English ways." Her nasally voice dropped to a hoarse whisper. "You shouldn't let those savages into your cabin. Oh, I know Roger befriends them. He even raised Absalom as his foster son, but they're not to be trusted. They're filthy. They live in skin huts and pile their bones and scraps outside. They don't clean their dwellings. They just move on when the scrap piles grow high." She tightened her grip on Grace's hand. "And who can understand their language?"

Grace pulled free of the woman's grasp. "Roger can. We've learned a few words, too."

"Wait till summer. Then you'll see. They go about in loin cloths and bare feet. Even the women go half naked."

"Do you not remember we arrived here in the summertime?" Grace asked. "I saw their feet. They looked like ours. The rest of their bodies did, too."

Emma's jaw fell open. "That's a shameless thing to say. Nothing about them is akin to civilized people. They're *animals*."

Like hackles, the hair rose on the back of Grace's neck. She dragged her stool so close to Emma their knees touched. "Why are the Indians not worthy of your regard?"

In an ice laden voice, Emma said, "You should know the answer."

"No, I don't. We need the Narragansetts. Roger said without them the colony wouldn't have survived the early days, and we'd be in jeopardy even now."

Emma sniffed up a drop of moisture. "Roger coddles the savages, treats them as equals."

"He keeps the peace by so doing. Other colonies have been attacked by the natives, but not Providence."

Losing her battle with the drop, Emma rubbed at her damp nose with the back of a hand. "Peace is an illusion. War will come. Roger won't be able to stop it."

"I pray you're wrong."

The woman shrugged as if her threat of war were of little consequence. "Without a struggle, how can we claim more than a few acres at a time? As it is now, the sachem, as they call him, parcels out a bit here and a bit there. It's not right for these ignorant heathens to control so much. They don't subdue the land, and they don't improve it. They build no houses, no farms, no towns." She sat up straighter on the stool, conviction firming her back into a board. "The New World is a wilderness waiting for white men to tame it."

Unsmiling, Grace asked, "Why did you and your husband come to Providence? You must have known Roger William's colony was different from the others."

Emma's eyes shifted from Grace's frown to the flames.

"Well?"

"My husband, Caleb, believes as Roger does."

"And you?"

"I do not, and others agree with me. And besides, despite Roger's claims, all the colonies are chartered by King Charles."

"True, but Roger's charter gives him the right to govern Rhode

Island as he deems fit. It prevents other colonies from imposing their laws on us."

"Laws are man made. They can be changed. Or broken." Eyes squinting as if to block out the brightness, Emma's eyes took on a faraway look. "Strangers, women more so than men, need take care. The talk of witchcraft is not unknown in the colonies. Some years ago, over to Northampton, Goody Parsons was accused. She escaped the fire and the hanging, but Northampton is not so far from here. A day's journey, perhaps. On a good horse."

"What has Northampton to do with us?" Grace asked, puzzled. "'Tis part of the Massachusetts colony."

"You spoke of laws. Women who speak of the law had better be cautious. One with fiery hair and fiery opinions could be seen as a devil's spawn. If she be Papist as well, who knows what might become of her? I'd bind up my hair, if I were you. Keep it from the sight of all. It burns like the fires of hell. No good can come of that."

Grace moved back on her stool, putting a space between herself and Emma, not wanting so much as their skirt hems to touch. The woman was evil.

Grace looked up at Owen, who stood behind Emma's stool. He shook his head in silent warning. Say nothing, he was signaling. But the woman had threatened her with death. With hanging like her Da. And she was to say *nothing*?

She took a deep, shuddering breath. Owen was right, of course. What could she say, except words that would inflame their differences? Wisdom lay in silence. But, dear God, that was hard. Grim-faced, she looked up at Owen again.

"The tea is steeped," he said, his expression matching her own.

"Good," Emma Harris declared. "I'll take two spoons of honey in mine. I like a sweet taste in my mouth."

Chapter Twenty-Two

"Emma Harris behaves like a Rushmount in skirts." Grace paced back and forth in front of the fire, over the bearskin, over the rough floor boards, from the side of the bed to the table on the opposite wall.

"Come rest by me," Owen said.

"Sure and I'm that angry, I can't sit still. The woman is greedy, Owen. Greedy for land. Greedy for wealth. Greedy for what doesn't belong to her. And she can't be the only one. Did you listen to her? She said others here think the same. Dear Lord, 'tis Ireland all over again. The Indians will be robbed of what's rightly theirs. Just as we were. And anyone who opposes her should be hanged for a witch. It maddens me to think of it."

She swirled to a halt in front of him. "Have you nothing to say for yourself?"

"I'm glad you've stopped moving. You'll be wearing out the soles of your new boots."

"How can you jest? There's no humor in this."

He grasped a handful of her skirt and tugged her close. "Sit on my knee."

"I can't sit."

"Oh, but you must. So we can talk."

"Will you be serious, then?"

"Aye."

She settled herself comfortably and nestled against his chest.

"You shouldn't fear for the Indians," he said. "There's so much untapped land here, it staggers the mind. There's plenty for all to share."

"Emma Harris doesn't know that, nor those like her." She gripped his shirt front. "We must not do evil to the Indians. Not even to make our own lives better. Not even for that."

"Grace, look at me." Finger beneath her chin, he tilted her face until her eyes met his. "Can we prevent the king from issuing royal decrees and deeding land he doesn't own? Can we deflect the power of England?"

"What is the—"

"Can we?"

"No."

"Agreed, but I believe in time England's arm will grow weak and we colonists will grow strong. Then we'll be left in peace to raise our families with food in their bellies and hope in their hearts. In Ballybanree, we had a sea at our backs and nothing before us but misery. Here we face a continent filled with possibilities."

"But what if England doesn't weaken? We'll keep running, then? Well, I won't, nor will I cheat the natives. Here I stay, to the death if need be." She went to get up from his knee, but he held her fast.

"So passionate, *mavourneen*. 'Tis glorious to hear you."

He tangled his hands in her hair. He loved touching it, weighing it in his palms, caressing it with his fingers, reveling in the feel of it, so thick and luxuriant about her shoulders. He had no wish to frighten her, but the viper-tongued woman had issued a warning, and for Grace's sake, she must be heeded.

"Perhaps you should wear your hair loose only when you're going about the cabin. Outside, you might plait it."

He steeled his arms about her, expecting her to wrench free at his words. She didn't disappoint him, but he was ready and tightened his hold. "No," he said. "Be still and listen to me. A man with a weapon in his hands, or a fist, I can fight, but an aging woman with a vicious mind . . . there's little to be done except take care." He felt her resistance lessen and loosened his grip. "Do you understand?"

"That she could wish to see me hang? Aye. I know the meaning of such a threat."

She pulled her hair free from his fingers and stood. "We've had our first visitors, and both brought trouble along with them."

"Did you expect the New World to be perfect?"

"No. I expected it to be *just*." She reached for her da's heavy old shag cloak hanging from a peg on the wall. "I'm wanting some fresh air."

"There's more, Grace," he said, his mouth firm, his jaw tight. "Mistress Harris was not entirely wrong."

"What?" The cloak in her hands, she whirled around to face him.

"Hear me out." He paused, struggling to find the right words then shrugging in defeat when none came to him. He'd simply say what he had to say, flat out. "I wouldn't be encouraging the Indians to visit here, especially Absalom. 'Twould be best to keep him outside when he's about."

"I can't believe what I'm hearing." Grace flung the cloak over her shoulders. "You're as bad as that woman. Are you afraid he'll murder us in our bed?"

"No. My fear lies elsewhere." His voice emerged ragged with the telling, harsher than he intended. But he had to make her understand.

She didn't stay to hear. Quicker on her feet than he, she slipped through the door and ran out into the winter day. He followed her, peering into the nearest stand of trees, but fleet as a deer, she had already disappeared from sight.

Good God, he'd bungled it. With a sigh, he returned to the cabin. She'd be back as soon as the anger left her. When she did, they'd make peace with each other. He had no doubt of that, just as he had no doubt she was right in trusting Roger's vision for their colony. But the moment had come and gone when he could easily tell her what he had seen in Absalom's eyes. He would keep the knowledge to himself for a while. Perhaps forever.

The woman's witch talk he'd share with Roger, though he doubted anything would come of her threat. She was just a loose-tongued old woman. Still, one never knew. Grace had no true idea of the effect her beauty had on others. How it enflamed both men and women, if in different ways. *A witch?* Emma Harris had spoken the truth in one sense: Grace had him bewitched for certain and now Absalom as well.

He sat warming his hands over the lavish fire. No more huddling over a few peat coals as he had in Ballybanree. Yet even so close to the blazing logs, he felt chilled in a room without Grace in it. As he watched and waited, the flames lapped at the wood like tongues of fire. Like tongues, they spoke to him. *A savage is drawn to your woman.* They said more as well, disturbing him greatly. *He's given her a gift far finer than any of your own.*

The realization stung, and the question that followed it burned straight to his gut. What gift *had* he given Grace? The answer shamed him. None. He slumped lower on the stool. He had never had anything to give her. No, he shook his head in disgust. He was lying to himself. He simply had not done so, not a flower plucked from a tree in springtime, not a ribbon from a fair, not a thing she could hold in her hand and say this is from the man who adores me. Nothing.

"Good God," he exclaimed, rising to his feet. "How could I have been so stupid?" He paced the room trying to think of something he could do for her. They had very little, yet surely he could think of *something*. He pounded a fist into his palm. *Something.* And then he had it. The most perfect gift of all. He'd surprise her with it, and soon. He grabbed his cloak off a peg and tossed it on. He'd find her wherever she was and bring her into the warmth with him where she belonged.

———————

Grace's anger gradually faded, her pulse slowed, and her pace through the trees slowed as well. Despite her distress, she couldn't deny the comfort of her new boots. They were nothing short of miraculous. They didn't slip on the ice patches or let in the damp. She wriggled her toes. There was ample room for them to move about inside the soft, fur lining. What a wonderful gift, as wonderful in its own way as the English Bible Kath Mann had given her back in Ballybanree, or the copper combs that had once belonged to great grandmother Granuaile. A spurt of anger shot up again. For Absalom not to be allowed inside their house was unthinkable. He meant no harm. Why couldn't Owen see that?

As for Emma Harris and her talk of witches, the woman babbled. An empty kettle is what she was. There had never been a witch hanging in Providence and there never would be. Roger wouldn't allow it.

Moment by moment, the peace of the forest entered her being. The deeper she plunged into its heart, the deeper its silvery silence became.

The druids would have loved this copse. Though there were more pines here than sacred oaks, the untrammeled woods reminded her of a holy place, far more so, in truth, than Roger's austere meeting house. On an impulse, she dropped to her knees in the snow. Blessing herself, she murmured aloud in Gaelic, the language of her earliest prayers. "Oh Lord God, keep this place, this Providence, safe from the acts of evil men. And heal me, oh Lord, of my anger and my old hatreds. Heal me, too, I beg you, of my disappointment in Owen this day. Amen."

Her prayer ended, she brushed the snow from her skirt and stood, unmoving for a moment, listening. Had she heard a branch crack, or was it the soughing of the wind through the trees? Or the brush of frozen limbs one against the other? No birds twittered, no creatures scurried under foot. Snug in their homes they all were, as she should be.

But not yet. With her grand new boots and the shag cloak wrapped about her, she was warm enough and not ready to return to the cabin. She regretted not bringing her bow and quiver of arrows. To be alone and unarmed in the deep woods wasn't wise. She had heard wolves howling in the night.

Dodging the low-hanging branches, she hurried along the icy path leading to the village. If she found no one to talk to, she'd watch the sea. Ever restless it was, like herself today.

At the shore, the landing place bustled with activity. Three beached canoes had been pulled up onto the sand, and a group of Wampanoags was busy emptying them of their boxes and bundles. Providence had a visitor. Whoever would brave that hostile sea in the dead of winter must have a serious purpose for doing so.

And then she saw him.

Acting like the king of the New World, Lord Rushmount stood in the midst of the activity giving instructions to his man, Thomas, and ordering the Indians about as if they were his personal property. As she drew close, she overheard a cluster of curiosity seekers mutter amongst themselves.

"Here for his taxes."

"Bloody hell, I say."

"The English king be damned."

"Aye."

"He'll not get much from me."

Rushmount would find his task difficult, Grace thought as she listened to the disgruntled murmurs. Good. Independent men should not pay tribute to an indifferent king.

Grace held Da's shag cloak snug about her, but the cold had begun to creep beneath her clothes. Time to go home. Surely Owen had spoken in haste, concerned for her safety, nothing else. She'd take the dirt path back to their cabin. 'Twould be faster that way.

───────────

GRACE O'MALLEY, BY GOD, IN THE FLESH.

Though busy directing Thomas and the savages—not one of them could be trusted—Rushmount spied her the minute she joined the knot of people crowding the sand. How could he fail to, with her hair flaming in the sun, her back erect, her feet gliding over the ice as if it were a ballroom floor? She had a heavy old rag wrapped about her for warmth. She was the only woman he knew who could overcome ugly clothes simply by wearing them.

As he watched the natives emptying the canoes, his mind fled the shore to the vision of her in that green velvet gown—a memory he would never be able to suppress. The pale, fine skin of her breasts and throat, her rich hair gleaming in the candlelight, her green eyes flashing fire. Yes, fire! He'd swear he had ignited a spark within her that night. And come heaven or hell, he would make it flame again.

To his disappointment, she turned, suddenly, and strode away. Should he follow her as he had done in Liverpool? Like a stupid schoolboy? Yes. Like a schoolboy, he needed a measure of satisfaction.

He beckoned to Thomas, struggling with the bags, the effort turning his breath into puffs of vapor. "Take the luggage to Roger Williams' house. You know the way?"

"Yes, milord."

"Good. Announce my arrival. Then come back here. Make sure the savages follow with the madeira and foodstuffs. Tell Master Williams I'll be along shortly."

"Very good, sir."

As Thomas started up the hill by a spring that splashed free despite the freezing air, Rushmount ignored the louts standing about and quickened his pace along the slippery path leading out of the village. Grace was wasting no time in her hurry to wherever she was going, but he'd soon catch up to her.

He was glad, after all, that he'd come to this forlorn outpost. He'd cursed having to travel in the dead of winter, but time was of the essence. When his business in Providence ended, he'd return to the Massachusetts colonies. Based on what the governors had collected since summer last, he'd restate the crown's demands, and in early spring, take a further payment in furs. There was little coin in the colonies. Furs, especially beaver, made an excellent substitute. Later, after harvest, he'd take the remaining difference owed in grain.

These colonists were a chary lot, unwilling for the most part to pay the crown's levies, but pay they would. He'd brook no refusal, not if he wished to return to his estates without his tail between his legs. The

Seafarer left for England at leaf falling. He had until then to carry out his assignment.

But in truth, more than the king's taxes had brought him to Providence. In Newport, he'd heard the O'Donnells had settled here, and he wanted to see that for himself. He hated leaving old scores unsettled . . . or unconsummated. He hurried faster, his quickened breath visible in the frigid air.

The bitterly cold ride in the canoe from Newport had chilled him to the bone. He longed for a goblet of wine and a seat by a blazing fire, but those pleasures would wait. First, he'd warm his eyes, and his hands on Grace. God, she walked like a queen, fearlessly over the uneven terrain, the shag cloak he could see clearly now swinging with each step she took. Only a short distance more and he would have her.

Without warning, she cut off the dirt path and ducked into the woods. He hurried, risking his footing on the ice, his heart beating fast, until he glimpsed her up ahead. Excellent. They'd be hidden by the trees.

A few paces behind her, almost near enough to grasp that tail of shining hair, he called out. "Grace!"

Instantly, at the sound of his voice, she whirled around.

He saw a sliver of fear shoot into her face before she caught it, smothering it from sight.

"You?" she said, her fear already replaced by a familiar haughtiness. "What do you want with me?"

"The same as always. Some time in your lovely company."

She blew out a breath.

"God, if you ever smile at me I won't know you," he said.

She gave him a sneer worthy of a duchess and tensed, ready to flee deeper into the trees. Quick as a snake's strike, he grasped a fistful of her heavy cloak and pulled her close, so close he could see the pale freckles dotting her nose and the green glare of hate in her eyes. He welcomed the hate. Anything but the indifference she'd shown him on the ship the day she lay there so ill, so wan.

"Do you know I saved your life?" he asked.

"Aye. After nearly destroying me in Liverpool. I owe you nothing."

"Liverpool? Your life was never in danger there. I wanted to have you, not kill you. What good would you be to me then?"

She raised her head high, jutting out her chin at him. "Your plan didn't succeed, though, did it?"

He loved her defiance. "Not quite, I must admit." He gripped her tighter. "Now you admit something."

Her eyes narrowed.

"You wanted me. For a moment that night, you were on fire."

"You're confused, your lordship. I *started* a fire."

"Yes, and a pretty penny it cost me. But that's not the fire that interests me. Just the one I lit in you."

"You're a bloody liar."

Look at her, he thought, enflamed with anger. What a glorious sight. "If I hadn't been so careless, I could have had you. Easily."

"*Had* me? *Ha.* What you did was outrage enough. Think of your lady wife. Would you want her snatched off the street, imprisoned against her will? Not knowing if she would be injured, or killed or . . . or worse."

He smiled. "You are not a lady."

"You seek to insult me? Don't bother. 'Tis not possible."

He clasped her so near the very fringe of her eyelashes was revealed to him, each golden lash clear and distinct. "No, you're not a lady. You're the most exciting woman in the world." He laughed. Moving his arms around her back, he pressed the length of his body to hers. "Both worlds. Is that an insult?"

She twisted in his grasp but couldn't free herself. "Take care. If Owen ever learns what you did to me, he'll kill you."

He raised an eyebrow. "You never told him of our little sojourn? I did wonder if he knew, and if so, why he hadn't confronted me with it. Interesting. I thought you shared everything with him, but apparently not. So there's hope for me yet."

"Hope for hell. I wouldn't add to Owen's worry with such a tale."

"You lie. Your ambition got in your way." He allowed himself a lazy, slow smile, knowing the sight of it would infuriate her even more. "Had he attacked me and been caught, the New World would have been lost to you. That's really what you wanted, not his ease. We're the same, you and I. We both pursue what we crave, relentlessly."

"I'd rather be dead than be like you."

"You are, nonetheless. And you're a fool as well. I could give you anything, luxuries such as you've never known. All you'd have to do is—"

"Lie with you?"

"For now, a kiss will do. I remember the last one well."

She struggled against him, tossing her head from left to right, whipping her hair back and forth. She could do little else. With the cloak covering her arms and hands, unable to rake his cheeks or beat on his chest, she was as good as imprisoned once again.

He lowered his face. From deep in her dry throat, she tried to summon enough saliva to spit in his face. Before she could, his grasp on her loosened. As his fingers slipped away, she stumbled back out of his arms' reach. Following the direction of his eyes, she slowly turned around not sure of what she would see.

"Absalom."

He stood a few paces behind her, unmoving, silent, his gaze riveted on Rushmount.

"Christ, what a place." Rushmount retreated a few steps, beckoning to Grace with a shaking hand. "Come away from that savage."

She shook her head. "He's my friend."

Rushmount's eyes widened in disbelief. "Your *friend?* And I'm not?"

"You never will be."

"Not true. We'll have our day." He looked beyond her to an Absalom carved of ice. "But this is obviously not it." He swept off his hat and bowed. "Until we meet again, Grace." Spinning on his heel, he ducked through the trees, hurrying back toward the dirt path that led into town.

"God, I hate that man," Grace said. When she turned around, she found herself alone in the forest.

The short winter day had begun to fail. She ran through the woods, dodging the snowy branches, in a wild hurry to get home to the warmth and to Owen. And then she saw him coming for her, his gait uneven as always, dogged and faithful, stubborn and determined, hurrying to reach her, to keep her safe, to embrace her, to forgive her, to welcome her, to love her.

"Owen," she cried out, "I'm here! Oh, Owen, I'm here!"

Chapter Twenty-Three

Winter clamped down like a fist of iron. January came and went, and still the cold held them tight in its grasp. With the constant need to cut and stack wood for their fire, Owen, always strong of back and shoulders and arms, grew more powerful than ever. Day and night, the fire burned. In the evening, banked low, it gleamed in the dark while they watched, warm, from their bed.

During a night of extreme bitterness, Grace insisted on covering them both with the bearskin. After an initial resistance—were the Indians to keep him warm, then?—Owen agreed, and every night thereafter, as long as the weather remained unbroken, they slept underneath it, nestling together, spoon fashion. All through the dark hours, she would rest her knees against his back, cradling her arm under his, and when, in their sleep, they turned, his legs would entwine with hers, and his hand would cup her breast.

In the frigid air, they made love under the coverings. It seemed furtive that way, Owen thought, hampered by the weight of the bedclothes, the sight of Grace hidden from him. One night, rather than let the fire burn low, he stoked it, piling log upon log as if it were early morning and the day just beginning. When the flames blazed high and hot, he pulled the bearskin off the bed and spread it on the floor before the hearth.

Grace had already removed her woolen skirt and doublet and the fur boots and stood shivering in her linen shift. She watched him, a smile starting up on her lips.

"Come here," he said.

Her smile grew wide. "Are you about to do something shameless?"

"Not at all. I just want to set you on fire."

"The bearskin *is* close to the hearth," she said, trembling.

"Come. There's no warmth to your garment."

"Then why keep it on?" With one fluid movement, she whipped the shift over her head and dropped it at her feet.

His gaze swept over her, lingering as if he had never looked on her before. "Loosen your hair."

She shrugged off the green ribbon holding her tresses back from her face, and with her fingertips, combed through the strands, arranging them to flow about her like a curtain.

"Come to me," he urged. She stepped forward moving slowly, deliberately, letting him feed on the sight of her.

"You've not undressed." She drew close.

"Oh?" He looked down at himself, at his boots, his breeches, his rough wool tunic, and he grinned. "I've forgotten entirely. No wonder. I go mad at the sight of you. And there's more I must see."

She laughed. "More?"

"Aye. Lie here before the fire. I've been dreaming of you there."

She obeyed, dropping to her knees on the soft fur.

"Lie back," he said, his voice turning hoarse. "Make a fan of your hair."

She lay as he wished, and lifting her hair in both hands, spread its rippling satin over the bearskin.

"'Tis a shower of gold." Owen stood, fully dressed, unable to move. The firelight flickered over her, playing about her form like random fingers. Against the black fur, her skin, sculpted by the light, glowed white as marble. He couldn't tear his gaze away. "I could look at you forever. You're my moon. My sun. My stars."

She glanced up at him through half-closed lids. "Is there such pleasure in that, then?"

"Aye."

She raised her arms. "There's more to be had. Much more."

In a fever, he began pulling at his clothes. But when finally freed of all garments, he lay beside her, propped on one elbow, touching her only with his eyes. They caressed her everywhere—her hair, her breasts, her waist, her flat belly, her long thighs, her slender calves, her small, narrow feet. Every inch, his eyes made love to.

"Are you not touching me?" she asked.

"I'm ashamed, love," he said. "You're perfect, and I'm so flawed."

"Not so very," she said, reaching for him.

After a moment, gently, he lifted her hand and pressed it to his lips. "No need, love, to excite me. I'm already where I need to be." He smiled down at her upturned face. "Are you?"

"What an unfair question."

"That means no. Not yet." He laughed and seized her to him. "But you soon will be."

He began to kiss her. He started with her eyelids.

———

Deeper into the night, he said, "Now that you've made love on a bearskin like a wild creature, the time has come to make an honest woman of you."

"Was I so wild?"

"Aye." His teeth gleamed white in the expanse of his dark beard. "I found it hard to remember you're a proper married woman."

She drew in a quick breath. "What a thing to say."

"Not to fear. I have something to seal our vows."

"Sure and our vows were sealed by Father Joyce well over a year ago."

"But our neighbors know nothing of our marriage. They may suspect we're consorting in sin." He grinned at her, enjoying himself immensely.

"You're toying with me."

"Am I now?" He stretched an arm out from under the bearskin folded about them and reached for his breeches lying nearby. His fingers dug into a pocket. "Well, to dispel any suspicion that might arise, I thought to dismiss it with this."

He opened his palm. Cupped in its center, something shone bright in the dying firelight.

"A ring?" Grace sat up, letting the bearskin fall away, oblivious to the chill night air.

"Aye, but not just any ring."

"A wedding ring!"

"Exactly."

"'Tis beautiful, but wherever did you get it?" She peered closer at his palm. "Gold?"

"Indeed."

"But—"

"You said gifts people make are the best of all."

Her gaze moved from his hand to his face and back to his hand. "You made this? From gold? For me?"

He nodded. "I'll answer all your questions, but first, shall we see if it fits?"

"Aye." Her eyes shining, she held out her left hand. He slid the gold band on her third finger and found it a faultless fit. Stretching her hand out to the low-burning fire, she wriggled her finger so the light played off the metal, causing the hammered surface to gleam like the facets of a gem.

"I love it," she said. "And I love that you made it just for me."

"Now the whole world will know you're mine," he said, pleased with her pleasure, unable to keep the satisfaction from his voice.

"That's as it should be, for I am yours." She grinned at him, then leaned over and tugged a flap of bearskin over them both before lying back in the circle of his arms. "Now tell me how you came to make this treasure. I want to know everything about it."

"Do you recall the gold coin, the crown, we had left after paying the Narragansetts for our acreage?"

She nodded, taking her hand out from under the covering for another look. "You used the crown to make this ring?"

"Aye. I hope you agree 'twas the best use the coin could be put to."

"Oh, I do." She rolled over on her side, facing him. "Where did you make it, and how did you get it to fit so perfectly?"

"For fit, I wrapped a piece of ribbon around your finger one afternoon. You thought I was playing a love game."

"And you were."

"Aye. I fashioned it on the forge, of course, but first I had to make tongs small enough to hold the softened metal. Far different it was from shoeing a horse or patching a plow. To solder the jointure, I shaved some copper from a farthing and melted it with a few grains of gold left from the crown. The mix strengthened the bond. It worked well, but not on the first try, I will admit."

She twisted the ring around on her finger. "You polished it so carefully I can't see the joining place. Beautiful 'tis and I thank you from my heart."

"You've already thanked me, love." He bent over her with a kiss. "Now, what is your pleasure? Shall we spend the rest of the night here, or go to our bed?"

"Let's stay where we are, so forever more we'll remember our night by the fire."

He kissed her softly once again. "I love you."

"I know. I've always known, and now my ring tells me so as well." Her face dreamy with the future, she said, "I feel the same, Owen O'Donnell, and one day the birth of our son will be my gift to you."

By mid-March, a thaw set in. The snow receded, melting into the ponds and streams, creating puddles along the paths and in the fields. The days grew longer, the sun grew stronger, and miniature buds appeared on the trees.

Sadly, by mid-March, Grace knew there would be no son. For days she cried bitter tears, giving in to them after Owen left the cabin to work at the village forge. Before he returned each night, she managed for his sake to brush her hair till it shone and tie it with a pretty ribbon, and to smile when she served his evening meal, the gold band glistening on her hand for she had never removed it and never would.

They loved each other so thoroughly it was strange no child came to them. Without a child, their love seemed dead-ended, all for naught. To Grace, the linking of the generations gave each life its meaning, its unique contribution to the great chain of being. She wanted that fulfillment for Owen, for herself, and wondered, in her prayers, the reason why God denied them.

CHAPTER TWENTY-FOUR

"LILIAWA IS COMISE'S WOMAN NOW. You waited too long to claim her." Anger thickened Canonchet's voice. "Riana tells me the girl is already with child. It could be yours she carries, but no, you would not listen to reason. *Bah.*" He turned his back on Absalom and stretched his hands over the burning firepit, holding his aging bones close to the warmth.

Absalom circled the fire stones until he stood facing his uncle. "Comise is a good man."

Canonchet raised hooded eyes. "I know Comise as well as I know you. Better. And I know his worth. But he has little knowledge of the light-skinned ways. You know the whites better than any of us. You could guide our people through the evil days ahead, and your son could follow you." His gaze returned to the fire.

"No man can foretell the future."

"No?" The sachem's eyes snapped open. "I see war. The whites are greedy. They don't understand the land is theirs only while they walk the earth. They want to possess it beyond the grave. What nonsense." He stared back at the coals. "Every year, their ships keep coming. Every year. Some day our people will try to stop them. What then? Who will lead them? The sons of Comise? What of *your* sons?" He spat, his spittle sizzling on the hot stones.

"You're angry with me, uncle, but I could not mate with Liliawa."

"Foolish words. A man does what he must."

Clearly, there would be no reaching him today. Absalom strode out of the longhouse, flipping the rawhide entrance flap behind him. Today, the sun warmed the air, and the sweet odors of spring swirled around him. The women had left to work in the fields, and Comise and his younger brothers had gone hunting, leaving him alone with Canonchet. A rare privacy in the winter longhouse where the entire family lived together in the dead season, sharing fire and food and the raised bed platforms lining the walls. He had heard Liliawa and Comise in the night. He was not surprised they had made a son.

Summer would soon be with them, and when the tribe moved to its fresh growing fields, he would build a new wickiup and live in it in peace and solitude. Only two more months, he promised himself as he walked up the hill by the bubbling spring. Roger had sent for him. He must have something he wished him to do.

About to tap on Roger's door, he heard voices raised in anger and hesitated. A woman's nasal voice came to him muffled through the wood. "They're not English. Why should you take their side against me?"

"I'm against evil. Is that your side, Emma?"

An indistinct reply. Absalom stood frozen in the warm sunshine.

Roger's voice again. "I first heard of this witch talk weeks back. I said nothing to you then, hoping your words were a single indiscretion. But your threats to her have resurfaced."

"I don't have to listen to this."

Roger's voice again, louder. "*Quiet.* You must listen."

Silence.

Roger's voice, softer now. "Should I hear more of this talk, you and Caleb will be asked to leave Providence."

"You threaten me?"

"I advise you, Emma, to take care."

Were there tears in Roger's voice? Surely not, but sorrow for certain. Brisk footsteps sounded on the wooden floorboards, but before Absalom could slip away, the old woman called Emma Harris rushed out the door.

"*Aaaah.*" She screamed at the sight of him and brushed past, running down the hill faster than he had ever seen a white woman move.

It was too late to leave. He knocked and entered. Roger sat on his carved chair, his head resting on one tented hand.

"Roger," Absalom ventured.

"Ah, Absalom. Come in, my boy, come in. Take a seat." Roger's face warmed with one of his frequent smiles. *Smiles.* Another way the races differed. Canonchet's face seldom lit up in that fashion. To do so would be a sign of weakness. This time, even Roger's smile faded quickly.

"I'm worried about the O'Donnells," he said. "The woman, especially."

"Why?" The question leaped free before Absalom could contain it. Roger sent him a quick glance. It was not the way of the Narragansetts to question elders so abruptly, but he had to know. Was Grace in danger?

"A woman in the village is full of loose talk. Owen tells me she's threatened Grace."

"How?" *Another abrupt question.*

"She's spoken of witches and hanging. Told Grace her hair is a reminder of hell fire."

"Is such a thing possible?"

"It's idle gossip, nothing more, but I can't allow such talk to escalate. Women have been hanged for witchcraft and burned at the stake." He shuddered. "I haven't heard of any witch trials in years now, nor would I tolerate such evil doings. I tell you all this because you get about the village. You hear things, Absalom. Should you hear any gossip of this nature, come to me immediately."

"If anyone speaks of it, I will. But sometimes the villagers stop their talk when I approach."

Roger nodded. "Sometimes. Not always. Not everyone is aware of your command of the language." He paused to massage his knees with his palms. "But that isn't the only reason I sent for you."

Grace was in danger, what could be more important than that?

"The O'Donnells have never worked virgin land. It's far different from farming in Ireland. The first crop, especially, will be a struggle."

"What has this to do with me?" Absalom asked, fearing he knew.

"I'm asking you to help them. Of all your people, only you speak their language." Roger looked serious, aware, of course, that Narragansett men hunted their food and left planting to women.

"You're asking me to embarrass myself before my people."

Ever honest, Roger nodded. "I am. We can't let the newcomers starve."

"There's little danger of that. Shellfish are plentiful. The woods team with game, and the woman is an excellent marksman."

Roger sighed. "They can't live on meat alone. Help them, Absalom. For my sake."

Both his foster fathers were making impossible requests of him. And both concerned women. He had disappointed Canonchet. He couldn't disappoint Roger as well. Nor did he want to, he realized, pleased at the thought of being near Grace again, the excuse to be in her company given to him by an impeccable source.

He rose from his stool. "Since it is you who asks, I'll see them today. Our women have already begun the spring burning. We'll start with that."

Roger walked him to the door clasping his shoulder affectionately. "You're a good son, Absalom. I thank you. You won't be sorry."

As he made his way back down the hill, Roger's last words echoed in his mind. He could, he knew, be very sorry. But he wasted no time in getting to the parcel of land the O'Donnells now called their own. Ever since he and Liliawa delivered the gifts, he'd wondered how they fared. He'd regretted leaving abruptly that day but took with him the memory of the woman's pleasure in the boots, and the admiration flaring in her eyes when he stood in her doorway in his finest regalia. And her gratitude later when he found her in the grip of the arrogant stranger and frightened the man into releasing her.

As he drew close to their land, a smoke spiral rose above the treetops sending the pungent odor of pine sap into the air. They must be burning one of those oversized fires. He sighed at the waste. Even pines took a generation to reach full growth. At the rate the colonists chopped them down for fuel, his people's winter homes would have to be built farther and farther inland.

Perhaps Canonchet was right. The whites were not only greedy, they were unstoppable. Yet here he was, eager to come to their aid. Did wisdom lie in fighting them or in acceptance? For that he had no answer, nor to the question of which people he belonged: His skin said Narragansett, but all too often his mind said something else.

He halted at the edge of the green meadow surrounding the small log cabin, noting anew the stream flowing in the north corner and the field's lack of tree growth. An acre or a little more could be plowed and sown with minimum effort. This year, an acre might be all they could manage, but next growing season, they would need to cultivate at least two acres and add to them thereafter. A formidable task. Most of their land was densely forested.

To give the earth a chance to rest and renew itself, the Narragansetts moved their summer camps to fresh fields every three or four years. Not so the whites. They wanted enough arable land in the same holding to let some fields lie fallow while they put others to the plow. They turned forests into farms. Of the two, who had the better method, his people or the newcomers? He gave a mental shrug. Both had merits; both had faults.

Still hidden by the trees, he looked across at Owen hard at work in the meadow. Sweating with effort, he had taken off his tunic and rolled his shirt sleeves to his elbows. With a heavy, iron-tipped pick, he was attempting to pry a boulder out of the ground. From the size of the stone, Absalom doubted one man alone would have the strength to move it.

He stepped out from the trees. "Owen O'Donnell," he called. No cause to appear in sudden silence in front of the man. He might let the stone slip and injure himself.

Owen looked in his direction and frowned. *Not a warm welcome.* Well, Roger had sent him to help, and judging from the way the man was struggling, help was needed, even from a savage. He tamped down the bile rising in his throat.

As he approached, Owen stabbed the pick into the ground and mopped his forehead with a shirt sleeve. "You have a way of surprising a man," he said by way of greeting.

"Roger sent me. I know the land."

"Do you know the stones as well? They're plentiful as raisins in soda bread."

Absalom scanned the field. It would be impossible to plow in the straight lines the whites favored without removing most of the stones. "You have enough of them to make a low wall."

"Aye." Owen bent down to pick-ax at the dirt.

He'd force him to talk. "My people say the stones were carried here by a great sheet of ice."

Owen looked up, startled. "A great sheet of ice, is it? We have elaborate tales in Ireland, too. Have you heard of the little people?"

Absalom shook his head.

"Well, some day after I've this field cleared, you can tell me about the sheet of ice, and I'll tell you about the leprechauns. But for today, I'd best keep digging."

He turned away as his uncle had done earlier. Irritated, Absalom moved so they could speak face to face. "Let me help. What one man can't lift alone, two can." Before Owen could refuse, he stripped off his fringed shirt, dropped it out of the way, and bare to the waist, bent over the boulder. "You've loosened it well. Now if we can lever it out of the hole, between the two of us, we'll be able to carry it to the edge of the field. I'll take the pick, you take the shovel."

Owen eyed him without warmth, but after a moment's hesitation, did as suggested. With much grunting and effort, they finally rolled the stone from its bed and onto the grass where they could grasp it.

"No need to carry it," Owen said. "We'll roll it in the wheelbarrow here."

"You made this?" Absalom said, eying the barrow carefully.

"Aye. There's wood aplenty for crafting."

The barrow was a simple contrivance with one wheel that rotated on a short, metal shaft—simple but clever. His people had much to learn from the whites as well as much to teach. Perhaps their ties were stronger than their differences.

Together they loaded the boulder onto the barrow. Owen grasped the handles, bumping its burden along the uneven ground to the edge of the field. Absalom followed and helped lift the stone and place it alongside a few others.

"The beginning of that wall you spoke of," Owen said. He was civil enough, but just barely.

Puzzled, but determined to see his task through, Absalom said, "Even with the help of your barrow, clearing the stones will take weeks. Before the season becomes too hot, you'd be wise to burn your field."

"What?" Owen stopped in his tracks. "Start a fire? Risk burning down my cabin? A fool notion." He reached for the shovel, dropped it in the barrow and wheeled over to another boulder.

Owen was proving as stubborn as the sachem. His blood starting to boil, Absalom followed, pick in hand. "My people burn their planting ground every spring."

"For God's sake, why? We never did so in the old country."

"Clearing away grass and low brush makes planting easier and stunts tree growth." Absalom pointed to a sapling. "Look there. Pine seedlings have already taken root, and I see maple and oak sprouts scattered about. If left unchecked, in a few years, they'll fill in, and you'll have a meadow no more. And there's something else about the burning, something mysterious."

"Ah, a mystery." Owen stopped his digging.

"Yes. Crops grow taller and fuller in land that's been spring burned. No one knows why exactly, but it happens."

Owen leaned on the shovel. "There's another mystery I'd be happy knowing. How do you stop the fire from burning down everything in sight?"

"We choose our day with care. A day like today would be good. Sunny with little breeze to fan the flames, and the ground still moist from the snow. We follow the flames with dampened rawhides so we can smother the fire where we need to. Low brush like this burns off quickly. There's little danger."

"Little, but some?"

Absalom nodded. "Some."

"You're an honest man. I'll say that for you."

Warmth had come into Owen's voice. But why had it disappeared at all? Absalom wondered. Truly, white ways were not as transparent to him as Canonchet believed.

Owen's skeptical look faded a bit. "Roger knew you would suggest this burning?"

"Of course. He knows our customs."

Owen eyed him thoughtfully before squinting up at the sky. "The sun's already high." He glanced toward the woods. "Grace is away from the cabin. I wouldn't start any of this burning business without knowing where she is, though she's bound to be somewhere in the copse nearby. She enjoys going after small game, but the wild creatures here are different from those in Ireland." Worry knitted his brows together.

"She's skilled with the bow," Absalom reassured him though the image of the stranger who had followed Grace through the woods flashed into his mind.

"Aye, but I fear for her when she's out of sight," Owen said, the worry still on him. "The freedom to hunt without reprisals is so wondrous to her I can't deny her the right."

Once more Absalom hit a stone wall in his knowledge of white men. No Narragansett would allow his woman to go against his wishes regardless of the reason. But this was a matter between a man and his wife.

He glanced up at the sky. "Should tomorrow be calm like today, I'll return at sunup for the burning. That will give us a month to remove most of the stones. Then if you can borrow a team of oxen . . . Caleb Harris has the best team in the colony . . . you'll have your field plowed and ready for planting by mid-May. Once that's done, we can begin leveling a wooded section.

After we fell the trees and cut them up for fuel, the stumps will have to be burned out." He grinned. "After that come the stones."

The stubborn expression had returned to Owen's face. "You're saying 'we' like you intend to help me work the land. Have I asked you for your help?"

The man has pride. "No. But Roger Williams is my foster father. He sent me to you. A man can't always do what his father asks, but when he can, he must."

"I see." For the first time in the past hour, a smile creased Owen's face. "Your thought is a kind one, and God knows I can use the help." He held out a hand. Absalom grasped it then turned away quickly as if considering how best to remove the boulder embedded at their feet. It would not do to openly show his pleasure at Owen's offer of friendship.

He reached for the pick. If Grace didn't return within the hour, he'd make an excuse to leave and begin searching for her. The arrogant one had long since left the colony, but Owen was right. Many dangers lurked for a woman alone in the woods.

But as they sweated and strained to remove the stone, Grace called out to them. Wiping sweat from their eyes, they both stopped their struggle and looked up to see her emerge from the trees. Hair flashing in the sun, cheeks flushed, she had the bow in one hand and a turkey, a good-sized tom, raised triumphantly in the other.

Chapter Twenty-Five

ON A BRILLIANT MORNING IN MAY, Owen splashed water from a bucket onto his face and chest and dried off with a clean cloth. He raked his fingers through his hair and buttoned on a shirt over still damp skin, though more than likely he'd be removing it to work bare-chested as the day grew warmer.

The aroma of frying eggs drifted out to him.

"You're just in time," Grace said, her voice brimming with excitement.

As he took his place at the table, she lifted the three-legged skillet from the hearth to the table and slid the sizzling eggs onto his plate next to slabs of yesterday's corn bread. From an ironstone jug, he helped himself to a mug of fresh water.

While Owen broke his fast, Grace washed her face and rubbed it with scented oil the Indians used as protection from the sun. She braided her hair into two long plaits and tied the ends with strips of rawhide. In her oldest blouse and skirt, her feet bare, she was ready to seed her land.

Absalom's shadow fell across the open doorway.

"Good-day," she said, her excitement bubbling up anew. "Will you come in and have a bite to eat with us?"

He shook his head. "I've broken my fast. I'll wait outside."

His meal finished, Owen got up from the table. Grace took a straw hat from a peg, tied it under her chin with a green ribbon and followed him outdoors. They found Absalom crouched next to the baskets of seed, running maize kernels through his fingers. "This looks to be of good quality. It was well dried." He stood. "So we begin. We plant the corn first of the three sisters."

"The three what?" Grace asked.

At her puzzlement, Absalom smiled. "The three sisters. Corn, beans and squash. We plant them together."

"You mean we divide the field into three separate growing areas," Owen said.

Absalom shook his head. "No, we plant them all together. In the same holes."

"That's not the way of any farming I have known," Owen said.

"Perhaps not, but it is the best way. Planted together, the sisters nourish each other. As the corn grows tall, the bean shoots twine around the stalks, and the squash leaves spread between the rows and keep the roots moist."

"You're sure?" Owen asked, skeptical but already half convinced. So far, everything Absalom had shared with them had proven valuable.

"I am. Plants are like men. We grow best when we support each other."

"Amen to that." Owen grabbed a basket of corn kernels. "Let's begin."

"Aye," Grace said. "I'll pop in the beans."

"I'll follow with the squash seeds and cover them over," Absalom said. "This soil has never been put to crops. It should yield a rich harvest. But it wouldn't harm to pray for rain."

"To Earth Mother?" Grace jested.

"To Her and to Christ," Absalom answered.

"You pray to both?" she asked, serious now.

"Why not? Let all the gods look after the sisters."

"Why not, indeed? With two religions to call on, we can't help but succeed." She gave him a dazzling smile before bending over to drop in her first seed.

The following day dawned radiant with sunshine, and with the field planted at last, Grace yearned to escape the confines of the farm and rove the woodlands. After gaining Owen's reluctant agreement, she waved good-bye to him from the edge of the meadow, suspecting he would be worried for her until she returned. But he had no need to fear. The woodlands were her home, her first love after Owen himself.

The spring air, damp and filled with the odors of the awakening earth, caressed her skin. Nature, the Great Mother, had emerged from Her winter sleep and was making Her presence known in the softening ground, in the unfolding green leaves, in the music of the birds. Nothing could hold Her back, nothing could stay Her fulfillment.

Bow in hand, arrows in a quiver slung over her shoulder, Grace plunged deeper into the forest, into its heart, heading northwest, past familiar woodlands into the common ground that lay unclaimed beyond them.

What riches this fallow land held as it burst forth with emerging life. She would never get used to its largess, its wild beauty.

She glanced up beyond the treetops. In hours that fled like minutes, the sun had passed its zenith. Time to circle back toward home and Owen. With the green bark on the tree trunks verifying her direction away from north, she kept a steady pace, although hours of sunlight were still left to her.

She hadn't raised her bow once today, not even when a hidden covey of quail fluttered up in her path, nor when rabbits, ears alert, went rigid at her approach. Somehow, she hadn't wanted to bring death into all this new life. Stepping lightly, she quickened her pace, avoiding the scrub brush growing between the trees. The land here she hadn't traversed before. If anything, the boulders strewn about were thicker than on the farm, huge outcroppings no man could hope to remove with a pick-axe and a barrow. Maybe Absalom's tale of the gigantic ice flow was true. How else could such stones have been carried over the land?

A sudden snapping of limbs and an eerie shuffling broke into her reverie, and then a deep growl. Dear God in heaven, what had made such a noise? She'd never heard its like before, and the hairs on the back of her arms rose up in shocked awareness.

She stood still for a moment to listen. The shuffling and growls sounded closer. Working quickly, she slipped an arrow out of her quiver, fitted it to the bow and held it in front of her in striking position.

The growl rose to a roar followed by a crashing through the underbrush. She felt the shock of heavy footfalls through the soles of her thin moccasins. Dear Mother, the creature must be enormous. An image of the bear skin spread over the cabin floor, its fangs and claws still intact, flashed into her mind. Was it a bear? Surely not. Canonchet had said they were rare hereabouts.

Keeping her bow at the ready, she stepped behind the nearest tree trunk. For the first time, her weapon felt puny in her hands, and her heart began a violent drumming. How could her slender, graceful arrow fell a bear?

The growls grew louder. The beast was heading straight toward her. More snapping of branches, a loud outcry, and then a series of screams knifed through the air. That was no wild beast. An instant later, a panting, fear-crazed man came scrambling through the undergrowth. She knew him and called his name. "Caleb Harris, over here! Over here!"

Her voice startled him into a stumbling halt. Then like a frightened deer, he stood motionless too terrified to risk a single step.

"Come, Caleb, over here!"

A flash of recognition lit his eyes, and he staggered toward her, his shirt clawed to shreds, his chest bloodied, strips of flesh hanging loose and oozing gore. "Help me. For God's sake help."

"Get behind me, Caleb."

Red-eyed, outraged, the bear, vicious after its winter fasting, roared into view. Grace gasped at the sight of him, a force of nature so powerful, her every instinct shouted *"Run."* But running from such a fearsome monster would be useless. They couldn't hope to outrace him. She would have to shoot. Shoot as never before.

A head shot had the best chance of bringing him down. Aye, the head, the smallest target, the most dangerous. She stepped out from behind the tree. He saw her, and rising up on his hind legs, he paused in his onslaught, a split second only, but enough time for her arrow to flash out. It struck him near the left eye. With a howl of pain, he swiped at it with a thick claw, but the arrow stayed fast.

Maddened, he dropped to all fours and began a clumsy charge through the underbrush. Forcing herself to move with deliberation, Grace took a second arrow from the quiver. Coming head on, he moved fast, quickly closing the distance between them. *The chest this time.* Aiming between his forepaws, she shot again, the arrow penetrating quick and true, clean into where his heart must lie.

He slowed but kept coming. *Dear God, will nothing stop him?*

Roaring his anger for all the woods to hear, he opened his maw wide, exposing his great yellow teeth, his tongue, his throat. *The throat, then.*

But if she missed?

She would not.

"Are you a bear, then?" she shouted, snatching another arrow from her quiver. "Come get me if you can! Come! Come! Show me how brave you are, Sir Coward Bear."

She kept provoking him, urging him to howl, to open his maw wider and wider, to turn his anger to frenzy. Goaded beyond endurance, he rushed forward, crushing the underbrush beneath his paws in a frantic haste to destroy his tormentor.

Willing her arms steady, she pulled back the bow. As he hurtled toward her, screaming defiance, her arrow soared and flew deep into his throat. He was almost upon her, so close she could smell his foul breath and see the veins in his eyes. Then in a gush of blood, his claws outstretched ready to rake her flesh, he crashed to the ground at her feet, angry no more.

Hands shaking, Grace dropped her bow and ran to Caleb, lying slumped behind an oak trunk. He was badly mauled. The claws had carved furrows deep into the underlying muscles of his chest. Was he dead? Grace approached him slowly.

"Caleb, can you hear me?" She touched his face, willing him to respond. "Caleb."

His eyes opened a slit and quickly closed.

"Can you walk, Caleb?"

No answer.

He had fainted. She glanced up at the sky. The sun was riding toward the west. They were at least an hour away from the village. He couldn't walk, and she couldn't carry him. She would have to leave him and run for help. There was no other way.

She prayed the bear had been hibernating alone, with no killer mate coming in search, nor a cub. Caleb would be helpless before either one.

"Caleb. Listen to me. Please. Open your eyes."

His lids fluttered.

"I have to leave you to go for aid. But I swear, I'll return." She squeezed his hand, then leaped to her feet and began running.

This was strange new territory, and above all, she didn't want to lose her way. Before the bear, she had curved from the north to the southwest. She continued in that direction, running, then walking when the stitch in her side became too hurtful to breathe. An hour later, the trail between the trees began to look familiar, and she soon came across a dirt path leading to the village. At the outskirts, she cried, "Help, help! Bear attack. Help!"

Cabin doors sprang open, and alarmed faces peered out. In minutes, after she gasped out her tale, several village men followed her, one with the presence of mind to bring along a woolen blanket for carrying Caleb. After a few false turns, she found her way back through the woods. In her haste to reach the village, she had broken off twigs and stripped leaves marking a trail that led them unerringly to where Caleb lay babbling and semi-conscious.

———————

Owen sat on the edge of their bed the next morning and looked down at his hands. For the first time in his life, they trembled. Grace could have been killed, and he would have lost her forever. No wonder he trembled. He glanced over to where she lay curled under the covers, her hair spread over the pillow, a hand under her cheek, the gold ring shining on her finger. God, she was utterly marvelous. Beautiful and brave beyond all measure.

As always, the sight of her warmed him. All was well in the world as long as Grace was alive in it. He blew out a breath and stood. Let her sleep the day away, if need be.

He stepped outside the cabin softly closing the door behind him. Another perfect day, the sun shining full on the planted field. A few more days like this and the sisters would soon stir into life. For today, he would stay close by and forget his plan to chop timber. The sound of his axe would ring in the air destroying the peace, waking Grace from her much-needed rest.

He'd leave her just long enough to fetch water from the stream. He picked up the empty bucket when a stirring from the edge of the trees caught his attention. Shielding his eyes with a hand, he peered across the sunlit meadow. Surely his eyes deceived him. Absalom and Emma Harris? Walking together, talking like familiar, friendly acquaintances? He lowered the bucket. A more curious sight he had seldom seen, and he waited, fascinated, for them to come closer.

"Good morning to you both." He grinned, making no effort to disguise his amusement.

Emma sniffed. "It's not you I've come to see."

"Grace?"

"Yes. Is she about?"

"She's still abed."

Emma drew in a shocked breath. "At this hour? The sun's high in the sky."

"Aye," he acknowledged. Whatever had brought Emma here hadn't changed her vinegary ways. Or had it? Though unsmiling and austere as ever, her expression held something more than its usual disdain.

"How is Caleb this morning?" Owen wondered why she'd left him to come calling.

"He's sleeping. The Indian women . . ." she upped her chin at Absalom ". . . his aunt and cousin are with him. Can you believe they covered his wounds with moss? Green moss from under the shade trees? Mary and Roger Williams are with him as well. Mary said to let the native women have their way. They know things we don't." She paused, uncertain, he would swear, about how to go on. "Roger said to speak to Grace while Caleb slept." Her voice dropped off completely, and she stared at the hard-packed earth fronting the cabin as if it were a compelling sight.

Roger had sent her. It was important, then. "If you would wait a moment, Emma, I'll rouse Grace. She'll want to see you."

"Yes."

The woman had no doubt of her welcome. Owen winked at Absalom and entered the cabin.

"I heard voices," Grace murmured.

"Aye. You have a visitor, love."

"And here I am, still abed." She sat up and went to throw off the covers.

"No," Owen said. "Stay where you are. 'Tis rumored the queen of England receives royal visitors while lying in her bed."

"Is royalty coming to call, then?"

He laughed. "I swear she thinks so."

Grace raised the sheet to her shoulders and fanned her hair over her pillow.

"Ready?" Owen asked, his eyes bright with humor.

"I can't imagine who it could be."

He held the door wide open and stood aside. "Welcome to our home, Emma. Please step inside. My lady waits."

"Emma Harris?" At the sight of her, Grace's mouth rounded into a perfect O of surprise.

"I'll leave you ladies alone." Owen closed the cabin door and went out to the yard where Absalom awaited him. They exchanged broad grins.

"Something tells me we've a new Emma Harris on our hands," Owen said. "A gentler, kinder one. At least after a fashion. Most interesting, to see you come across the field together chatting like old companions."

"Hardly that." Absalom stiffened with a touch of the sachem's dignity. "Roger asked me to accompany her. She's more terrified of the woods now than ever." His posture eased, and for a fleeting moment his grin returned. "I doubt she'll come calling often."

"Praise God."

Absalom grew serious. "Canonchet sends a message. The bear meat has been parceled out to the people. It's a rare feast, fresh bear meat. My uncle thanks Grace for it, and for the hide. It will make a magnificent covering. Nothing will be wasted."

"I'm glad some good came of the beast. We cared not to see it again." Owen frowned, worry lines creasing his forehead. "I had no idea bear roamed the woods hereabouts."

"We're convinced this one was a rogue. Judging from his coat and teeth, he wasn't young. Nor were there signs of a mate. He might have been forced from his territory by a younger male. Or had roamed for food, found a good wintering place and stayed. Odds are against finding another so close to Providence. It was a mishap as Roger would say."

"Good." Owen pointed toward the cabin. "I wonder what they could be talking about."

———

"I am that surprised to see you, Emma," Grace said.

"I knew you would be." Emma stood stiffly at the foot of the bed.

Grace patted the coverlet. "Do sit."

"No. I'll stand."

Grace wondered why she would leave home with her husband so ill. "How is Caleb this day?"

"Asleep. We hope he will live. His wounds are fearsome."

"Aye." Grace shuddered, remembering.

"While he sleeps, Roger bade me come speak with you."

Grace nodded. Whatever Emma wanted to say, she was having great difficulty getting it past her tightly held lips.

A lengthy moment passed before Emma took a deep breath, clenched her hands and stepped to the bedside. "If he does live, it will be due to you. You saved him. The men told me the bear fairly bristled with your arrows. All well placed, they said. You were brave, Grace, like a warrior. No man could have done more. And most less." Her voice wavered. "They found Caleb's musket on the ground. The ball still in the chamber. He hadn't shot at the beast. Not even once." Tears sprang into her eyes. "He hadn't tried to save himself." She lifted her apron to her face.

Grace tossed the covers aside and leapt up to put her arms around Emma's thin shoulders and draw her close.

"Caleb is a brave man," she said. "The bear surprised him, knocked the musket out of his hand before he could fire. Caleb fought him. The wounds are on his chest, not his back. When I came across them, they were locked in mortal combat. Caleb distracted the beast, gave me time to take aim. Without him . . ." Grace's voice trailed off into silence. Let Emma believe her husband had been courageous. It was a good lie.

"You speak truly?"

Grace nodded.

"You're an angel from heaven."

"Not otherwise?"

Emma shook her head. "I've learned better. For anything I may have said against you, I am sorry. It was wrong of me."

"Sure and that's all over now. Shall we celebrate? I'll make tea."

"Another day. I must return to Caleb."

"Very well. And I must dress for the day. The sun is high noon and here I am still in my bed gown."

Emma sniffed. "Yes, it is very late."

Grace laughed. Some things would never change. She walked Emma to the cabin door and flung it open not knowing Absalom would be there. A look of shocked surprise crossed his features at the sight of her standing in the sunlight, dressed in nothing but her thin bed gown.

Chapter Twenty-Six

BY WEEK'S END, GRACE FOUND TINY GREEN SEEDLINGS dotting the field. Within a fortnight, the greens took hold in earnest, shouldering through the soil, thriving in the wet spring warmth. By June, she and Owen no long spent most of their days shooing away the birds and rabbits eager to feast on the tender new sprouts. With the help of the scarecrows Owen fashioned and dressed in rags that fluttered in every breeze, the bulk of the crop seemed destined for survival.

With the three sisters thriving, Absalom left for the Narragansetts' summer camp to erect his wickiup. And with the field no longer needing his full attention, Owen began clearing a section of the woodland adjacent to his crop. It was slow work. The trees were tall, their trunks thick as a giant's thighs. They had been growing unhindered for longer than anyone could remember and, initially, he felt daunted by the task before him. He knew the strength in his arms and shoulders and back would stand up to the strain, but what of his accursed leg? Would it fail him now that he and Grace had their place in the sun?

No. He'd die first.

He raised his axe for the initial strike. With a loud whack, it bit into a pine trunk. Again and again, he raised and cut, raised and cut, raised, cut, raised . . . cut . . . until the odor of fresh wood chips filled his nostrils and, finally, with a shudder of release, the pine fell, crashing against its neighbors, shearing off their branches in its descent.

He paused to catch his breath and gulp some water from the wooden bucket he'd brought with him. Next he'd trim off the branches, save the light limbs for kindling and chop the rest into good-sized logs for fuel. Thank God for the large stone fireplace; he wouldn't have to chop the pieces too fine. Heartened by his first success, he thought: One tree at a time, one day at a time.

Ignoring the gnats swirling about his head, he began swinging at the limbs. A year from now, he'd plant twice the acreage, produce enough to sell part of his crop to the next English ship plying these waters, and buy goods for their home. He'd ask Grace what she'd like to purchase first. He grinned. Colored cloth for bed curtains most likely and fine woolen thread to knit into baby clothes. When he had enough land cleared, a pair of oxen would be grand, and some day, God willing, a horse of their own—a chestnut stallion, he vowed. As he sweated and dreamed, the woods rang with the music of his axe.

Summer deepened, and by late July, the corn had sprouted waist high, the bean shoots, as Absalom had predicted, clinging to the stalks, their green pods plump with seeds. Between the tall rows, the squash leaves fairly covered the ground hiding their small, hard gourds, so many gourds Owen decided to stop felling trees for a while and begin readying a winter storage place.

In the spring, Absalom had told him a storage pit should be dug at least four feet deep to get below the frost line. Padded with grass and leaves, the crops would winter well there.

DAYS LATER, AFTER HE'D READIED THE PIT, Owen returned to felling trees. With the crop now shoulder high, neither crows nor rabbits could stunt them. Nor could Grace wait any longer to tell Owen what she had in mind.

Picking her time carefully, after a satisfying meal of roasted quail and dandelion greens wilted with vinegar, she said, "There's something I need to tell you, Owen."

He looked up from his plate. "Aye."

"I wish to travel to Newport village."

He lowered his knife. "Newport? Why?"

"To see Sara Duxbury, the woman who aided me the night I lost the babe."

"Ah." He stared across the table, searching her face for another answer. Finding none, he asked again. "Why?"

"For talk I cannot share with you. Or any man."

"I see." He ate a few more bites before pushing his plate away. "I'll go with you."

"You know you can't." She rose from the table to dip the wooden plates in a bucket of water. "Not with harvest time so near. And besides," she avoided his eyes, "I'll speak freer to Sara if we're alone."

"Oh, I see. This has to do with no babe in our cabin."

Hearing his distress, she glanced at him over one shoulder. "I must do this. Please try to understand."

"There's something *you* must understand." He got up from the table and went over to her. Ignoring her dripping hands, he turned her to face him. "If for the rest of our lives, we live alone, just the two of us, with no child to call our own, I'll still be the happiest man on earth."

She didn't raise her eyes or speak.

He stared down at the top of her bent head. "But you wouldn't be the happiest woman." He put a finger under her chin, tilting her face upward so he could see her eyes. They were filmed with tears.

He sighed and let go of her chin. "How would you get there? By canoe?"

"Aye." The tears spilled over to run down her cheeks. She tried to wipe them away with her wet hands.

"Let me." He pressed her to his shirt, letting her sob against him, letting his heart and his linen absorb her sorrow. "By canoe," he said into her hair, "with Absalom?"

"Aye." She stood back a little, the better to look at him, and gave out a shaky laugh. "Sure and I've your shirt all damp."

His hands slid from her back to her arms. "By canoe with Absalom?"

"Aye, he's going to there and—"

His hands dropped from her arms. "I can't allow it."

"But you must."

"No. My wife is not traveling about the countryside alone with a savage. Absolutely not. 'Tis not fitting."

"You don't understand."

"So you just said. What cannot be changed must be accepted. *You* understand that."

His voice must have carried to the very treetops. She hurried to close the cabin door. Someone might hear him. That no one was about with dark falling fast didn't matter. The sound of Owen shouting at her in anger had to be sealed off from everyone, everything.

The latch secured, she leaned on the plank door, her cheek pressed against the wood. She felt him come up behind her, his breath warm on her nape.

"I'm so sorry, love, but I grew wild for a minute thinking of you alone with him." He reached out to her, but she shrugged his hand off her shoulder.

"He is not a savage."

"He's a man who has looked at you in a certain way."

The shock of that turned her about. "I've not been aware of such."

"Then you don't see him as you think you do. As a man in full."

Dear God, is that true? She'd never mistaken the intent in Rushmount's eyes. She was not an innocent maid any longer, yet every instinct she possessed told her Absalom was a good man. Not Christian, nevertheless a good, well-intended man. That is how she saw him.

"He will never harm me," she said.

Owen exhaled. "I know that, Grace, but be that as it may, I don't like what you propose. Think of the talk."

"There will be no talk, not if Roger goes with me."

"Is that the plan you've hatched?"

She flinched at his tone and at the kernel of truth it held, but she was not ready to give up, not even, she realized, to please him. "You make it sound like a scheme. I overheard Roger say he was going to Newport to meet with Governor Clark. When I asked, he said he would make room for me, if you agreed to let me go."

"You know I don't want you to. And you're right, I can't leave the land now with harvest so near."

At the lost expression on his face, she came to him and laid her head back on his damp shirt front. "I beg you to say yes. I must talk to Sara to see what the matter is." She raised her head. "She's the only one who might know." He pulled her in closer. "I'll be gone only a day or two."

He caressed her back, running his finger tips along her spine. "Very well. If it means so much to you, I can't refuse, and you'll be safe in Roger's care." His hands stopped their idle rubbing. "So tell me, when do you plan to leave?"

"Tomorrow. At dawn."

"God, you've out-foxed me. What a vixen!"

He let out a laugh, and lifting her in his arms, whirled her about the room. When they were both dizzy with turning, he lowered her down on unsteady feet. "There's a price, of course, for everything." He stripped off his shirt. "And now's the time to pay up, Mistress O'Donnell, before I change my mind."

———————

THE WATER SPARKLED WITH THE SAME BEAUTIFUL blue-green of a year ago. The flash of fish, the lapping waves, the sun gilding all with its rays she recalled with crystal clarity. The memory had been emblazoned in her mind the afternoon she lost her hatred of the sea, the afternoon Absalom took her on that first canoe trip home to Providence.

This time, traveling in a smaller dugout, he sat slightly forward of center and she behind him. Without heavy supplies to weigh them down, he dipped the oar mere inches into the water, barely skimming the surface as he guided them toward Aquidneck Island. Comise and Roger followed in a second dugout. As the afternoon wore on, she turned once or twice to wave and reassure herself that they were within sight.

Although she'd tried to deny it, Owen's concerns had lodged in her mind. Absalom was her friend, nothing more. Still, how much did she know of this silent, capable man, whose bare, muscled back rippled in front of her? He revealed so little of himself. His words were well formed, but he spoke seldom, and kept his face impassive rarely showing care, or joy, or humor. Yet when they needed him, he seemed to appear out of the air to offer his aid. Surely that spoke louder than language or laughter.

Well, she could keep her silence, too, and sat quietly watching him and the water and the soaring sea birds. Soon, too soon, the sloping shore of Newport harbor came into view, its snug houses ascending the hills just as she remembered. Now all she had to do was find Sara Duxbury's farm.

It lay, as Roger had instructed, two miles west, on a clear-cut path from the shore and Newport village. She glanced in that direction and reached for her bundle with its extra shift and bodice and a loaf of soda bread she'd baked as a gift for Sara. Two miles she could walk easily and be at the farm long before dark. Her pulse quickened. She could hardly wait. They would have much to talk over—what had befallen each of them in the year since they'd last met—as well as the other matter.

"Absalom will go with you," Roger said, as she picked up her bundle. "I'd go myself, Grace, but two miles on these old knees would do them in for certain."

Owen's warning flashed through her mind. "No need for Absalom to go all that way. I'll be fine alone."

"He'll go with you, Grace."

"But, there's no need."

"I insist. I promised Owen I would keep you safe."

A solitary stroll through the woods with Absalom was hardly what Owen had in mind for her, but she couldn't protest further without an explanation, and that, above all, she couldn't give.

At the shore, the Indians slid the canoes up onto the sand away from the pull of the surf. Roger called out to Absalom and beckoned. He came toward them, his face unreadable as always. "Before you make camp, will you take Grace safely to her friend's home?" Roger asked.

He nodded. "Of course."

Had his expression changed? Grace couldn't tell whether the task pleased him or not. But as for herself, the seed of doubt Owen had planted in her mind pleased her not at all. Once easy and carefree in Absalom's presence, she now felt awkward and self-conscious, aware of his every glance, every trace of tension, every effortless motion of his supple, dark-skinned body. Dear God, what power words possessed if they could turn an easy friendship into a guilty awareness.

With little choice left to her, she bade farewell to Roger who was eager for his visit with Governor Clark and followed Absalom along the rutted path out of town. He strode ahead until the path turned and they were hidden from the village. Once out of sight, he turned back to her.

"I'll carry that." He took the bundle from her, swung it over a shoulder and stayed to walk by her side.

She knew the natives never carried their women's burdens, nor did they walk beside them as equals. For her sake, he was doing what no proud Narragansett would ever do. Touched, she looked at him and smiled. "Thank you."

He nodded, noncommittal as usual, sharing nothing of what he felt. He might be made of stone, she thought, and glory be to God, alone on this path with nothing but chirping birds and chattering squirrels for company, it was just as well. She wished to God Owen had never told her how Absalom troubled him. It had changed everything.

They walked on in silence until the scrub pines and scruffy shrubs gave way on either side of the path to fields planted with corn and beans and potatoes. Here, too, the crops were full and thriving, a satisfying sight, all the more so since the harvest would belong to those who had labored for it and had paid a fair price for their acres, not to a thieving landlord. Not to a Rushmount. As his name snaked into her mind, she wanted to spit in the dirt and pretend it was his face. But the urge could not be given in to, and she continued on as calmly, on the surface, as Absalom by her side.

Around a second bend, a good-sized cabin stood under a wide, spreading oak, a tail of smoke curling out of its chimney.

Grace stopped. "I'll take my bundle now, Absalom, and go the rest of the way alone. Thank you kindly for your protection."

He bowed slightly, a half-naked courtier. The sight made her want to smile, but she wouldn't risk offending him.

He placed the bundle at her feet. "I'll return at noon two days from now," he said. "I'll be waiting here at this place."

Before she could do more than nod, he slipped away between the trees. She had only gone a few feet more when she saw Sara come out of the cabin and behind her a sight that took her breath away, a young woman, hugely pregnant, supporting her swollen belly with her hands as if the weight of the child within was too heavy for her belly alone to bear.

With a whoop of surprised disbelief, Sara caught sight of Grace and ran toward her on spindly shanks as fast and wiry as a little terrier dog. Grace held out her arms and they met, the force of Sara's jolt nearly knocking them both to the ground.

"You haven't changed a bit," Grace told her when she caught her breath.

"Have you?" Sara asked searching her face for an answer. "You're as comely as ever, more so, if anything, but there's something else."

"Aye, there is, that's why I've come. I'll save it for later, when we're alone."

Sara patted her hand and pulling her by the arm brought her over to the girl, for that's what she was, hardly sixteen, Grace guessed.

"This is Carrie. My new daughter-in-law. And my grandson, too, I warrant."

Carrie blushed.

"When is your babe due to be born?" Grace asked.

The girl shrugged. "Any day."

"Aye," Sara said. "Judging from the way the babe has shifted of late. Getting ready for his journey into the world, he is."

Grace stared at the girl who looked hot, and cross and unhappy with her condition. She had conceived a babe quickly, and from the look of her, it was one she didn't want. It wasn't fair. Not fair at all.

Stop, Grace chided herself. You sound like a whining, spoiled child. Are you defeated so easily then?

At dusk, subdued as much by her own thoughts as by the day of travel, she sat quietly at Sara's supper table eating rabbit stew, longing all the while for night so she might seek her bed. They had been too busy recalling the events of the past year to talk yet of why she was here, but in the morning she would broach the subject.

Later, after dark fell, she lay awake on a straw pallet in the cabin's open loft, listening to Sara and John snoring in their bedstead near the hearth below her. The young couple, Carrie and Jack, as was befitting, slept alone in the small bedroom where their babe had most likely been made. Grace tamped down the spurt of bitter regret, then with a sigh and a soft prayer for Owen, she gave it all up to sleep.

———————

MIDMORNING, WHILE THE MEN WERE BUSY in the fields and Carrie, obeying some silent signal from Sara, had wandered into the meadow to sit under the oak and doze, Sara drew Grace to the cabin table. Setting a mug of tea before her, she said, "You've come a ways to see me, lass, so what brings you?"

"You're still the same, Sara, not one to waste words." Grace smiled despite herself.

"Then you do the same." Sara sat herself on a stool and hiked her skirt up to her skinny knees. "August is a bear in this New World. England was never so hot."

"And never so free."

"You have the better of me there." She leaned forward and peered into Grace's face. "Is that what you want to speak of?"

Grace shook her head. "No, not this time."

"I didn't think so. Well, I'm waiting."

"It's the getting started that's hard."

Sara leaned so far forward her scrawny rump lifted off the stool. "Out with it."

She had come seeking this woman's counsel, and however much she didn't wish to talk of what troubled her, she had to. "I can't conceive a child," she blurted then burst into tears.

Sara patted her hand. "Take your time, lass, I'll wait." Good as her word, she picked up her tea and let Grace sob in peace for a while until wiping her streaming face on her skirt, she went on. "For . . . for all the loving Owen gives me, it doesn't happen. Month after month, it doesn't happen." Grace laid her arms on the table and buried her flushed face in them.

"And?"

The word hung in the air until Grace looked up, puzzled.

"Go on," Sara said.

"And I wonder why."

"Do you expect me to know, child?" Sara's words were blunt, like most of her speech, but her voice was kind.

"That night. The night on the ship when I miscarried—"

"Aye, I remember it well."

"Was anything amiss with me? Anything that made you think I could never have another?"

Sara shook her head. "What happened I put down to the sea. You had been retching for weeks. On land, I daresay you would have carried to term. Many a woman has lost a babe and gone on to have others." Suddenly, as if a new thought had struck her, she reared back on the stool. "Perhaps the reason is not in your body."

"Whatever do you mean?"

"The mind, it's said, can play tricks."

"I don't understand."

"Look at Carrie."

"I have."

"The last thing on that girl's mind was the *result* of lying with my Jack." Sara's own words turned her wrinkled cheeks pink. "If you know what I mean?"

Amused, Grace nodded.

"By not thinking on it, the body is at ease."

"I'm at ease." Now Grace felt her own cheeks heat.

Sara smiled. "But not enough, I think. Your mind makes demands. And we cannot command a child into being. Or a flower. Or a sunny day. The will of God alone does that."

Sara clapped her hands on her knees and stood. "So my advice, young Mistress O'Donnell, is to enjoy your life as it is and trust in the Lord to change it in His own good time."

"I've been greedy then? Wanting too much? I've wondered about that from time to time."

"Maybe. Maybe not. Life is harsh in the New World, for all of its freedoms. For a reason not known to us, you're not ready yet. When you are, the babes will come whether you wish them to or not." Sara's wrinkled face lit up in a grin. "Ask Carrie."

Grace laughed, her heart lighter than in months, her trust in Sara complete. As she sipped her tea, Owen's words came into her mind. *I will be the happiest man on earth with you alone.* And to think she hadn't answered him.

It would be a long day's wait until Absalom came tomorrow to take her back where she belonged.

Chapter Twenty-Seven

HE THOUGHT HE WOULD GO MAD. Of all the tasks Roger had put to him over the years, this had been the most trying. Walking alone by her side without speaking, without smiling, without touching any part of her, not even her finger tips when he took the bundle, or her arm when the path narrowed, or her hair that rioted around her shoulders and down her back. He'd like to ask Roger what such hair was called, but he wouldn't. No one must know the turmoil this woman created within him. Not even the woman herself. She belonged to another man, one she loved with shining eyes.

He fisted a hand, banging it into a tree trunk, bloodying the knuckles, enjoying the pain. Ignoring the blood, he turned and leaned up against the tree. The cabin was in sight from where he stood in the shadows. Soon Grace would appear, tormenting his senses once again. Her husband wasn't the reason he had no hope of her. Marriages end, as he himself had learned. All manner of accidents befell men, some of evil intent, some from the will of the gods. With time and patience, who knew? So if fate should make her free, what then? Would she turn those shining eyes on him, Absalom, a man from an alien race? He let out a long breath.

No, she would not. She had never looked at him as Naomai had before they mated, or as Liliawa still did, with longing and a smoldering heat. Never anything but a sisterly concern, though there had been brief moments on the path when he had sensed an unease in her manner, and his hope had spiked momentarily before he put it from him.

Her unease was fear. To have her fear him as a *savage* was worse than mere friendship.

Nor would he force himself on her like the tall, arrogant one. His blood still boiled remembering the icy day the man had seized her in the woods. If the weather had been warmer, if the man had not alerted him by tramping through the brittle undergrowth, Grace might well have suffered a harsh fate. His jaw clenched. That was not the way to take a woman—with violence. Despite what the whites might think of the eagle feather jutting from his hair, his loin cloth and fringed leather tunic, the moccasins on his feet, and the wampum necklace around his throat, he was a man of honor.

While he waited on the edge of the farm in the shadow of the pines, he knew what he must do. He would leave the home of the Narragansetts, put distance and time between himself and Grace. That was the best solution open to him. Canonchet had Comise to help him lead and soon Comise's son to train. Yes, it would be better to leave. Since Naomi's death, he had endured a bleak procession of days and nights, and now this hopeless craving.

If he stayed, he couldn't trust what might happen. Should he weaken, give in to his urges, chaos would result. The whites prized their women's virtue as highly as their land, though neither one was truly theirs forever. His uncle didn't know it, but for once they were in complete agreement, and he found himself stifling the impulse to smile.

He would see for himself if land stretched to the far western horizon as Roger claimed. See if it was vast enough to accept all men. Afterward, he would return to tell many tales, or not return at all.

The cabin door opened, and a wizened old woman walked out into the sun. His pulse quickened as Grace followed her, carrying a bundle and smiling in a way he had not seen her do in a long while. The two women embraced, then with a farewell wave for the old one, Grace began walking toward where he stood concealed, as if she had every confidence that he would be there waiting for her. *She trusts me.* Perhaps she should not. How could she be so certain that alone in the woods with her, he would not act as the arrogant one had?

She approached, her hair aglow in the sun. He soaked in the sight without moving a muscle. Before she reached his hiding place, a disturbing thought crossed his mind. The arrogant one was due to return to Providence for the final tax payment that so angered Roger. When he did, it would be wise to track his every move. Grace loved to wander through the forests alone and might run into him. For her sake, it would be best to delay his own leaving until the *Seafarer* sailed for England with the man aboard her. Yes, he would wait for that; it would not be too many weeks now.

For an instant, he wondered if his decision was just hope stirring once more. Hope that she might notice him and turn to *him* with her eyes shining? Who knew? Whatever the reason, he would stay through the leaf-falling season. His decision made, a calm came over him as he stepped out of the pine shadow to meet Grace and take her back to Providence. Back to her husband.

"Damn it."

Owen stripped off his shirt. Just as he thought, he'd ripped open the back of a sleeve while chopping the trees. Like most of their clothes, the linen was old and thin, well nigh worn out. He should have worked bare-chested, but the gnats and mosquitoes were troublesome in the deep woods. Once he had the harvest safely reaped, he might be able to barter some of their grain for a few lengths of linen so Grace could make them some new clothes. She hadn't had anything new for so long now.

In the meantime, he needed a fresh shirt. Grace kept their garments folded in the sea chest. He must have another one stored in there somewhere.

As he flipped open the lid, the pleasant odor of lavender rose up to greet him. Inside, a small packet tied with blue ribbon lay on top. Curious, he untied it. The ribbon fell away revealing tiny garments, a gown, a cap and swaddling bands. With a pang, he laid them aside. He found a stout linen sheet, and a shift edged with lace, and a clean blouse. Ah. He lifted it up. Too small, it was Grace's. His best shirt lay next to it, too fine for chopping wood. Maybe some day they'd have a special occasion to wear their finest, but for now he needed a simple work shirt. He came upon his good woolen breeches and a black wool skirt, their winter doublets, the fur boots, and underneath them, the old shag cloak that had belonged to Grace's da. Grace was so like her da, independent and brave, and the best shot with a bow he'd ever known. So unlike most women. Though doubting he'd find a clean shirt under the heavy cloak, he lifted it out. As he did, his hands brushed against something so soft and smooth it reminded him of Grace's skin.

He reached in to the bottom of the chest and pulled out a green garment, a gown he had never seen before. Even to his untutored eye, it was passing fair; velvet, the color of emeralds, and fashioned with a cunning skill. The whole lined with matching green silk, the sleeves and bodice—what there was of a bodice—edged with satin trimming.

Where had such a gown come from? And why had Grace never shown it to him? He stroked it, enjoying the feel of the fabric between his work-roughened fingers, but not the questions he had no answers for. They would have to wait until she returned tomorrow or the next day, a long wait, for the gown disturbed him. Why hadn't Grace mentioned it? Or ever donned it for him? That she would be beautiful in it he had not the slightest doubt. But doubts aplenty as to where she had acquired it assailed him.

Leaving the gown out, he piled the rest of the garments back into the chest, willy-nilly.

The devil take it, he'd wear the ripped shirt. Then his glance fell on the tail of one hanging on a wall peg underneath Grace's apron. Why hadn't he seen it in the first place? he wondered, as he laid the gown carefully over the top of the closed sea chest.

———————

"Owen, I'm home." She could hardly wait to see him and called out again. "Owen!"

She cupped her eyes and looked toward their cabin. Yes, there he was in the doorway, but he wasn't hurrying toward her. After a day of hard work, his leg must be aching. She'd have to run to him. She did, as fast as she could without spilling the pail of milk she carried. But as she hurried over the rough ground, the milk slopped over the pail's edge. It was too precious to waste, and too eager to wait, she set the pail and her bundles on the ground next to a corn row . . . had the stalks grown even higher since she left? . . . and ran to Owen's embrace.

She flung herself at him. His arms came around her and held her tight. "Lord, I've missed you so," he said, his face in her hair.

"No more. I'll go away no more."

"Did you learn what you needed to know?"

She nodded. "Sara helped as much as any woman could. She put my mind at ease."

"I'm beholden to her then."

Though he pressed her close, his arms not loosening their hold, she sensed something amiss. It wasn't the crops. They were taller than she and, from her quick glance at them, about ready to be harvested.

She pulled away a little to gaze full in his face. He'd trimmed his beard and neatly combed his hair, but he hadn't smiled, nor had his eyes lit up in welcome. He must be angry about her leaving. Well, she'd make it up to him. Beginning with a fine meal.

"I stopped to dig clams at the shore. I have a whole apron full of them. Abigail Martin was doing the same and bade me come by her barn on the way home for a pail of milk. Did you know they have a bull and five heifers now? Maybe some day we could buy a cow from them. Wouldn't that be grand? Abigail told me the receipt for making Indian chowder too. 'Tis delicious, she said, and I'm that anxious to try it." She tugged him by the hand. "Come help me carry my things to the cabin."

Once inside, in the half light, she didn't spy the green gown draped over the sea chest, not until she went to put her bundle on the bed. In that instant, she drew in a shocked breath.

Dear God, I should have destroyed it.

She shot a glance at Owen. He was watching her, his expression unreadable.

"Oh, you found this old thing." She tried to keep her voice even as she picked up the gown. "I don't know why I bothered to pack it along. To use the fabric in some way, I suppose."

She opened the chest's lid ready to toss the garment in out of sight and be done with it. Before she could, Owen took it out of her hands.

"I've never seen you wear this. Is it yours?"

"In a manner of speaking."

"Where did you get it?"

"I bought it."

"Only a lady of the gentry would own such a gown. It must have cost the value of a year's work." He ran his hands over the fabric. "Not as much as the chestnut stallion, but a great deal."

"New made perhaps it might have, but I found it already well used at a stall in Liverpool. When I saw the color and felt the cloth, I couldn't resist." She was looking at a spot beyond his shoulder, a chink in the wall where a ray of evening sunlight fingered into the room.

He bent to spread the gown out on the bed. Straightening, he turned to her without a smile. "You forget I spent a winter traveling from fair to fair up and down the English coast. I saw the goods in those stalls. Most of them poor and worn, offered for a tuppence or two. Nothing like this, ever."

She felt a flush rise into her face.

"I want to see you in it."

"But—"

"Now."

"I've been mucking in the sand, and I'm travel stained. This is not a time for the showing of fripperies."

"There's water in the wash bucket. I'll go outside for a bit. Call me when you've the gown on." Without another word, he turned his back on her and walked outside."

She had no escape from what lay ahead, but Mother of God she'd tell lies as long and hard as she could to spare him from knowing how she acquired the wretched garment. For no good would come of telling him that she'd fled before Rushmount could harm her. All that would matter to Owen would be Rushmount's evil intent.

Her mind awhirl, she stripped off her soiled clothes and washed herself with the cool water. In the hope it would calm her, she held the wet cloth to her fevered cheeks, but it did no good, and with a sigh, she dropped the cloth into the bucket. From her bundle on the bed, she removed her brush. Bending over, she flung her hair forward stroking it until it flamed out around her. Then she stood, raised her arms, and slipped the gown over her head. It fit as she remembered, snug in the sleeves and at the waist, the bodice cut low and revealing.

She'd been a fool not to be able to part with it. Even knowing she'd never have its like again with its deep, rich color, its luxurious feel against her skin, and the daring cut of the bodice that displayed her in a way no garment ever should, none of these had been reason enough to risk Owen's peace of mind. Aye, as she had long suspected, as she had asked Sara this very day, she was a greedy witch and look where her greed had brought her.

When Owen saw her clothed in velvet, she'd better have a new tale at the ready. No, not another tale, she corrected as she walked over to open the door to him, the same lie repeated over and over until he believed every word.

Her heart pounding, she lifted the latch and let the door fall open. He sat waiting nearby on an overturned bucket. At the sight of her standing still in the doorway, he arose in one slow, astonished motion. "My God, look at you. I can't believe what I'm seeing." With a gasp, he abruptly sat again, as bereft of air as a sail on a windless sea. "I never could have dreamed . . ."

To her astonishment, tears filmed his eyes. She was sure they were tears and went to go to him, but he held up a palm.

"Stay, so I can gaze at you longer." He stared at her until she grew uneasy. "You look like a queen of the realm," he said at last. "And to think

I will need you in the fields tomorrow to help strip the corn." His hands went up into the air then fell back by his sides. "I can't ask that of you."

"Sure and we have no queens here. Nor is there any need to ask. We've a life to build together, Owen O'Donnell. This gown is nonsense."

Again she moved to go to him. Once more his palm stayed her. "Go in and take it off. There's a clean shift and blouse in the chest."

As if she didn't know, she thought as she went in to do his bidding. She dressed in clean clothes before rolling the gown into a ball and stuffing it in the chest. Now for the chowder.

Before she could begin following Abigail's instructions, Owen came into the cabin closing the door behind him. His face held no smile. "I want you to sit at the table and tell me how you came by a gown fit for a queen."

"But I have a meal to make ready."

"The truth, Grace."

"I've already told you, at a stall in Liverpool."

"I said sit down and tell me the truth."

She eased onto a stool, his relentless eyes, like knife blades, pinning her to the seat. She had no choice but to stay with her tale. If she changed it now, he'd know something was awry. She sighed but didn't speak.

"I'm waiting."

"Aye."

"If you lie I'll know."

"How would you, when I've never told you a single word of a lie? Not once."

"This would be a bad time to start then."

She glanced across the table. "Sure and the clams are waiting."

"I'm waiting as well." Exasperated, he raked a hand through his neatly combed hair roughing up its smoothness. "I know you didn't have the coin to purchase such a garment. I regret that bitterly. You should have dozens of gowns in every color of the rainbow and jewels and every sort of finery. For no woman on earth could set them off as well as you do, but the simple truth is we are not so favored by fortune."

Her chin came up. "In that I differ. We are very well favored, indeed."

His fist banged on the table, rattling a bowl to the floor. "You never purchased that gown. It was given to you, was it not?"

How close he had come. Her pulse beat faster for a second. "No, certainly not."

He ignored her protest as if she hadn't spoken. "The question, of course, is who gifted you."

"No one." She hadn't lied this time, she told herself. In a manner of speaking, she had stolen the gown, but to explain why would be to tell him the whole sorry story. Instead, she stared at him in silence. He got up to pace about, his limp more pronounced than usual. He must be tired. She went to rise off the stool. "Sure and I'll start our meal."

"I'd rather you answered my question. That's what I'm chewing on at the moment."

"Owen, you're making a great to-do over a piece of woman's frippery. I don't understand it, and I won't have it."

She stood, put the bowl back on the table, and went to brush past him on her way to the hearth.

He took her by the wrists holding her at arms' length. "We've never lied to each other, Grace, and we'll not start now. You can tell me the truth. Do we not share all things?"

She nodded. "Whenever possible."

"'Tis always possible." He released her so abruptly she stumbled back a step.

She felt no fear, but still she flashed a quick glance at him. Like the night before she left for Newport, he was raising his voice to her, anger replacing love on his face. Dear God, what was happening to them? What could she do? How could she stem his questions? *Only with the truth.* Sooner or later, Owen might stumble on it himself, if he hadn't already. But he'd have to hit on the answer alone, for in this she had no intention of helping him. She looked into his iron face. He would never understand.

Another lie then. "I bought it at a stall on Market Street, two blocks from the quay. Perhaps it was stolen goods, I don't know. But I regret the buying of it, for the strife it's causing between us."

"Your eyes give you away, love. They've not looked directly at me since I raised the question. You're concealing something. Whatever that may be, your lack of trust wounds me more than any truth ever could."

Before she could think of a response, he turned from her and went out into the dusk shutting the door softly behind him.

Night had fallen as he stumbled along in the moonless dark. His leg ached something fierce. The work of felling trees and hauling branches and logs had strengthened his torso, but for the leg's sake, it would be a relief to begin the gentler work of harvesting.

As he walked the path edging his field, the cornstalks rustled, and he heard the scamper of a wee creature scurrying between the rows, and in the far distance, the hoot of an owl. Tomorrow he'd begin the gathering.

It should be a day of triumph over the many powerful forces they had prevailed against, but the thought of waking the next morning beside a secretive Grace had taken the heart out of him.

Why? Why had she lied to him? That she had, he was certain. Her face, her open, beautiful face, registered her every thought and feeling. He had watched the lie form, heard her spout it out at him. So she didn't trust him with her secret. What could be so bad that he couldn't be told of it? If it was an innocent purchase, why hadn't she shared it with him?

Anger and puzzlement came together in his mind and kept him walking despite the aching limb. He trudged on until the owl's hoot became faint, the roar of the waves louder. He picked up his pace, nearly dragging the leg now, in his haste. Months had passed since he'd had a swim. Though he'd wanted one, the work had kept him from it. Now with the salt scent strong in his nostrils, he hurried like a lemming toward the shore. He'd swim away his aches, all of them.

On the deserted sand, he wasted no time in stripping. No one was about. Like the last man on earth, he stood alone letting the sea breezes flit about his skin, cooling and soothing him. The villagers must all be asleep. The houses were dark, their roof lines hardly discernible against the sky. Ah, no, he saw the wink of a single candle. Someone was awake, by the bedside of a sick child perhaps. Unless Roger sat up reading into the night. Aye, the light came from a hill, it could be Roger.

No matter, he stumbled into the water, gasping at its coldness. Unlike Ballybanree's rocky coast, the shore here felt smooth as glass against his feet. It sloped downward gradually so a man could walk into it, letting the water lap at him until he readied himself to take that first shallow dive into the surf.

God how he had missed this. Without hesitation, he gave himself up to a rolling breaker, plunging in head first, cutting into the water's tumult, wanting it, not fighting it, cresting the wave, riding its force like a wild, bucking stallion back to shore. Over and over he plunged and rode, plunged and rode, until tiring of a game that could not wash his hurts away, he began to stroke parallel to the beach, left to right in a steady pattern, the rhythm of the strokes calming him, the wink of light on the high hill guiding him back to where he had begun.

When he'd had enough, he stumbled onto the sand, by sheer accident coming across his boots and clothes where he'd left them. He dropped down beside them, naked and solitary, heavy with thoughts he could no longer swim away from. Fog had begun rolling in obscuring everything, the pinprick of candlelight, the waves, the sleeping village at his back, everything except his question: Why?

Why couldn't she tell him what she was hiding?

What had she done?

And with whom?

No, not that. Not with anyone. She wouldn't have. But she was so beautiful. Even in her shabby clothes, men turned their faces to her in the streets as if she were a sun and they needed her warmth. In the green gown she had shown him a glory such as he never expected to see . . . and the heart and spirit of her . . . her courage that had drawn her across an ocean to a strange new land . . . with a cripple for a husband.

Of course, something had happened. Common sense told him so. It must have been during the winter he'd traveled with the tinsmith. What a fool he'd been to leave her. She had looked so pale and wan when he'd returned. He'd thought her ill at the time, and then the babe on its way . . .

No!

He rose into the enveloping fog, brought to his feet by the power of a black suspicion.

No.

And yet.

He fell back onto the sand. His heart sped as his mind tumbled through long forgotten facts. She'd been ill on the ship long before the night she lost the babe. Afterward, she'd been slow to recover. As much as he despised the man, Rushmount's food had saved her life.

Rushmount. The name flooded his mind until he thought he would drown in it. *Rushmount.* Who else could it be? What an idiot he'd been not to see it sooner. The lust had ever been in the man's eyes when he looked at Grace. Before they fled Ballybanree, he had tried to make her his own, and on the ship, his willingness to help her. Doing without himself for her sake—like a lover.

An even blacker suspicion nearly gutted him. He could hardly breathe. Had the babe she'd carried been Rushmount's?

Chapter Twenty-Eight

"Stop!" Grace screamed. "Don't go, stop!"

The ship was disappearing. Though she called and called, her voice hoarse with effort, it sailed deeper into the mist, its running lights fading in the distance. In another instant, it would slip away forever.

"Grace, wake up. You're having a nightmare."

Owen's voice pulled her from the mists into a lonely bed. She sat up and looked over at him in disbelief. He lay rolled in a blanket by the hearth.

Half awake, she asked, "You've spent the night on the floor?"

"Aye." He raked a hand through his beard and tousled hair then stood in his smallclothes and reached for his breeches.

"I was frantic with worry for you. I waited outside by the door for hours." She sat up against the bed pillows. "Did I fall asleep there?"

He nodded. "I found you on the doorstep when I came back. I put you into bed."

"I remember you helping me." I must have fallen asleep again." She looked down at the rumpled shift twisted about her legs. In the early light beaming in through their one small window, she could see the rest of her clothing neatly folded atop the sea chest. "You helped me to bed then slept on the floor when you could have held me the whole night long?" Even to her own ears, her voice sounded accusing.

He continued dressing in silence.

She scrambled to her knees in the center of the bed. "Are you not speaking?"

Seated on a stool, in the act of putting on his boots, he paused, the high boot in his hand. "I begin harvesting today."

"That's not *talk*, that's *information*." She jumped from the bed and ran to him. Kneeling by his side, she looked up to see what his face revealed though her heart already knew. "Are you so angry over a silly gown that you'd sleep on the floor?"

Silence.

"Are you?" she asked, the question shrill, out of control, her hands cold and shaking. Without Owen to love her, what was she? *Nothing that mattered*. The thought was unbearable.

Without speaking, he continued lacing his boot. She could live with his shouted anger but not with this quiet indifference. She had to make him understand. Fisting her hands, she began pounding his chest and shoulders, his arms, his thighs. He ignored the blows until he had the boot laced on his foot. Then he straightened, turned to her, and grasped her flailing hands.

"Stop, Grace."

"Aha, he speaks." She swung her head back and forth, all the while trying to wrench her hands free.

"Stop. You're acting like a mad woman."

"You're the cause of it."

He scowled, his grip tightening on her hands. "No, I am not. We're each responsible for our own behavior."

She glared at him through her tangled hair. "Fancy words, but what meaning do they have for us?"

He released her hands with a sigh.

Fearing what he might say, still she had to hear it. "For God's sake, Owen, speak to me."

He nodded. "Aye. You've asked, so I will, but hear me well." With his eyes never leaving her, he paused for a breath. "Whatever happened that you refuse to tell me about, I forgive. No matter what it might be. Do you hear me?" He took her by the shoulders and shook her gently. "No matter what."

In the long silence that followed, his dark gaze became a troubled stare. When she stared back without speaking, he looked away from her. "What I cannot forgive is your lack of faith in me."

"I have all the faith in the world in you."

"Then show it to me. Trust me with whatever it is you're hiding, or our life as man and wife is ended."

The blood drained from her face. "Sweet Jesus, you don't mean what you say."

"I've never meant anything more. Without trust there can be no life between us." He stood, leaving her on her knees by the stool. "I'll take the barrow and start harvesting the corn."

"I don't care about that. All that matters is you."

"We'll strip the ears and dry the best for seed. The rest we can grind for meal." He moved toward the door. "Call me when you have our food ready."

He went out, leaving the cabin open to the chirping bird song and the sunlight, to all of nature's lush warmth. She sat where he had left her, hearing the morning sounds, but not listening, watching the sunshine on the trees, but not seeing.

How could she tell him Rushmount had seized her off a Liverpool street with every intention of raping her? Only the burning candelabra, a chance opportunity, had prevented him from doing so. Owen would want to kill him for the intent alone, and then what? Be hanged for murder?

The memory of Ballybanree's hanging tree, with her father's body swinging lifeless from a barren branch came back with a vengeance. She couldn't risk that happening again to someone she loved. Not to Owen, her beloved Owen. Surely, with time, he would forget his hurt and come back to her heart and soul, and back to her bed as well. She had to believe that. She had nothing else to cling to.

In her shift and bare feet, she went to the woods in back of the cabin to relieve herself, returning to brush her hair, wash, and finish dressing for the day. Though all she wanted to do was return to bed and draw the covers over her head, she had Owen's food to prepare.

Tea today, she decided, and quick bread baked with milk instead of water for a change. The eggs she'd found in a bowl she'd beat into the batter as well. Owen must have taken them from the chicken roost while she was gone.

She eyed the clams ruefully. She'd not made the chowder after all. All that digging in the sand for naught. By this time, the clams had lain wrapped in her apron far too long. Festering they were now like her secret. Before their odor spoiled the air in the cabin, she'd add them to the compost heap at the edge of the field. She'd have other days for chowder making, she thought, striking the tinder box over a clump of dried moss. Or perhaps not. It would always remind her of the morning she found Owen sleeping alone by the hearth.

From the sparks, she built a small fire, just enough to cook their food. Though the day had hardly begun, the breeze blew warm, bringing out beads of perspiration on her forehead. She wiped them away with the edge of a cloth, dreading the moment the meal would be ready and she'd have to call Owen inside.

When the water boiled, she lifted the pot off the spit and dropped in a generous pinch of tea leaves. While the tea steeped, the corn bread's aroma began scenting the air. If only they had a cow, she'd add a lump of butter to the bread and let it melt over the crust, but the cow would have to wait until next year, or the year after, or the year after that.

Overwhelmed by a future of days without end and no talk, no banter, no love in any of them, she wanted to weep, to pound the walls, to fling the food, the tea, the boiling pot about. But she did not. Her ancient ancestress, Granuaile, the pirate queen, would be ashamed of such weakness. And rightly so. Grace lifted her chin, proud at the thought of Granuaile who had fought like a warrior against the English, against the Spanish, against her own countrymen when she had to. Even against her own husband and son. She had been heroic, for certain, but lonely at the end of her life.

Satisfied that the pan bread had baked to perfection, Grace carried the skillet to the table along with the pot full of tea. She'd have to call Owen now, but she'd eat nothing, not with the nausea gnawing of a sudden at her belly.

Silence at their shared meals began and continued that day, and the day after, and for a host of days. All the while, the fine weather held steady. Out in the sunshine, with few words between them, they worked, stripping the corn from the sheaves a row at a time, piling the harvested ears in a mound in front of the cabin and together pulling off the husks and tassels and laying the ears out on Indian mats to dry in the sun. After several days in the blazing heat, the kernels could be rubbed free into a basket and kept in the cabin until the weather turned cold. Then the filled baskets would be stored for the winter in the underground pit, a pit that would not be any colder or drier than existence above ground.

The beans they harvested in much the same wordless way, opening the pods with a finger, tipping out the seeds into baskets. Most of the ripened squash, Owen piled in the storage pit as well. The rest he chopped open with an axe, and Grace spent a day scooping out the seeds in their concave centers. Some of the seeds she reserved to roast by the hearth. Sprinkled with a bit of salt, they would make a fine-tasting treat.

Owen knew they'd been fortunate in one respect; the September rains hadn't begun until after the crops were safely in. But not every year would be the same, and he realized his dream of a larger cabin would have to wait. First, they would need a storage shed. But until they had farm animals to shelter, a cow to start with and sooner or later, a stallion, a *wickiup* such as Absalom lived in during the summer months would be enough to keep the gathered crops dry during harvest time. He might well sleep in the *wickiup*. A thought, if need be, for the future, but for now, he had land filled with trees to clear.

And a home filled with a loud silence.

To ease his sleep, he spread his blanket over the bearskin near the hearth, trying not to remember the night he and Grace had lain on it together making a heaven out of their rude cabin. When such thoughts came to him, he found sleep impossible and lay awake for hours listening to Grace's restless tossing on the bed in the corner, longing to go to her, waiting for the words that would let him do so. But no words came. She clung to her secret, and it grew larger the longer she told him nothing.

One weary morning, shortly after harvest, he went to the copse to find Absalom already there, an axe in hand, cutting off a ring of bark several inches wide from around the maple trunks.

"This will kill them, so they'll not leaf in the spring," he said. "Your work will be easier."

"I've heard of doing such," Owen said, "though I've never seen it done. In Ireland, the fields had been cleared for centuries. Besides, the forest land that remained belonged to his lordship and his peers." He laid his hand on a maple trunk, running his fingers over the bark, over *his* tree. "Having this land to call my own is still a wonder to me."

Absalom lowered the axe to his side, his face as impassive as always. "Your saying that makes what I've just done seem less evil." Before Owen could respond, he disappeared into the trees.

A strange one, Owen thought. After not calling at the cabin for weeks, suddenly appearing here in the woods and just as suddenly disappearing. He shrugged and picked up his axe.

———

As he slipped away, Absalom felt a stab of guilt knowing he should stay longer, help more, as Roger would wish him to do. Owen had looked fatigued. Work on untamed land was hard, very hard, and the whites obeyed no natural rhythm in their labor but continued on from sun up to sun down regardless of how their bodies protested. In this, his own people were wiser; in this, and in their protection of Mother Earth's gifts.

Is that why he had walked away? The sight of Owen stroking the tree as if it were a woman, calling it his own even as he prepared to destroy it? And he, Absalom, by all the gods in the sky, lending his hand to the destruction. It did no good to tell himself what Roger and the other whites would claim: the forests had to die to make room for planting. The Narragansetts had planted since time began, but this wholesale slaughter of trees had never been part of their custom.

Canonchet had been right all along. These permanent farms, as they called them, would sooner or later usurp all the woodlands, leaving nothing for his people to call home.

Taking no care for once to move silently, he roamed like a crazed man striding noisily through the undergrowth, snapping twigs, viciously brushing branches out of his way, taking out his anger on the very things he revered.

Soon, very soon now, he would begin his journey west toward new lands and untouched forests. He saw no other life for himself, so why this puzzling rage? White ways were not new to him. The great ships had been sailing here since before his birth, the threat they posed always clear to those wise enough to see into the future.

He slapped a pine branch out of his way, hoping it would recoil and snap at his back. When it did, he felt a satisfaction in the sharp whiplash on his bare skin. He must be stupid to have underestimated the white threat. Or blinded by Roger's teachings. With a foot in both races, like a man straddling a fence, he stood firmly on neither side. Torn between two worlds, at times believing in one, at times in the other, he was never convinced that either was entirely right. Yes, he needed to get away from everything and everyone he knew. Maybe then he would know which world he belonged to. And which world would call him back.

As he made his noisy way through the woods, squirrels scampered up the trees. Disturbed in their den, a mother fox and her half-grown kits ran through the heavy undergrowth, and a quail rose up, fluttering, from its hiding place in the tall grasses.

Look how they run from me. I'm walking like a white man, frightening the small creatures.

Ashamed, he slowed his pace, pausing between footfalls, seeking out a quiet way through the trees, slipping from one to another without direction, wandering free, but careful not to startle any of the creatures.

The Narragansetts believed they were his brothers. For too long he had considered his uncle wrong in many matters. Now that he was about to leave, perhaps forever, he respected him as never before. He let out a pent-up breath. The leave-taking would not be an easy one. Nor would it be easy to bid farewell to Roger. He had two fathers from two different worlds. Few men could say the same or, as a result, feel such confusion.

Ahead, the stream widened. Birches leaning over the bank shaded the water with their yellow-tinged leaves. A few more cool nights and the yellow would become scarlet then shrivel into brown at the approach of winter. But for now, and for the next one or two fortnights . . . no, until the next full moon, he corrected, amused a little by his lapse into the white man's time keeping . . . the whole earth would be golden, glowing with ripened life like Liliawa these days, with her son at her breast.

The sun shone hot upon his head. After a drink from the stream, he'd go to his *wickiup* to sit for a while and consider how best to tell of his plans.

He stopped abruptly. A young deer, a hart, had come to water at the stream. Bending to drink, front feet in the shallows, ears alert, eyes darting about, it sensed danger. Hidden in the birch shadows, Absalom stood stark still. He had his axe in hand but not his bow. For once, he was glad to be weaponless. Let the creature live. In a day so filled with life, he wanted to cause no more death.

On impulse, to release the animal from its tension, he clapped his hands, the sound like musket fire in the still woods. At the sudden report, the hart leaped into the safety of the trees. Good. Now for his own drink. He walked into the sandy shoals ready to kneel when he saw Grace, bow in hand, glaring at him from across the water.

"Sure and you frightened him off," she said.

He straightened. "Yes, I did."

"I thought Indians were quiet in the woods. You clapped your hands."

"I could see he sensed danger. And I wanted to drink."

"There's a whole river here." She waved her arms in a wide arc, a bow, his bow, in one hand, an arrow in the other.

"I wanted him to live."

"You're a fine one, you are. I won't get another chance like that again. You've probably frightened him off for good."

He had never seen her like this, angry, out of sorts, the lovely lilt gone from her tone as she spoke to him in a way no woman should ever speak to a man. Even a man who was not her husband.

Her feet were bare, her linen sleeves rolled to the elbows, her skirt of blue cloth tied at the waist with a green sash and another piece of green around her hair. In the sharp morning light, she looked pale and, like Owen, tired and thinner than he remembered.

Something was amiss with his white friends. He sensed it just as the hart had sensed danger. Wading through the knee-deep water, he crossed to the bank on her side of the stream. She stood tall, knuckles on hips, clenched hands still gripping her weapons.

He ignored her warrior stance, and looking into her green eyes, saw they were filled with pain. "You are troubled."

"No, I am not."

"Eyes don't lie."

"Sure and I've never told a lie in my life."

"You're lying to your own spirit. It is making you ill."

"How do you know such things? You know nothing."

His face grave, he said, "Something is wrong, but you're correct, I know not what."

Without a warning, she sank to the grassy bank, and dropping the bow and arrow, hid her face in the blue skirt.

After hesitating, he sat beside her, listening to her weep. It went on for so long he finally dared raise a hand to her heaving shoulders. It was the first time he had touched her, and the shock of her firm flesh against his fingers scalded him. He jerked his hand away.

At his quick movement, she raised her head. Avoiding his gaze, she stared across at the opposite bank. "Sorry I am, Absalom, that you should see me thus. But in God's truth, I cannot help myself."

"What troubles you?" Would she tell him? Could she trust an Indian with her deepest concerns? If she did, he would take that knowledge with him to warm his journey.

Yes. Eyes, wide, she turned to him. "I have to tell someone or die. And you're my friend."

Friend.

"It concerns Owen."

He nodded, somehow not surprised.

"I've kept a secret from him."

"Ah."

She bent over her tented knees again, hiding her face.

"Something you can't speak of?"

"Aye," she said, her voice muffled in the skirt. "It happened a few weeks before we boarded the *Seafarer.*"

"You can't tell your husband what it is?"

She sat up straight and shook her head sending tears flying off her cheeks. "No. For the very reason that he is my husband." Breathing in ragged gulps, she added, "It concerns Lord Rushmount."

"The arrogant one who came at you in the woods last winter?"

"Aye. I never told Owen about that day."

"I saw what happened." He frowned. "The man took a great liberty."

"There's more. Another time in England."

"I see."

"No, you don't." She swiped at her tears. "I escaped before . . . before . . ."

"Then all ended well."

"Owen won't see it that way. He'll want revenge, and I fear for what he'll do. Rushmount is ruthless. He's an Englishman with friends in high places, and this is still an English colony for all that Roger governs justly." She paused to catch her breath. "Rushmount killed my father. I cannot risk Owen's life. Not for any reason. Not even if he never loves me again."

A permanent estrangement? Was this his chance? His pulse quickened but as quickly calmed. Of course, Owen loved her. How could he not? He would, for certain, be outraged at the thought of any man touching her, as he would be himself.

He glanced at Grace's streaked face, feeding on the sight of it. It would have to nourish him for the rest of his life. The dusting of light tan dots across the bridge of her small, straight nose, her eyes spaced wide and the color of the sea, her mouth full, her white teeth caught in the bottom lip as she struggled to regain herself.

"You have only one choice," he said. "And you already know what that is."

She met his gaze without flinching. "I have to tell him." She spoke the words reluctantly, with hesitation, but as he watched, her jaw firmed with resolve.

He nodded and got to his feet. "Go to him. He's felling trees in the copse next to your plowed field."

"He won't listen."

"Yes, he will." Absalom smiled. "I would."

"A mighty chance I'll be taking."

"Trust him with the truth. He must be waiting to hear it."

She sighed. "Aye, he is, I know that for fair." She reached up and held out her hand. "I thank you, Absalom, for your friendship."

He took her hand, holding it for an instant only. She smiled and stood, brushing her skirt free of leaves and grass, tossing her hair over her shoulders. As he watched, she disappeared into the trees hurrying, he knew, to her love.

——————

"OWEN."

He looked up, startled by her approach, and struck the axe into a maple where it vibrated to a halt, suspended in the tree limb like a barrier between them.

She stepped closer. "I need to talk to you."

"Talk then." He wiped his forehead with a sleeve. "I'll not stop you."

So he wasn't going to make this easy for her. Very well.

"I stole the gown from Lord Rushmount. 'Twasn't a gift." She could see questions springing into his face, but he said nothing, just stood facing her, waiting. *Like a judge he is, and a jury.* "You have to promise me you'll not place yourself in danger if I tell you the rest."

"I'll make no such promise." He reached for the axe. "If that's all you have to say, I'll go back to my work."

"That's not all." The stubbornness of the man. He was leaving her no choice. She'd have to take the risk. She'd have to trust him utterly.

With the axe between them, she told him everything. In the end, as she had known all along, the tale amounted to nothing. Nothing worth spilling their lives over. She prayed to God he would see it that way, too.

"Are you finished?" he said when she stopped speaking and only birds broke the silence.

She nodded, her eyes brimming with tears.

He rushed to her. Coming fast, he was upon her in an instant, seizing her in his arms, pressing her to him, the closeness of his body, its strength and warmth overwhelming her with memory and need.

"Oh, Owen," she murmured before he began kissing her as if he would never stop, *could* never stop, never wanted to stop until, finally, he tore his mouth away to speak. "I love you so. I love you so. I love you."

She let her own kisses answer him, and together they sank onto the carpet of fallen leaves.

Though Owen asked no questions of her in the days to come, she knew what she had told him lingered in his soul. A proud man always, he would not forget Rushmount's violation no matter that she had sworn he had not had his way. So now he knew everything, except for the single moment in Rushmount's arms when a spark of response had flamed through her. That secret she would take to her grave.

CHAPTER TWENTY-NINE

Like the year before, when autumn began, Owen and Grace watched in wonder. As if brushed with a magical hand, the trees turned yellow and orange and russet, and finally a breath-taking scarlet.

In Ireland, winter announced its coming with cooler, damper days, and the dead leaves hung sodden from the tips of the oaks before falling colorless to the ground or clung to the branches until spring when the new buds pushed them off. Here the growing season didn't die with a whimper but with a shout as befit a triumphant land.

One day when hoarfrost lay white on the fields and the scarlet glory had begun to fade, Owen packed the last of the harvested grain in the winter storage pit, sealing the opening against vermin curiosity with stones jammed tightly together.

Roger had asked him to start work at the blacksmith forge again. It seemed, Roger said, his eyes twinkling, that every pot and pan in the village had sprung a leak. And there were plowshares aplenty that needed mending before spring, and horses and oxen with faulty shoeing.

Owen agreed to cease cutting trees for a while and man the forge until the villagers' needs were satisfied. He could use the earnings for some lengths of linen and another pair of English shoes for Grace. His own clumsy boots he fashioned himself. No one knew his special needs as well as he. He glared down at his feet, the usual disgust at what he saw sweeping through him.

Later this winter, when foul weather kept him at home, he would make himself another pair of boots from deer hide; as always, one boot with a high wooden sole, the other one low and of leather. Except for Grace, he kept that part of his body covered from prying eyes. That she could know of it yet love him, showing him so with every look and word and act, was as miraculous as the trees in their scarlet coats.

He set out for the forge on a cool, brilliant October morning and found someone had stacked a cord or more of dry wood next to the blacksmith shed and left a basket of kindling and a bucket of water beside it. Roger had seen to the supplies, most likely.

Owen opened the creaky shed door. The musty smell of neglect wafted out, and in a corner, he spied the same rough twig broom he had left last spring. Along with his tools, a few derelict pots and a broken plow awaited him on the work bench. Warmed by his walk, he removed his doublet, tied on a protective leather apron, and began laying logs in the stone fireplace next to the anvil. Once the villagers heard his hammer on the metal, they would know the smithy had returned and bring their goods for mending, but to get the coals hot enough to be useful would take a while.

He struck the tinderbox, breathing on the sparks until they burst into tiny flames. So fast did they ignite the handful of dry leaves he'd bunched under the kindling he hardly needed the bellows. A fine day it was for the work, sunny, but with a stiff, salt breeze blowing. In this weather, he'd not be perishing hot leaning over the fire.

While the flames licked at the fuel, he took up the broom, sweeping the shed free of the season's leaves, dust and cobwebs. He imposed order on the work bench, rubbing a bit of tallow he'd brought with him into the rust on the tools. When he had all at the ready, and the coals white hot, he took up one of the old pots and began heating it, softening the metal so it would receive a patch. After he had the vessel leak proof and useful again, he'd see to the broken plow tip.

He found himself smiling. Enjoying himself he was. Life was good, better than good, the best a man could hope for. He began humming a sea chantey he remembered from boyhood, never for a moment letting up on the patch.

He'd nearly forgotten how the strike of hammer on anvil could fairly raise the dead from their graves. A farmer in truth now, he was a blacksmith but seldom. Still the old work satisfied him mightily, absorbing him, keeping his attention riveted on his task so that he didn't notice passersby or see the man approach until he came nigh upon him, standing as close as anyone ever did to the noise and heat.

"O'Donnell."

At the sound of his name shouted above the din, he looked up from the anvil, his arm stopping mid-strike when he saw who had called to him.

Ah. His patience had been rewarded. The bastard had returned.

On his way to collect the last of his taxes, Rushmount had dressed well, in black from head to toe, his snowy white linen in sharp contrast to the rest of his clothing, his knee high boots polished to a glossy luster. Neither sole thick, both boots the same. Owen's jaw tightened. He struck the metal harder than necessary.

"No 'good day' for me, blacksmith?" Rushmount taunted. "It may be your last chance. I leave for England as soon as my business here is finished. In this wretched place, that shouldn't take long."

Owen stared across the fire. "I've more than a 'good day' for you," he said, "but first, I'll complete the task I've begun."

Rushmount glanced at Owen's leather apron, letting his gaze wander slowly, insolently, over him. "Do so." He smiled his derision. "Farewell."

"Rushmount." Owen paused, hammer in hand, the urge to strike out with it barely held in check.

Half turned to take his leave, the Englishman glanced back with careless condescension.

"Our farewells will come later this day," Owen said. He brought the hammer down with all the force of his muscled arm. "Count on it."

Rushmount shrugged and started up the hill to Roger Williams' cottage, his man Thomas following like a beast of burden laden with bundles and packages.

As he watched Rushmount climb the hill, Owen knew the coals he stood over were not the cause of the heat surging through his veins, a heat that strangely enough left him icy cold.

He finished sealing the patch, then lifting the red hot pot with iron pincers, he plunged it into the bucket of water. The cold bath would stiffen the joining, making the vessel good as new. If only a man's life could be repaired so easily, he thought, as he removed his leather apron and hung it on a peg on the shed wall.

The plow tip he'd intended to mend next would have to wait. He lifted the cooled pot out of the water and set it on his work bench for the owner to claim. Shameful to waste a fire heated to perfection, but he saw no help for that and doused the coals with the water remaining in the bucket. If rain fell in the night, the bucket would fill by morning, or by the next morning, or not at all, nor did that matter.

He latched the shed door and walked back through the village nodding to his neighbors, not pausing to speak to anyone, driven by a force so primal it was impossible for him to stop.

He hurried along the main street, past houses and sheds, moving down the slope toward the water. At the docking place, three large dugouts had been pulled up on shore. The Algonquins who had oared them from Newport were nowhere in sight. They would be off visiting their cousins, no doubt. The dugouts themselves were empty, awaiting the goods Rushmount had come for. The tax pickings would be lean this time. Grain mostly. He had paid his assessed amount to Roger, both of them hating the obligation. But it could be worse, as Roger had pointed out. Pacifying England helped keep the colony at peace.

Aye, it could be far worse Owen acknowledged as he strode along, the memory of rent-racked Ireland and its half-starved children chilling his icy resolve even further. He hurried his step. He had to rid himself of what remained from his life in that time and place—Rushmount—a man who had usurped his ancestral home, who had impoverished his friends and family to desperation, who had killed Grace's father, and hounded her brother to suicide. The listing infuriated him.

Yet from every one of those wrongs he, Owen O'Donnell, had fled, fled to the New World. *Fled.* No other word could describe what he had done. He could have stayed and fought and died. But he had chosen to live . . . with Grace . . . *for* Grace. He still wanted that life with every fiber of his being, but the need for justice—no, be honest, man, he chastised himself—the need for *revenge* swept everything else aside.

Some violations a man could not simply accept and call himself a man. In seizing Grace, Rushmount had crossed an invisible line. Owen's hands balled at his sides. Seeing the sneer on Rushmount's face again this day, he knew he couldn't ignore what had happened, not if it cost him his life.

He hurried so fast his crippled leg dipped in the awkward way he hated, but he didn't slow his step. Haste had him in its grip.

At the cabin, Grace was nowhere in sight. For once, not seeing her, he found himself relieved. Were she there, she would try to stop him. He flung open the sea chest. The green gown lay on top of their garments. The sight of it rolled into a careless ball cheered him somehow. Grace must have dropped it into the chest without a thought except to conceal it from view. He lifted it out and, shoving it under his arm, hastened back the way he had come.

Happier than ever before, Grace tramped through the woods, drinking in the beauty of the trees, the sunshine, the bird song, the rich aroma of the earth. Above and beyond all these, she gloried in the bond she and Owen had forged. It was stronger than ever, something a short time ago she would have thought impossible. Yet like the seasons, their love had ripened beyond springtime.

She'd have good fortune today. She felt it in her bones. Bow in hand and the quiver of arrows slung over her shoulder, she made her way to the stream where the sandy bank widened forming the shallow watering place the animals favored. The very spot where she had seen the hart a few weeks past, the day Absalom purposely startled it into fleeing. A strange, good man, Absalom.

If she dared, she would have begun whistling like a rogue lad on his way to mischief. But quiet is what the hunt called for, and today she wanted a strike. With winter coming, they needed the meat.

The moccasins helped her move through the woods without a sound. She looked down at them, pleased by their intricate purple and white beading. *Wampum* Riana had called it the day she had traded them for a knitted shawl. The better part of the bargain was mine, Grace thought with a pang, for the moccasins were beautiful.

Now for the difficult part. Waiting. At the stream, she stopped by a leaning birch, its low branches nearly touching the water. Shifting the quiver off her shoulder, she eased it to the ground and glanced up at the sky. The morning was still young, but a dawn hunt would have been better. The deer were more likely to drink at daybreak before bedding down to rest. Yet the last sighting she'd made had been in the afternoon, so there was no certain telling. She would just have to wait and see.

She removed a single arrow from her quiver. The deer reacted so quickly one shot is all she would have, if even that. A low juniper grew beside the birch. She positioned herself, bow and arrow on her lap, between the shrub and the tree, well concealed from any eyes.

In this sheltered place, the air lost its tinge of autumn chill. The sun beat down warm and golden on her head and shoulders, caressing her skin, soothing her into reverie. How long she sat dreaming she didn't know, but at the slight sound of a gently slapping branch, she awakened, stiffened, instantly alert.

Something moved.

Grasping her weapon, she peered over the juniper. *A hart.* Could it be the same one? No matter. As he bent to drink, his eyes on the water, she carefully raised her arms, and with a silent hand, fit the arrow to the bow. She studied her prey for a moment without moving a muscle. If she tried for him in a sitting position, the arrow might fall short. She needed to stand. But would she have that vital split second before he heard her or saw the pattern of leaves on the water shift and be off before she could let fly?

The chance of missing was great, but she had to take it. Slowly, she tented her knees and tightened her thighs. She would jump up and shoot in one fluid motion. Her speed against his. Concentrating her effort, she gathered her strength and leapt to her feet pulling back on the bow in the same instant. The arrow arced across the water, striking the deer in the neck just as he raised his head, alarmed, scenting danger a heartbeat too late.

With the arrow deep in his flesh, he fell into the stream like a thrown rock, half in, half out, of the water.

Grace glanced across the shallows, the flush of victory swiftly dying within her. A moment earlier, what had been so quick and alive now lay deathly quiet. No matter what her need, the killing of such a beautiful creature struck her, suddenly, as wrong. She dropped her bow to the ground and crumpled next to it, covering her eyes with her hands, blocking out the sight of what she had wrought. Good God, was this what life meant? Kill or be killed? No more than that? Was it for this she longed to bring a child into the world?

"Again I find you weeping."

Startled, she looked up to see Absalom standing beside the fallen deer, his bow in his hand, a slight smile playing about his lips. "You took him before I could," he said. When she didn't answer, he pointed to the hart. "You weep for him?"

She nodded, unable to speak, feeling foolish at being caught again in tears. Why now? This was not the first deer she had slain. "He was very beautiful," she finally said, a bit uneasy that once more Absalom had appeared from out of the trees without warning. Was he following her about the forest?

His expression pensive, he gazed down at her kill. "Mother Earth made a gift to you. His life will not be wasted."

"True. It will not be." Relieved, she scrambled up, glad he had found her after all. "We'll make good use of every bit."

Hopping on one foot then the other, she pulled off the moccasins, stuffed them in the quiver with her arrows, and slung the quiver across her shoulder. She picked up the bow, raised her skirt to her knees, and waded across the stream.

Beside the hart, knee deep in water, she said, "In Ireland, I would have butchered him here and now and distributed the meat as fast as ever I could." She wrinkled her nose. "I hated that part, all the blood and gore. But I had no other way. People were starving." She frowned, remembering. "If they had caught me in the doing, I would have been hanged. Like my da."

Absalom slid his unused arrow into his quiver. *No wonder they come here in their giant ships.* "You won't die for taking this one. He'll be hung, not you, and properly prepared."

She nodded, heartened. "I'll fetch Owen. Perhaps he can dress him right here."

"No need." Absalom bent over, pulled her arrow out of the deer's neck and handed it to her. His own bow and quiver he hung from a birch branch. Leaning down, he grasped the hart's hind legs and pulled him out of the water. Once he had him on the bank, he gained purchase beneath the animal's belly, and placing his heels firmly apart, lifted the carcass with one great grunt and flung him onto his shoulder, letting the head and front legs dangle over his back, the rear legs over his chest. "Come," he said, "It isn't far."

Grace walked ahead easing branches out of the way, taking the shortest route through the woods. Wait till Owen saw her kill. He'd be that pleased. They'd have meat for weeks to come and plenty to share.

Absalom was right. Killing the deer had been a good thing, for she had killed in accordance with God's plan, to live, not for any other reason. Comforted, she hurried along until they reached the cabin clearing. With a heavy sigh of relief, Absalom dropped his burden to the ground. "If you have some rawhide or rope, I'll hang him from that nearby maple until Owen can dress him down."

"Aye." Grace left her bow and arrows by the cabin door and hurried inside. A moment later, skirts whirling around her legs, she ran back out, panic glittering in her eyes. "I can't wait," she said. She reached into the quiver for her moccasins, jammed them on her feet, and seized her weapons. "I have to find Owen."

"But the deer?"

"Not now," she shouted over her shoulder, already tearing down the path to town.

Stunned, Absalom watched her disappear into the distance. Why would she need her weapon in the village? There'd be no prey there. It didn't make sense. What had she seen in the cabin that made her so frantic?

He went inside the house and looked about. Everything appeared to be in order: the fire banked low, the bearskin spread before the hearth, a Bible centered on the tabletop . . . the bed smoothed and ready for the night to come . . . and at its foot a sea chest with a raised lid.

He saw nothing out of place, nothing amiss. But clearly something had upset Grace to the point of panic.

What?

He scanned the room a second time. The only hint of disturbance might be the chest. If it contained their most valuable possessions, shouldn't it be kept closed? Yet the lid gaped open. Had Grace noticed something missing? Something Owen had taken? A weapon? A musket? Although he had never seen Owen shoot one, that meant nothing.

She'd raced toward town without a second's hesitation. So she suspected trouble. But how could she be so certain? He knew little of what went on in their marriage, only the one trouble she had spoken of. Standing still in the quiet room, he let his mind play with it until, *of course*. The arrogant one had returned. Something in the cabin told her so and that Owen had gone after him. Nothing else would have sent her racing wild-eyed along the path.

He hurried out of the cabin, leaving the deer where it lay, and began to run. As he ran, he cupped his eyes, but caught no glimpse of her. Terror must have made her fleet as a deer. At the docking place, he saw the beached canoes. So he'd guessed correctly. His cousins had delivered their passenger and by now would be busily feasting with their kin.

Sprinting lightly on the balls of his feet, he raced through the center of the village, ignoring the townsmen's alarmed glances. They preferred to have their Indian neighbors move slowly among them. No doubt they thought his haste menacing, though they'd never think the same of the Englishman. How little they knew of their own kind.

His body had so heated from the run, he could smell his own sweat, yet he picked up his pace. Where *was* she? Up ahead, on the steep slope leading to Roger's cottage, he saw bright hair flashing in the sunlight. Tumbled free from its ribbon, her hair flew behind her like a brilliant banner calling him to battle, a battle he would have to wage without his best weapon. His bow and the arrows that matched it were hanging useless on a tree near the stream. So be it. He had his skinning knife, his people's wiles, his white language. They would be enough.

A pace behind her, he called, "Grace!"

She turned without stopping, her face flushed and strained, her breath ragged. He grasped her arm. "Don't stop me," she gasped. "I have to help Owen."

His grip tightened, slowing her to a halt. "Not like this. You need your wits about you." As she tried to wrench free, he asked, "Has this to do with the arrogant one?"

"Aye." She took in great gulps of air and struck at his hand with the edge of her bow. "Let go of me, or I'll scream for aid."

Their eyes met, and an unspoken message passed between them. She was rushing toward the man she loved just as he was rushing after the woman he loved.

He let his hand fall away. Freed, she dashed ahead straight for Roger's cottage. Without seizing her in his arms, he couldn't stop her. As much as he wished it, she was not his woman. He had no control over what she could do.

He cursed and hurried after her.

She burst through Roger's door without knocking. Following close behind, Absalom peered in the open doorway.

"Is Owen with Lord Rushmount?" she blurted, almost breathless, struggling for air.

"Yes," Roger said nearly startled out of his chair. A bowl of hot stew slipped out of Mary Williams' surprised hands and splashed onto the table top.

"Where are they?" Grace asked, her voice hoarse with effort.

"I don't know," Roger said, attempting to rise to his feet.

"Oh God." With a sharp cry Grace dashed across to the settle and held up the green gown. "Owen left this?" She whirled around to Roger. "What did he say of it?"

Roger gave up the attempt to stand and fell back onto his seat. "He threw it at Lord Rushmount's feet."

"He said nothing?"

"Yes, he said, 'My wife has no need of your rags.'" Roger looked puzzled. "A strange statement for such a beautiful garment."

"Then what? Hurry, I implore you."

"He said, 'We'll settle this like gentlemen, Rushmount. In private.' Lord Rushmount laughed, but he left, rather unwillingly, I think. It was either that or discuss their difficulty in front of me." A trace of anger began to color Roger's cheeks. "What is this about, Grace? How are you and Owen involved with Lord Rushmount?"

"Oh God, 'tis a long story," Grace said, and without a further word, flush-faced and distraught, she ran out of the cottage, her glance frantically taking in the hillside, searching it for a sign of the men, but finding none.

Before she could dash off, Absalom said, "They weren't below. They must have climbed the hill. Come with me, I'll find them for you." She gave him a look of such trust his heart turned over. He hurried from Roger's cottage, and she followed him without protest. A few paces away, the marks left by Owen's uneven gait were as clear on the dusty lane as writing on a page. At the crest of the hill, they heard voices. Grace sprinted ahead the last few yards.

"Get away from me, O'Donnell," Rushmount was shouting. "I shouldn't have come here. There's no talking to you."

"Of course not. I'm done with talk." Owen laughed, a sound without humor in it. "Now there's a fine Irishman for you."

With his long-legged stride, Rushmount was trying to put some distance between himself and Owen, but his greater stride made no difference. Owen kept coming, unhurried, relentless, narrowing the space with every footfall.

Under a leafless tree, a few feet before the slope dropped off into a steep ravine, Rushmount turned to face his pursuer. "I'll have you prosecuted, you madman. I'll see you chains."

"I'll see you in hell, first" Owen grasped the linen stock under Rushmount's chin. His expression read war.

Grace gasped. She had seen that same cold, determined look on Owen's face once before, on their last night in Ballybanree when he had beaten Rushmount senseless for attacking her. He'd do the same now. Worse, he'd kill him if he wasn't stopped. She took a step forward ready to intervene. Absalom gripped her arm. "No. Stay back. Owen must do this alone."

As she hesitated, torn between running or staying, Owen fisted his right hand and struck Rushmount on the jaw. The impact, with the power of Owen's hard, muscled body behind it, echoed across the clearing. Lifted off his feet by the blow, Rushmount staggered, swiftly rallied, and long arms flashing out, caught Owen in the midsection, pounding his gut, throwing him off balance. With his weight thrust onto his injured leg, Owen reeled back, growling as a shaft of pain shot up his calf. Quickly righting himself, he brought up a left and a sharp right. Closing in, he feinted with the left, jabbing once, twice, three times at

Rushmount's hawk nose, and spotting an opening, struck another solid right to his jaw. Blood pouring from his nostrils, Rushmount stumbled back. He raised his hands, trying to ward off Owen's punishing fists.

"Owen, no more," Grace shouted. "Let him go. He's not worth—"

"Grace!" At the sound of her voice, Owen turned away from Rushmount, leaving him on the edge of the ravine, bleeding and fingering his jaw. To her relief, Owen bore no sign of struggle except for the dark hair falling into his eyes, and the sweat-stained shirt pulled free from his breeches and flopping about his hips. He smiled as he limped toward her. Her heart went out to him. He had sorely tested his leg this day. They needed to go home together and put Rushmount and his evil deeds behind them.

As she watched him come close, a quick, furtive movement behind him caught her eye. A flash of sunlight on metal. Rushmount held a musket in his hand.

She should have known he'd be armed. Even on horseback in Liverpool, he'd held a knife to her ribs. He cocked the trigger, the sound of metal on metal echoing louder than Owen's blows to his jaw. His arm rose.

On instinct, without thought to guide her, she reached into her quiver and yanked out an arrow, its tip still covered with the deer's dried blood. As she fit the bloody arrow to the bow, she shouted, "Would you shoot him in the back, Rushmount?"

Her voice startled him, as she knew it would, and squinting along the musket barrel, his finger tensing on the trigger, he swiveled his aim away from Owen toward her.

"No!" Fleet as a deer, Absalom leaped in front of her.

Rushmount fired, the shot shattering the air, the musket ball striking with a force that sent Absalom slumping to his knees. Time stopped as he knelt suspended, then slowly, so slowly he seemed poised between rising and falling, he slipped to one side and with a sigh fell over, his face coming to rest on the earth.

As Absalom collapsed at her feet, Grace knew nothing but a rush of air, all other senses fell away. Then, as if though she were poaching a deer to feed a hungry village and would have only one shot, she took aim, careful, solid aim, and pulled back on the bow with all the power she could summon. Straight and vengeful, the arrow flew, impaling Rushmount in the chest. He fell to the ground, the spent musket sliding out of his hand, the arrow quivering in the place where his heart used to beat.

"Grace? Are you harmed?" Owen rushed to her, his face ashen with fear for her.

"I am not, love." She dropped her weapons to the ground and flung herself into his arms, needing to feel him pressed against her for an instant, alive and well and strong.

Reassured, she pulled out of his embrace and knelt by Absalom's side. His eyes were open and sightless, his body motionless. She looked up at Owen, stricken. "He took the shot meant for me."

"Aye, he did." Pale as death himself, Owen got down and turned Absalom gently onto his back.

"He's breathing," Grace said.

Owen nodded. "For now."

To Grace's horror, a bloody froth bubbled up between Absalom's lips. She wiped it away with the hem of her skirt and lifted his head onto her lap. With fingers as light as a dream, she caressed the smooth copper skin of his face, his thick, coarse hair. The bubbles frothed up again, and again she wiped them away. Lifting his hand, she pressed it to her lips.

"Absalom, my friend, my dearest friend."

Whether the touch of her lips or her murmuring voice aroused him, she would never know, but his dark eyes opened to stare into hers.

"Promise me," he said, "promise me." To hear his faint voice, to not miss a single word, she bent close to his bleeding mouth. "Promise . . . me."

"Anything, Absalom. Anything."

"Say I killed him."

"But—"

"You said anything . . ."

His wide, dark eyes continued staring into hers though she knew he could no longer see her.

Owen's hand gripped her shoulder. "He's gone, Grace."

"I know. Dear God, I know."

"Stay here, love," Owen said, "I'll see to Rushmount."

Hardly aware of what she was doing, she gently slid Absalom's head from her lap and closed his eyelids. She folded his hands over his chest hiding the wound with his arms, and sitting stunned beside him, let the horror wash over her.

Back in Ballybanree, she'd sat by her brother Liam's body like this, folding his arms to hide his wound, telling herself she wasn't responsible for his death, that he'd died by his own hand. But could she have prevented him, somehow? Even now she didn't know for certain. Nor did she know, for certain, if Absalom's death would be counted against her soul.

But of Rushmount's death, she had not the slightest doubt. She had killed him deliberately, with all the passion and determination God ever placed in a human heart.

No matter what Rushmount had done, she had no right to seek such vengeance. No right at all. When she pulled that bow, she had taken a man's life and jeopardized her immortal soul.

A shadow fell over her. "Rushmount's dead," Owen said. "Two men gone from one heartbeat to the next. 'Tis hard to believe."

Grace looked down at a patch of earth. She couldn't raise her eyes to the accusation she was sure to find in Owen's face.

He crouched beside her. "Look at me, Grace."

"I cannot."

"You saved my life."

She kept her eyes hidden.

"Do you hear me?"

"Aye," she managed to whisper.

"Would you rather I had died in Rushmount's place?"

She didn't speak. He well knew the answer to his own question.

"Would you?"

Her head snapped up. "Never in God's world."

"Rushmount shot first. You did what you had to do."

"I did what I *wanted* to do. Sure and I'm as guilty as sin." Her expression challenged him to deny it.

Owen shook his head. "I wanted my hands on his throat. If you hadn't called to me, I might have finished him. But you did call. You took the guilt from me and placed it on your own shoulders. I'm sorry for that. I know how heavily it will weigh on you."

"I cannot deny that." Her gaze swept over Absalom's body stretched out next to her. She knew she would weep bitter tears for him and for what she had done to Rushmount, but for now she could find no release in weeping and looked up at Owen dry-eyed. "Have we brought evil into the New World, then? Only evil?"

"You can't believe such a thing of yourself. Or of me. Evil as well as good is everywhere. This is the New World not paradise."

"Aye," she said, a bitter note rising into her voice. "After my work of this day, I may never see a paradise."

Before Owen could respond, agitated voices reached them. Roger and Rushmount's man, Thomas, both panting with effort, were mounting the hill.

"Say nothing, Grace," Owen warned as they approached. "I will do the answering."

"But I must tell what happened."

"*Nothing*."

Hobbled by his knees, Roger painfully made his way toward them, his face pallid, his bottom lip trembling at the scene spread before him.

When he spied the arrow in Rushmount's chest, Thomas rushed past them to kneel by his master. He picked up a lifeless hand, and getting no pressure in return, laid his palm on Rushmount's cheek, both privileges he wouldn't have dared take ten minutes earlier. He looked back at the others. "His lordship's dead. Killed by an arrow, 'e was." He pointed an accusing finger. "That Injun must 'ave killed him."

"No," Grace began.

"Grace," Owen interrupted. "Remember your promise."

"How in the world can I keep such a promise?"

"How can you not?"

"Help me get down to Absalom, Owen," Roger said, his face streaming with tears.

With Owen holding him under the arms, Roger lowered himself to his knees and bending over Absalom, he, too, took a dead man's hand, holding it between his own like a closed book. "Absalom. My son. My dear son."

He stroked the body with futile caresses before turning a wet face up to Owen. "Later, you will tell me what happened here. But first, you must bring Canonchet. Absalom was like a son to him as well as to me."

"Aye." Owen nodded, his own eyes blurry with unshed tears. "I'll go for him." He looked to Grace and softly said, "But before I do, your promise."

She shrugged, pale-faced, barren of emotion. "What more can I promise this day?"

"You must promise to keep your word to Absalom."

Puzzled, Roger looked from one to the other.

"I'm waiting," Owen said.

"I promise to say nothing while you're gone."

"That will do for now."

Owen hurried off, his crippled leg ready to buckle under him with every step. He had a walk of an hour or more to the Narragansetts' winter longhouse where it sheltered southwest of the village, well away from the ocean's roar. But the leg held up, firm and steady enough as he hurried along.

When he finally drew near the dwelling, someone within must have heard him approach, for Riana flipped open the entrance skin just as he reached it.

"Canonchet," he said, pointing into the dwelling. Then pointing to his chest, he said, "O'Donnell." Bringing his two hands together, he repeated their names.

To his relief, the woman understood his pantomime. She nodded, and holding the flap open, motioned for him to enter.

Chapter Thirty

IN THE DIM LIGHT, OWEN COULD BARELY MAKE OUT Canonchet crouched by the firepit, huddled in a fur cloak as if the dead of winter had arrived. A log shifted on the coals, and from its brief flare, he saw the sachem take a pipe from his mouth and raise his head, surveying him carefully from under hooded lids.

Owen came closer. "There is something you must know."

"Speak." The impassive face gave nothing away, not even curiosity.

"I fear I bring sadness with me."

The sachem stiffened.

"Absalom, your son in spirit, is gone."

Canonchet's hand dropped to his lap. "Gone?" His face, no longer impassive, bore a look of stunned disbelief. "He leave for the west with no farewell?"

Oh God, he was bungling it. Owen blew out a breath to ease his own tension. He'd have to say what he must bluntly in the simplest terms possible. "Absalom is dead. Shot." Owen pointed toward his chest. "Here."

The pipe dropped from Canonchet's hand and fell into the firepit. "My son? Dead?" He rose to his feet, the fur cloak slipping away unnoticed. "Where I find Absalom?" he demanded.

———

GRACE SAW THE SACHEM PLODDING UP THE RISE. Strange that none of his tribesmen accompanied him. Owen must have found him alone. And where *was* Owen? Why hadn't he returned with the sachem? Shown him the way? She sighed. His leg had been sore tried this day. He would return as soon as he was able.

Canonchet walked over to where she and Roger huddled beside Absalom's body. Bending down, he lifted up the arm hiding the wound as if he needed more proof than his eyes could provide. He studied the musket ball's entry point for a long, silent moment before folding the arm back across the chest. He raised his chin at Grace. "Her man come to my hogan. He tell me of this. He follow me slow, very slow. I did not wait. A musket, he say."

"Yes," Roger answered, "a musket shot."

Canonchet pointed to where Thomas sat keeping his own vigil over Lord Rushmount. "The fallen one, he shoot my son?"

"He did," Roger said.

Deliberately, without haste, Canonchet walked toward the body under the tree. Seeing him coming, Thomas scurried to his feet dashing back to safety at Roger's side.

The sachem stood over Rushmount's body, examining it as carefully as he had Absalom's. Satisfied with what he saw, he planted a foot on its chest, ripped out the arrow and walked back to Roger and Grace with it in his hand.

"Killed with that very same arrow 'e was." Thomas pointed a shaking finger at Absalom. "That Injun there done it. And the one that's comin' over 'ere got the proof in his 'ands."

As if Thomas were a buzzing insect, Canonchet ignored his ranting and handed the arrow to Grace. "Leave us," he said to the man.

"I take no orders from the likes of him," Thomas said from behind Roger.

His arm outstretched, the sachem pointed down the hill, his expression wooden, waiting to be obeyed.

"He won't ask again," Roger said. "Kindly do as he says, Thomas. Go to the house. Tell Mary to send for Caleb Harris and his brothers."

Mumbling but obedient, Thomas stumbled away. When he was out of earshot, Canonchet spoke to Roger in Algonquin. "Tell the woman I know Absalom did not shoot the white one. The weapon is hers. And I know of her great skill with a bow. She did the killing. Her."

He stood, unmoving, his dark eyes on Grace while Roger translated his words.

Close to despair, her head lowered, Grace nodded, but remained silent as Absalom had asked of her.

A sound too guttural to be grief alone arose from Canonchet's throat. "Now tell her no one is to know the truth."

When she understood, she raised a stunned face to the sachem. "Why not?"

He answered in Algonquin. "I remember what your gods say, Roger. 'An eye for an eye, a tooth for a tooth.' This my people will understand. And your people as well. If the whites hear the woman killed one of her own to avenge a Narragansett, they will need to know why. And the matter will continue." His jaw tightened. "Absalom did not act to save himself. He was unarmed when the white one killed him. This my people will not accept. It is far better to say the two fought and the gods spoke. The grievance will end there and without dishonor for my son."

"You wish to call what happened here a duel?" Roger asked, incredulous.

The sachem nodded once, a quick jerk of his head. "You use your words, I use mine. As long as we maintain peace."

"Amen," Roger said. He looked over at Grace who sat watching, her eyes shadowed with remorse. She had not understood what the sachem said, but the sorrow in his tone had bled through his words.

"So long as the sachem and I did not witness what occurred here, we can, in conscience, be silent concerning the circumstances," Roger told her. "I'll write to England and call this unfortunate tragedy a duel. For the greater good."

Grace looked straight into his face. "I'm guilty, Roger. Can you absolve me of my sin like a priest? Like Father Joyce in Ballybanree?"

"No. But I can forgive you as God will if you repent of your act." He rested a hand on her hair for a moment. "Can you forgive yourself?"

She shook her head. "Sure and I never will."

"You must, or your life is over."

Canonchet eased himself onto the ground next to Absalom. "I will guard him until Comise and the others find me."

"Canonchet." When Grace spoke his name, he glanced at her with a face of stone. "Absalom stepped in front of me. He took the shot in his own body."

The sachem didn't answer.

"He was the most beautiful of men," she murmured.

"And the most unwise," he retorted. Implacable, he turned from her to stare down at his nephew, his beloved adopted son.

Struggling to rise, Roger said, "Old friend, I leave our son to your care. I must see to Lord Rushmount's burial, perhaps here under the tree where he fell."

Yet another tree with a man lying buried beneath it, Grace thought, the memory of the hanging tree in Ballybanree flooding her mind. She had not been able to prevent her father's death, or Absalom's, or to keep her bow from its fatal flight into Rushmount's body.

Aye, remorse would eat her alive for certain. She had no escape from it. Yet she must take heed of what Roger said. If she didn't forgive herself, she would die and Absalom's sacrifice would have been in vain. Is that what she wanted for herself and for Owen? No, Mother of God, in truth, she did not. Nor is that what Absalom would have wished for her. She owed it to him to live. And she had so much to live for. Guilt alone was not all she carried beneath her heart.

She scrambled to her feet. "I'm worried for Owen."

"Go to him, Grace," Roger said. "Seek comfort from each other. You'll need it in the days ahead."

"Aye." She picked up her bow and the bloody arrow. The arrow she would keep forever as a reminder of this day—of its nobility and its vengeance. And glory be to God, there would be other memories as well from today. For she had something wondrous to tell Owen. Something that if she had to keep to herself any longer she would surely burst.

But the need to wait longer disappeared, for in the distance, she saw him struggling up the hill toward her. Her heart leapt at the sight, and she began sprinting toward him as fast as ever she could. Owen needed to know Absalom had saved two lives this day—hers, and the child she carried.

He had saved Absalom Owen O'Donnell.

Or, if God chose to send them a girl child, he'd saved his daughter—Absalom Grace O'Donnell. That name had a fine ring to it, too.

They could call her Abby for short.

Aye, Abby.

'Twould be her love name.

Sharon Yanish

AFTER A SHORT CAREER WRITING ADVERTISING COPY and a long career teaching college English, Jean Harrington launched a new career as a fiction author and since then has had ten novels published, including a Florida Book Award Winner. Another book is about to be published and a current work in progress has her excited. Nowadays, Jean and husband John are living in and exploring the Chagrin Falls area of Ohio.